The door slid shut behi... ...ame part of the wall. The lig... ...an instant and the restaurant was sudde... ...ansformed.

Ewart gazed around in total amazement. The room itself was circular, not very large, yet its surroundings were absolutely sensational. He looked up, looked down, and was almost too scared to move in case he was swallowed up by the infinite.

The roof was transparent, a window on the universe, with countless glittering stars scattered at random across the vast heavens.

The view beneath Ewart's feet was equally spectacular. It was as if he stood on nothing, that he was held suspended above the miniature star which burned with pure white brilliance in the absolute centre of Hideaway.

STARGONAUTS

DAVID GARNETT

ORBIT

An *Orbit* Book

First published in Great Britain in 1994 by Orbit

Copyright © David Garnett 1994

The moral right of the author has been asserted.

A CIP catalogue record for this book
is available from the British Library.

ISBN 1 85723 186 4

Typeset by Solidus (Bristol) Limited
Printed and bound in Great Britain by
Clays Ltd, St Ives plc

Orbit
A Division of
Little, Brown and Company (UK)
Brettenham House
Lancaster Place
London WC2E 7EN

For Frances

For Ever

PART ONE

Breakfast

Earth

CHAPTER ONE

It was going to be a great day.

William Ewart, the second richest man in the world, hated to waste a single minute. Time was the most valuable thing there was, and the only thing which he was unable to buy. Sleep was nothing but a waste of time, and over the years he'd managed to reduce his sleeping hours to a minimum. As soon as he awoke, he was straight out of bed.

But not this morning. Today was special. He lay without moving for an extra minute, and he smiled.

'Happy birthday.'

Ewart's smile vanished. That definitely wasn't the reason today was special.

He turned and looked at Zena. She was exactly what a man such as Ewart needed – and could afford.

'How did you know it was my birthday?'

'I know everything about you, sir,' she said. 'That is my job.'

At first, he'd told her there was no need to call him

'sir' when they were in bed together, that she should only address him as such when other people were there. The request had seemed simple enough, but it hadn't made any difference.

'When you get to my age,' Ewart said, 'you don't like to be reminded of birthdays.'

'Why not?'

There was no way he could explain. She couldn't even comprehend what it was to grow old, to have lived for almost two thirds of a century. Neither was there any need to explain, so he said nothing.

'You will not be celebrating your birthday, sir?'

'It's just another day.'

'No,' said Zena, 'it is not just another day.'

He smiled and nodded. 'Right, it isn't. I'm going to give myself a birthday present, the best present of all.'

Today the second richest man in the world would become the richest.

'Will you have any other presents, sir?'

'I doubt it.'

'Not even from your family and friends?'

'You should know by now that I have no friends. As for a family . . .'

'I know you are in dispute with your wives, sir, but surely your children will send their greetings.'

'Some of them might, but they don't mean it. All they're thinking is: "Another year older, you bastard, another year closer to the grave." What they want is my money. That's all everyone wants. But they'll never get it. Whenever I go and wherever I'm going, I'm taking it with me.'

4

'Is there anything special you require on your birth-day, sir?'

Zena was lying on her side, her head propped up on her left elbow. Her free hand reached for the buttons on the wall. The canopy above the antique four-poster bed rolled away; the curtains at each side were pulled back; the thermocover was drawn off their naked bodies. The room was hemispherical, its multifaceted surface composed of octagonal mirrors.

Surrounded by reflections of Zena's nude body – and of his own – Ewart shook his head and quickly climbed out of bed.

'Too much to do,' he said.

'Or you could have breakfast,' Zena suggested. 'This is a very special day, sir.'

That was a tempting offer, which Ewart considered for a moment. But he'd only recently cut down from three meals a day to two, and he should keep to his resolution. Tonight he would have a really memorable dinner. Although it wouldn't be his birthday that he was celebrating.

He shook his head again and stepped towards the wall to examine his face.

'How old are you, sir?'

Ewart gazed past his own reflection, studying Zena's mirror image. Her face was absolutely symmetrical. She was physically perfect, of course.

'Sixty-five,' he said, although he was aware that she must have known the answer.

'But you look exactly the same as when you were sixty-four.'

5

Ewart laughed. Zena was right, he supposed. What difference did a day make? The trouble was that the days added up to weeks, the weeks to months, and his birthdays were coming around faster and faster.

He'd reached what was probably halfway through his life, he realized. From now on, there would be less time ahead of him than he had already spent. He didn't like the idea.

But he was still fit and healthy, with most of his original parts. He looked good, or else he wouldn't sleep in a room full of mirrors. His enemies sometimes referred to him as 'the fat man', but he had never been fat. Not really. He had a large frame, big bones, and so he was naturally bigger than most other people.

He may have had a slight weight problem at one time, but that was the unfortunate price of being such a renowned gourmet, a connoisseur of the galaxy's finest wines and liqueurs. In any case, this was now solved by regular surgical attention.

Moving to the Moon with his fourth wife had also helped him lose some weight, because it was almost four hundred thousand kilometres to the nearest good restaurant. She had been born on the Moon, and Ewart suggested that was where they should take their honeymoon, a honeymoon which would last the rest of their lives.

Ewart shuddered as he remembered his fourth wife. Karis, right, that had been her name. He'd married again very recently, and he was curious about his fifth wife. He hadn't even seen a hologram of her, but it was very unlikely they would ever meet. Because they lived a hundred light years apart, it ought to be the perfect marriage. He'd always believed each of his marriages would be perfect. And they were. For a while. A very short while.

He studied Zena for a moment or two, then said, 'You can get ready for your daytime duties.'

'Very well, sir, if that is what you wish.' Zena stepped out of bed and pressed the button which opened her clothing cabinet. 'I should like to wish you a very happy birthday, sir, and I hope that your plans for today prove successful.'

'Thanks,' said Ewart.

He turned around, watching as she pulled on her red and gold bodysuit; it was the same colours as her streaked hair. Although Zena's words meant very little, because it was part of her job to say such things, he was very glad of them.

All his years of preparation and scheming were about to come to fruition. He was relying on so many different factors, but every minor part of his plan was dispensable because there was always an alternative. And every detail was kept in the most secure place of all, inside his head.

There was no one else he could trust, but the secret of what he intended had craved release, and last night he'd told Zena everything. She was a good listener, very easy to talk to, the exact opposite of any of his wives. Ewart knew it was stupid, but he had grown very fond of Zena during the months they'd been together.

It was only coincidence that today was his birthday; but he couldn't think of a more appropriate celebration.

7

The only thing better than making money was making even more money, while making a colossal amount was infinitely better. By the end of the day, he still wouldn't be the richest man in the whole solar system, because there were several crazies out in the asteroid belt who claimed to be far wealthier. But owning chunks of rock, no matter how full of ore they were, didn't really count.

True wealth was what you owned here, down on Earth.

Ewart owned the Ewart Communications Corporation.

By tonight he would also own his biggest competitor, Sol Global Network. And Hiroshi Larnvik, the man who was this morning the richest in the world, would be totally wiped out.

Ewart smiled at the thought of bankrupting his archrival. They'd had so many battles over the years, in the investment markets, the courts and the media, over the power beams and across the electromagnetic spectrum, once almost coming to blows, as they each strove for mastery of the planet's communications industry. Sometimes Ewart had won, sometimes it had been Larnvik; the day they'd attempted to assault one another, their respective bodyguards had intervened to prevent the tycoons hurting each other – and themselves. Ewart's personal psychopath, Grawl, had pulped Larnvik's mandroid, and Ewart claimed that as another ECC victory.

Today was the final battle, and again Ewart would conquer. Larnvik had no idea what was about to hit him. By the time he knew, it would be too late.

Ewart reached for the buttons above the bed, pressed a sequence, and part of the bedroom wall sank into the floor. Slowly, looking all around, Zena walked into the next room.

They were five hundred metres beneath the surface, but Ewart had to be very careful. A man as successful as he had countless enemies, and many would profit by his assassination. Zena came back safely, and Ewart went into the bathroom.

When he returned, Zena supervised his morning physcan. The readings were fine; he needed no biofix.

Zena fixed Ewart's medpack to her belt, then helped him dress. She passed him the console, and he punched in the day's security code. All the mirrors became screens, and he cautiously scanned every room. While she waited, Zena put on her jewellery, the ear-rings and bangles and necklace, and brushed her hair. Finally satisfied, Ewart coded the console again, and another part of the wall slid down into the floor.

Zena stepped through and started walking along the arched corridor. The wall slid back into position. Ewart watched on one of the screens, punched in the next randomized number, and the outer door swung down. Zena went through, on to the next screen, and the door slid back into place.

'Good morning, Grawl,' she said.

Grawl said nothing; he was unable to speak. Even if he could have spoken, he would not have replied. He didn't like Zena. He didn't like anyone. Anyone except Ewart, that was, although 'like' might be the wrong word. Did a dog 'like' its master? Grawl was fanatically loyal to

Ewart, which was exactly what Ewart required of him.

Zena and Grawl stood on either side of the door, their fingers poised above the security pads.

Seeing them together, they appeared to be complete opposites. Because Zena was so tall, she made Grawl look even smaller than he already was; and Grawl's width made Zena's athletic body seem so much slimmer.

A bodyguard was expected to be big and burly, with a physique boosted by muscle implants and chemically accelerated reflexes. Grawl was short, almost a dwarf, and he looked nearly as wide as he was tall. But he was tough and strong and very fast, and he owed his life to Ewart. Whenever he was in public, Ewart liked having Grawl around because he wasn't what was expected.

He liked having Zena with him for the opposite reason: because she appeared to be what was expected, the kind of attractive young woman to which a man of his status was entitled.

'One ... two ... three,' said Zena, and she and Grawl simultaneously entered their own personal codes.

'Secure,' the electronic voice of the defence shield said to Ewart.

Ewart punched the console and the inner door opened again. He made his way along the corridor, then the outer door opened and he went through. One advantage of this location was that he didn't have to travel far to work. Five seconds after leaving his bedroom, he entered the headquarters of Ewart Communications Corporation.

*

Ewart often thought that the best moment of the day was when he first walked into the hub of his empire and gazed at the gallery of screens which surrounded him. His, all his, and it always hit him with a sudden rush. This was power, literally and metaphorically, and the fix was better than anything . . . *anything*.

The first thing he always did was study the statistics, watch the data charts as they grew and grew, as more and more people linked to ECC. Every day there was a new peak, a new record.

Then he would look at the network screens. The top array was always changing, as every ECC transmission was sampled. All of Ewart's terrestrial networks, all his channels throughout the inhabited solar system, were displayed for a few seconds in a rotation system which lasted hours.

This was the glamorous side of Ewart's enterprises, and the enormous media network was the popular image of ECC. But there was more than entertainment, more than news, so much more. Communications was everything. It meant datadeks and InfoChek, sound-splints and SeeV. Without communications, there could be no power; without power, there could be no communications. They were indivisible. The world would seize up if energy could not be beamed from producer to consumer. There would be no transport, no one could go anywhere, do anything. They would all be trapped in their apartments because the maglevs had ceased to function, and they would freeze to death because there was no heat.

And all of this Ewart had built up from nothing,

because in the beginning that was all he had; he hadn't inherited his various enterprises, like Larnvik.

By tonight Larnvik would be gone, but this was only the beginning for Ewart. ECC would be the biggest communications network in the solar system. But beyond lay the stars, and Ewart had already begun to stake his claim out there.

It was going to be a great day – and he didn't have to do a thing. The wheels had already begun to roll, each one turning another as ghost companies and phantom nominees started to buy and to sell, to purchase various debts and to shed unwanted assets, to take on loans, to buy up options. It should be plain sailing. For the first few hours, all Ewart had to do was watch, although he might need to steer occasionally and alter course as things became rough. By this afternoon he would be in the eye of the hurricane, and when the typhoon struck . . . Larnvik would sink.

'Coffee,' he said.

Zena and Grawl had been standing behind him while he watched the screens, and it was Grawl who went for the coffee. They took it in turns.

Ewart sat down at his desk. It was in the centre of the room, and there was a single blank screen mounted in the middle. Before switching it on, Ewart spun around on his gravchair, surveying his domain. Very few people worked in ECC headquarters. Probably even fewer were necessary, they could have carried out their functions elsewhere and reported by SeeV, but Ewart liked to see people working.

'Good morning, sir,' said Joseph Abdenga.

It would make no difference, Ewart had often thought, whether Abdenga were a screen image or not. His face was always exactly the same, without any trace of emotion. Perhaps that was part of his job. He was Ewart's lawyer, personally indentured to him for another eighty-seven years.

'What do we have?' asked Ewart.

It was always best to start the day on a positive note, and Ewart usually enjoyed the meeting with his lawyer, because it was here that he discovered how many writs, injunctions and law suits he was about to initiate. A man in his position had to maintain his reputation against all his rivals and detractors.

'Something rather unusual, sir,' said Abdenga. 'You have received a summons to appear in court this morning.'

That didn't seem so unusual. Ewart switched on his desk screen, coded it, and watched the numbers begin to scroll. He nodded his approval as he absorbed the figures, all part of the inevitable progress towards victory.

'Get a postponement,' he said.

'A court appearance, sir,' Abdenga told him. 'You have to be there, in person, in an hour.'

'What?' Ewart turned to face him. 'You mean *go* to court? In an hour? I don't believe it.'

'There does appear to have been some error, sir, because you should have been given at least seven days' notice. The summons is, however, dated fourteen days ago, but it only arrived this morning.' He pointed to the date at the top of the document.

Ewart shrugged. 'They've made another mistake, what else is new? Those people are so inefficient. What a waste of taxpayers' money. Forget it.'

'As your legal adviser, sir, I advise that you obey the summons.'

'If I don't?'

'You can be found in contempt of court, sir, and heavily fined.'

Ewart had returned his attention to the screen, only partly listening to what Abdenga told him. Time was money and he hated wasting both of them, but a fine was absolutely nothing compared with the eventual profits from today's endeavours.

'They can't just expect me to turn up in court,' he said. 'I've better things to do with my time. Take care of it.'

Grawl placed a silver tray on Ewart's desk. On it was an antique porcelain cup and matching saucer, a silver spoon with the monogram *E* embossed upon the handle, a similarly marked silver jug of cream, and a cafetiere of freshly roasted and ground coffee. The coffee beans had been grown fifty metres from where Ewart now sat.

'I believe you should take this summons seriously, sir,' Abdenga told him.

Ewart gestured dismissively. 'It's meaningless.'

'If necessary, we could always argue that because of the unreliability of electronic communication you were unaware of the summons.'

'Unreliability! What do you mean? Ewart Communications Corporation is always reliable!' Ewart glared at Abdenga. Had anyone else cast such aspersions, he would have sued them for commercial defamation. Could he sue his own lawyer? If so, would Abdenga appear for ECC or for himself? 'Can a defendant act for the plaintiff if the defendant is the plaintiff's lawyer?'

'Sir?'

'Never mind. I'm not going to court, especially not today. Send a proxy.'

Ewart was a busy man, he couldn't do everything for himself. Proxies could be very useful. He'd married his latest wife that way.

'No, sir. No proxy, no relayed appearance. Your actual physical presence is legally required.'

'What do those tax bastards want off me this time?'

'It's a court summons on behalf of your wives, sir.'

'My *wives*! Throw it away, Joe, you should know that by now. Anything from one of my wives should be ignored.'

'It's from all of your wives, sir. They are jointly suing you for fifty per cent of your assets.'

'What? They want half my money?'

'They are each suing for fifty per cent of your assets, sir.'

'Ha! They were all calculating bitches, but none of them could ever count. How can they expect more than I have? They'll get exactly what they deserve: nothing!'

Ewart realized there was something very odd going on. His ex-wives hated each other almost as much as they hated him, so why were they colluding like this? It could be greed, that they were after his money. They always were after his money. But they had never brought a joint suit until now. Someone else must have

15

been involved, someone who had put them up to this, and it didn't take much to guess who it was.

'Larnvik,' said Ewart.

'Sir?'

'Nothing. Do what you always do. Appeal. I'm not being distracted by anything else until tomorrow.'

Ewart gently pushed down on the coffee plunger. He always did this for himself, because only he knew exactly the right moment. Pouring the coffee into his cup, he inhaled the rich aroma.

'And who am I taking to court today?' he asked.

Sometimes Ewart wished there were three of him, that way he might have enough time to deal with everything which needed his personal attention.

He spent the next two hours conferencing, summoning his staff from various parts of the globe, receiving a brief verbal report from each, then giving them their instructions. Ewart never said 'hello' or 'goodbye', it wasted too many seconds. Over the years, those seconds had added up.

All the while, he was keeping one eye on the financial data. Things seemed to move slowly, which was how they were meant to seem.

He was interrogating the zone co-ordinator on Venus when the override signal flashed on to the screen. Ewart didn't recognize the code, and then the screen dissolved into a shapeless pattern of stellar interference.

'What's this?' he yelled across the room to the input controller.

'It's from,' she began, hurrying towards him, 'your,'

she lowered her voice, 'wife.'

'You know none of my ex-wives has access to me!'

'No, sir,' said the controller, 'it's not one of your ex-wives. It's the other one, your new one.'

Ewart stared at the screen again. He'd never been in direct contact with his fifth wife. And, judging by the reception, it seemed likely to continue this way.

'Get a filter on this, boost the picture,' said Ewart. 'Find out what she's saying.'

He shook his head as he studied the garish images on the screen. Even across a hundred light years, reception should have been better than that. He changed the screen. The numbers scrolled, slightly larger figures than before, slightly faster, and he sipped at his second coffee, the one which Zena had brought him.

'Security alert,' announced the defence shield. 'This building is under attack. Surface protection seals have been breached and surveillance indicates that intruders are descending towards this level.'

'What?' said Ewart.

'This building is under attack,' the voice of the defence shield repeated. 'Surface protection seals have been breached and surveillance indicates that intruders are descending towards this level.'

Ewart spun around, staring at Grawl. Grawl was gazing up, as though waiting for the descending intruders to crash through the ceiling, then he hurried across the room towards the access shaft.

None of this should have been possible, that was why Ewart had a security system – and security guards to guard the security system.

'What about the escape exit?' he asked.

'The surface exit has been seized by hostile forces,' answered the shield.

Ewart looked at the screen again, but his eyes were no longer focused on the data flow. He was thinking. Zena stepped closer to him.

The screen suddenly changed, and the woman who appeared there said: '—unications Corporation head William Ewart, known as the fat man, has *defied* a legal summons to appear in court. But Candy and Mandy aren't going to let him get away with *that*! We have discovered that Ewart recently married again, for the *fifth* time! Although why anyone should want to *marry* a lump of lard like him we can't *imagine*! But what happened to his *previous* wives? The obese beast used them and abused them, then divorced them, and they were left with *nothing*! The four ex-wives intend to *claim* the alimony that the overweight ogre has *denied* them. After all they've been through, we think they deserve a *fortune*! But Ewart didn't turn up in court today as he *should* have done. In the interests of truth and justice, Candy is about to serve the *warrant* on Ewart! Will the corpulent crook *dare* to *defy* the law? Find out right here on the Candy and Mandy "Doubletime News Show", always *twice* as much of everything, now *live* and *exclusive* on *Sol Global News*. After this *important* message, it's over to *Candy* – and fat fugitive lawbreaker William Ewart!'

'What's going on?' whispered Ewart. 'What's happening?'

Whenever Ewart's name was mentioned on any

channel, it triggered an automatic recording in case legal action were necessary. Sol Global News always gave unfavourable reports on Ewart, just as Ewart Communications Corporation always had bad things to say about Hiroshi Larnvik. Some of it was to be accepted, but there were limits – and this, *this* . . .!

'Off,' he ordered, and the screen blanked. He wondered how the programme had got patched through directly to him.

What made it so much worse was that it was Mandy who had said those terrible things, and she wore the SGN logo on her blouse. Larnvik had stolen ECC's most popular presenters, stolen the whole concept.

Yesterday Candy and Mandy had worked for Ewart, but their defection could only have happened in the last few hours. No one at ECC must have known, or else Ewart would have been informed. Heads would roll for this. He shouldn't have had to discover their treachery in such a . . . *personal* way.

'Joe!' yelled Ewart. He'd sue SGN for every rupan.

Then he realized that he wouldn't be able to take legal action, because by tonight SGN would no longer exist. He couldn't act against the company, but he could make certain that the only media jobs Candy and Mandy ever found would be defrosting lenses on Pluto.

How could they be so disloyal after everything he'd done for them? Ewart had created Candy and Mandy, made them what they were. He had given them new faces, improved bodies, enhanced their eyes – especially the left ones, which were now opticam lenses. Candy and Mandy had become major celebrities, the most watched live show on Earth. They'd both been tough and ambitious, and now they had betrayed him. Their new badge of allegiance was the SGN logo on their breasts: the breasts which Ewart had also given them.

Ewart became aware that the security shield was making another announcement, but he didn't need to listen. Knowing the way that Candy and Mandy operated, he realized what was happening. They'd perfected their technique while working for him and it seemed he was about to become their next victim, their first trophy for Sol Global Network. There was little consolation in knowing that he would also be the last.

'Call my wives,' Ewart said to Abdenga. 'Whatever it takes, whatever it costs, get them to postpone this case until tomorrow. Promise them anything.'

'I think it's too late, sir,' said Abdenga, who must also have worked out what was going on.

'Just do it.'

Candy and Mandy took it in turns to go out on assignment, and whatever happened was transmitted live. They never went out alone, they were too valuable for that. A security squad always accompanied them. Today, Ewart realized, there were probably two security squads – one of which, like Candy and Mandy, had been his until very recently. No wonder ECC headquarters had been infiltrated so easily, it had been done by experts, the ones who operated the system. They would also pay the price of treachery, Ewart promised.

He was on his feet now, pacing the room, with Zena close behind him.

'It wasn't from your wife, sir, not as such,' said the input controller.

'What?' asked Ewart. 'What wife?'

'Your fifth wife, sir, the message which needed interpreting.'

'So? What did it say?'

'It was from your father-in-law, sir. The translation may not be completely accurate, but it seems that your new wife is on her way to join you. You must be pleased, sir.'

'Delighted,' muttered Ewart. What was she coming here for? That wasn't part of the deal.

'Intruders will reach this level in twenty seconds,' said the security shield.

Ewart coded the console below the nearest screen, watched as the numbers came up. They weren't quite right, he was sure. It was time to get involved.

'Something else, sir,' said the controller, watching her own screen. 'It's not too clear, but your wife's father seems to be saying that his final arrangements don't allow him to support his daughter in a befitting manner.'

'Final arrangements?' said Ewart. Then he froze. 'Or "financial arrangements"?'

'Could be, sir.'

He kept watching as the numbers continued to scroll. They were definitely the wrong numbers.

The controller concluded: 'And he sends his fondest regards.'

Ewart remained motionless, thinking furiously.

'Intruders at the base of the shaft. Security code for

the entrance being annulled.'

Ewart hurried to his desk. A few minutes, that was all he needed to delay everything here. If he could get through this legal charade within an hour or two, when he returned he could still salvage himself.

'Hold them!' he yelled at Zena.

Zena sprinted across the room to where Grawl was waiting for the door to open.

Ewart's monitor showed the view from within the shaft as the door slid back. SGN's cameras would soon be inside his headquarters!

He commanded the screen to clear and split, then began issuing rapid instructions.

And Grawl and Zena launched themselves into attack.

Violence was exactly what Candy and Mandy loved. Stunning and immobilizing were not very visual. They wanted those they tracked down to put up a fight. Ewart hated obliging them and their audience, but he needed every second.

Grawl thumped and punched the security guards, splitting their armour with his bare hands. He had his priorities right, Ewart noticed as he glanced around for a moment, it was the ECC team who were suffering most.

But Grawl wasn't alone. Zena was by his side, also laying into the invaders with her own combat techniques. Her feet lashed out, sending squadmen tumbling.

The fight was all being documented, mixed and immediately transmitted on the 'Doubletime News Show'. The implant in Candy's left eye enabled her viewers to see exactly what she saw. There was also an autocam, which always hovered within a few metres, to give the scene another perspective, and which also encompassed Candy.

Although it was Candy or Mandy who provoked the violence, they were usually immune from its consequences. Partly this was because of their security squad, but it was also because of their sex. Most men had reservations about hitting women, particularly if it was being shown live across the globe to hundreds of millions of people.

Grawl had no such inhibitions.

And neither had Zena.

'No!' yelled Candy, her voice trembling with terror.

She was cornered and alone, all of her squad horizontal around her. Zena moved closer. Candy glanced up at the autocam, hoping it would save her.

'Any *violence* perpetrated upon my person will be recorded and used in *evidence*,' she recited.

'Recorded?' Zena looked up and shook her head. 'Too late to do you much good.'

Ewart watched in horror as she suddenly leapt up, kicking out with her left foot, about to flatten the nose which he had paid for. But at the last moment Zena twisted away, her foot missing Candy's face by a few centimetres. She bounced off the wall, sprang even higher, somersaulted, brought down the autocam with her right foot, then caught and smashed it against the floor. She moved forward again.

'There's still *this* camera,' said Candy, and she quickly pointed at her left eye.

'Not for long,' Zena told her, reaching towards Candy's face, fingers aimed at her eye.

All Candy could do was shake her head. Ever the professional, she shook it slowly so that Zena remained in focus.

'Stop!' shouted Ewart, and Zena stopped.

Grawl also obeyed, although more reluctantly. He turned towards Ewart, back-kicking the helmet of one of the prone guards as he did so, and the guard stopped writhing. Ewart hoped Grawl had managed to restrain himself. If any of the guards had died, it would be the prison planet of Arazon for him. Grawl calmly surveyed the mayhem. He looked at Zena, obviously viewing her in a new light, and he gave a brief nod. He showed no expression, he never showed any expression, but it was the first time he had acknowledged her existence, and Zena smiled at him.

Cautiously, Candy walked past Zena and towards Ewart.

'In the name of *justice*,' she said, 'I have here a summons for you, William Ewart, to appear in court *immediately*.'

During any apparently hazardous assignment, Candy or Mandy's blonde hair would become artistically dishevelled. But Candy was genuinely shaken by her encounter with Zena. A few beads of sweat speckled her face, and her hands were trembling. Ewart was the only person who knew, however, because there was no other camera to spoil her familiar confident image.

Every screen in the room displayed what was being shown across the planet: viewed through Candy's opticam, Ewart accepted the legal document. He couldn't refuse, not with the whole world watching. The warrant was printed on a piece of paper, which was not quite as anachronistic as if it had been chiselled on to stone.

It was going to be one of those days.

CHAPTER TWO

'In the name of *justice*,' said Candy, 'I have here a summons for you, William Ewart, to appear in court *immediately*.'

Joseph Abdenga was a lawyer, and the word 'justice' was unfamiliar to him. The legal system had little to do with such philosophical concepts as 'right' and 'wrong' or the metaphysical idea of 'fairness' – because how could such intangibles ever be judged?

'Have you anything to *say*, Mr Ewart?' asked Candy.

'As your lawyer, sir,' said Abdenga, 'I advise you to remain silent.'

Although it must have been very difficult for him, Ewart said nothing. He appeared relatively calm, but inside he must have been seething with anger. He glanced around his headquarters, and his image appeared on every screen.

Abdenga's mother had always told him that a career in jurisprudence meant aspiring to the summit of human achievement. There could be nothing more honourable than being part of a noble tradition which could trace its ancestry back over the centuries; there could be nothing more fulfilling than the true interpretation of complex legal statutes originally laid down when the world was divided into countless different nations, each with its own distinct laws and judicial systems.

'Let's go,' said Ewart, and he headed for the elevator shaft. He obviously didn't want to appear as if he were being coerced.

What distinguished man from the lesser animals was his ability to think, and there could be no greater challenge than defeating an opponent in a battle of mental ability – and no greater victory than that of the skilled attorney against a worthy rival. Superior intellect would always triumph over inferior thought.

'OK, Bill,' said Candy, as they rode towards the surface, 'the camera's *off*.'

Abdenga thought, Bill . . .?

'We can *talk*,' she continued. 'It's just *you* and *me*.'

In fact it was Candy and Ewart and Abdenga and Grawl and Zena and a pack of security men.

'An opticam can't be switched off,' said Ewart.

'It *can*. I don't want it on when I'm doing *intimate* things, do I?'

'I don't believe you.'

'I can make sure the camera is off, sir,' said Zena, and she leaned towards Candy.

Candy took a step back, seeking the protection of her guards. They looked at Zena, looked at Grawl, and they also moved back.

It was not only creatures without the power of

rational thought who had to settle disputes by physical violence, however. The lower ranks of society also resorted to the law of the jungle as their way of resolving arguments.

'That won't be necessary,' said Ewart.

'Hiroshi Larnvik is an *ugly, evil, rotten, scheming bastard,*' said Candy.

'What else is new?'

'Would I say *that* if he could hear me?'

'Larnvik would probably take it as a compliment.'

'I know *you* would.'

'Except I'm not ugly.'

'It was nothing *personal*, Bill. Joining Sol Global was a *career* move, that's all, a better *opportunity*.'

'Breach of contract,' said Ewart, 'plagiarism, copyright infringement, whatever else you can think of. Got that, Joe?'

The higher orders preferred to adopt the rules of civilized behaviour in their conduct with one another, using attorneys as intermediaries.

Abdenga's name was Joseph, not Joe, and he didn't like being called Joe. He had never said this to Ewart, of course, but Ewart probably knew and that was why he called him that.

'Yes, sir.'

Nothing else was said, and when they reached the surface a police skimmer was waiting. It was painted in SGN colours and adorned with the SGN logo. Because he was going to court, Ewart was allowed his lawyer; and because Ewart was Ewart, he was allowed one bodyguard. Zena climbed in with Ewart and Abdenga. Candy joined them, and the vehicle accelerated away.

Abdenga was glad Zena was there, not Grawl. He had always been intimidated by the dwarf. That was a bodyguard's function, he knew, but he had never felt physically threatened. It was as if Grawl always seemed to know what people were thinking. Perhaps that was one reason why he was so good at his job, because he could pick up hostile thoughts and therefore anticipate danger.

There was a screen inside the passenger compartment. It showed Ewart, viewed from Candy's left eye. He turned away. There was also another camera within the skimmer, because then Candy herself appeared on screen.

'This is *Candy*, reporting *live* for this Doubletime Sol Global Network Candy and Mandy all day newstime *special*! And I'm escorting famous fat felon William Ewart to *court* where his four ex-wives are eager to testify! I know they're watching right now, so is there *anything* you'd like to say to them, Mr Ewart?'

'Mr Ewart will say nothing until he is in court.'

'And *what* will he say when he's in court?'

Abdenga said nothing, and Ewart maintained his silence.

'This is a *really* exciting special day for both myself and Mandy,' Candy said, very quickly. 'It's our *first* day with Sol Global Network, the biggest and bestest communications corporation in the whole *universe*! And we want *you*, yes every one of *you*, to stick with us all day for this *very* special Candy and Mandy Sol Global "Doubletime News Show", because we can *promise* it will be very *special* indeed!'

Candy was not allowed to be silent. If there was silence for more than four seconds, if nothing exciting happened on screen for more than eight, the channel would lose a statistically significant percentage of viewers. Candy would probably prefer to lose one of her eyes – not necessarily the one with the opticam.

'And right after this very special *message*, it's over to my very good *friend* and *yours*, the person without whom the Sol Global Candy and Mandy "Doubletime News Show" would only be *half* of what it is. So stay *exactly* where you are, then *Mandy* will be here with more special *exciting* news about today's all day absolutely *unique* and totally *exclusive* Candy and Mandy *Extra*time Sol Global news show!'

The screen flared into a whirling kaleidoscope of colours which rapidly coalesced into the SGN logo. Candy leaned back and pressed the pad on the inside of her left wrist. She sighed and closed her eyes for a few seconds as she relaxed, then she looked at Zena.

'I know you were only doing your *job*,' she said, smiling. 'And I was only doing mine. Can't we be *friends?*'

Zena mirrored her smile, but a moment later it had become the smile of a predator about to pounce upon its helpless prey.

Candy slapped her wrist and was immediately alert again. 'Any *violence* perpetrated upon my person will be recorded and used in *evidence.*'

'I thought violence was good for your ratings,' said Zena.

'*Bill!*'

Abdenga knew that Zena would do nothing to Candy unless Ewart ordered her to. Until he had seen her in action against the security squad, Abdenga had assumed that her secondary function was as Ewart's medic. What other talents did she possess?

Zena turned her gaze away from Candy – and towards Abdenga. She was like Grawl. It was as if she knew he was thinking of her. He quickly looked at the screen, trying to empty his mind of all thought. The images made little sense, the words even less, but that was exactly what he needed.

Another image came into view, another blonde inanely babbling away. The exciting new very special Candy and Mandy Sol Global Network 'Doubletime News Show' seemed as frenetically vapid as the old Candy and Mandy Ewart Communications Corporation 'Doubletime News Show' – until Abdenga's attention was captured by what was behind Mandy.

He recognized the impressive room, its walls lined with endless shelves of ancient leather-bound volumes, its tables and benches made from sombre dark wood. Everything was imitation, of course, but the effect was very imposing. It was the Central Law Court.

It had always been Abdenga's ambition to work there, to spend even a few brief minutes debating a legal point, his confident voice effortlessly demolishing the arguments put forward by his learned opponent. After years and years of training, even more years and years of practising law, he had never achieved that goal. Until now.

'What!' Ewart stared at the screen, his eyes wide as the full enormity of what was happening suddenly dawned on him. 'You've got to stop this, Joe. Call Larnvik. Make any deal. He can't do this to me!'

'It's the law, sir, the due processes of law.'

'I'm not going to serve as some form of entertainment for Larnvik and Sol Global!'

'Not only must the system of law be done, sir, it must also be seen to be done.'

Ewart opened his mouth to speak again, then realized that Candy's opticam was aimed at him and that his face was back on screen. Whatever he said next would be shown in countless millions of homes throughout the solar system. Abdenga didn't need to advise him to remain silent.

The Central Law Court. Abdenga's mother would have been proud of him. She had sacrificed everything to finance her son's education and training, determined that he would achieve the success she had once dreamed of for herself. To become the best meant learning from the best, and that had been very expensive. She had been deep in debt when she died. And Abdenga was still in debt. Eighty-seven years in debt.

He was very grateful for the opportunity his mother had given him, but sometimes he wished that he hadn't been so dedicated and ambitious, because then he wouldn't have become one of the world's top lawyers – and wouldn't now be working for William Ewart.

'This is where the *judge* will be.' Mandy was gesturing around the court. 'For some reason it's known as the *bench*. And this is where the corpulent *criminal*, William

Ewart, will be. It's called the *dock*. Pity there aren't any *bars* around it!'

Ewart glanced at Abdenga, frowning. Abdenga shook his head dismissively. Mandy didn't know what she was talking about, but that had never been any handicap. Ewart wasn't an accused criminal; this was a civil case brought by his ex-wives.

In all of Abdenga's years with Ewart, this would be the first time that his employer had ever made a personal appearance in court. Although that was a reflection of Abdenga's legal ability, he felt it was a waste of his skill. It didn't take a brilliant brain to keep a man with Ewart's wealth and influence out of court; it was all a matter of delays and deals, of knowing what could be postponed and when accumulated fees and fines must finally be paid.

'And by staying tuned to *Sol Global Network* for this very special Candy and Mandy "Doubletime News Show", you won't miss a single minute of the *trial* of the *century*!'

Ewart laughed, but it didn't sound very convincing.

Assisting Ewart to evade the judicial process was not where Abdenga's true talents lay. He wanted Ewart to win in open court, where the whole world could admire the legal skills of his handsome young attorney.

Or that was what he had wanted until very recently.

'At this very moment *Candy* is escorting the overweight *crook* to court. As you have already *seen*, the Candy and Mandy "Doubletime News Show" earlier tracked down Ewart to his underground *lair*, where he was hiding away like the ugly *slug* that he is!'

33

'As Mr Ewart's lawyer,' said Abdenga, 'I must point out that your colleague's comments are defamatory, and she and her employers will be issued with a writ for libel.'

'It's only *libel*,' said Candy, 'if it isn't *true*. Can you *prove* that Ewart *isn't* an ugly slug?'

She was trying to provoke some comment from Ewart, and she succeeded.

'This is too much!' Ewart hissed; but he kept his voice low.

'"*Too much*", claims Ewart!' said Candy. She was back on screen again. 'That's not what any of your *wives* could say, is it? You didn't give them *too much*, did you?'

Abdenga had worked for Ewart for five years, eight months and sixteen days, but, because he'd been advanced extra finance during that time, his debt had only decreased by three years, two months and four days. As of today, his contract would last another eighty-seven years, three months and twenty-one days. He was unlikely to live that long, although Ewart might. And if Abdenga did live that long, it would be because Ewart had paid for his rejuve. Which would mean that he would be in debt for even longer.

'Ewart *refuses* to speak,' Candy continued, 'but you can *watch* and *listen* to this *very* special message especially for all you very special people, and because you're tuned to the Candy and Mandy "Doubletime News Show" that means you're very special *indeed*! Mandy will be right *back* right *here* on Sol Global Network. See you in *court*!'

Zena leaned forward. 'Let me inflict severe pain upon her, sir.'

Candy gasped. She shook her head, unable even to utter her warning about violence perpetrated upon her person being recorded and used in evidence.

'I am only doing my *job*,' said Zena, smiling Candy's professional smile. 'Even if I hurt you, can we not be *friends*?'

'No,' said Ewart.

Zena shrugged and leaned back.

Whatever remained of Abdenga's debt would have to be paid off by his children. That had never bothered him until recently, because such a possibility had been very remote, but now things were different. If he had children, he didn't want them to live under the same burden he'd carried all his life. Their contracts could be sold against their wishes, and they could find themselves working for someone like Ewart.

'Welcome *back*!' said Mandy. 'This is the Central Law Court, home for *today* of this the very *first* Sol Global Candy and Mandy "Doubletime News Show", where *live* and *exclusive* we are pleased to present the trial of crooked corporate and *corpulent* boss of ECC – William *fat man* Ewart!'

Ewart held back his angry words behind gritted teeth.

'It's all fair *comment*, Bill,' Candy told him. 'You've heard of *freedom* of speech?'

'Nothing is free,' Ewart muttered. 'And you're all going to pay for this!'

On screen, Mandy continued, 'You've seen where the *judge* will be, you've seen where the *criminal* will be, but

35

what – I know you're all *anxiously* asking – about the *jury*? And here is the most *exciting* news of all! Everyone who watches this terrific trial in its complete and total *entirety* right here on Sol Global Network will be entitled to *vote* for the *verdict*! Yes *you*, all you very special Candy and Mandy Sol Global "Doubletime News Show" *viewers*, you are the jury!'

Abdenga wasn't a man who was easily amazed, but he stared at the screen in amazement.

This was the ultimate achievement of human evolution? This was the reason his mother had surrendered everything she had, everything and more? This was where all his own years of effort and struggle had led him? This was the pinnacle of his profession? This . . .?

'Any *comment*?' asked Candy, as Ewart's face filled the screen. 'How do you *feel* about millions of decent, upright, law-abiding viewers giving an honest *verdict* on your *criminal* activities? The people will *choose*, and they know a *guilty* man when they see one.'

Ewart shook his head slowly, lost for words.

'As Mr Ewart's lawyer,' Abdenga managed to say, 'I must object. He is here of his own free will. He has not been arrested. He is not accused of any criminal offence.'

'Nobody asked *you*,' Candy told him. 'So shut *up*!'

Abdenga had spent years and years learning the perfect riposte to any complex argument, but 'shut up' was an expression beyond the bounds of normal legal vocabulary. The only person who had ever told him to shut up was Ewart. Those two words, however, were so precise, so commanding, that they offered no ideal rebuttal. Perhaps he would have cause to make use of them in future. While he considered the idea, he shut up.

'It seems Ewart has *nothing* to say – but not for *long*. This is *Candy* on Sol Global Network and now it's back to the other half of the "Doubletime News Show". Here's . . . *Mandy*!'

And Mandy said, 'I've just been *informed* that Candy will be arriving with her *prisoner* very very soon. Let's go and *meet* them both. Because we've got another *surprise* for fat crook Ewart. Right after this *important* message.'

The windows in the back of the skimmer had been opaqued, but Abdenga felt the vehicle start to descend. Ewart was looking at him, his puzzled expression asking what Mandy could have meant. Abdenga kept staring ahead, trying to lose himself in the screen.

The skimmer halted. The door opened. Candy started to climb out. Zena sprang forwards, quickly thrusting Candy through the doorway, then shielding Ewart by blocking the opening with her own body.

'You can't stay in there for *ever*,' said a voice which came both from the screen and from outside.

Ewart sat still for several seconds, then he stood up. Zena stepped aside, and Abdenga followed Ewart out of the police skimmer.

'This is *Mandy* for Sol Global's "Doubletime News Show". And in the *name* of the Terrestrial Taxation Authority, I have been duly *appointed* to serve *you*, William Ewart, with this *warrant* for your *arrest*. You are hereby *charged* with *cheating* and *defrauding* the *people* of this *planet* of the *legitimate* sums duly *assessed* for *payment* over the past *twenty-six* years.'

Abdenga gazed up at the solemn stone facade of the Central Law Court. After all these years, he was finally to present a case in the world's highest court.

Mandy thrust the document into Ewart's hand. He was still clutching the first summons, the one that Candy had given him. If he had known about the latter fourteen days ago, it could have been dealt with on time and he wouldn't have been here now.

Abdenga's legal training had taught him how to hide any expression, which was why he did not smile.

CHAPTER THREE

'What am I doing here?' said Ewart. 'Treated like a common criminal, brought to court in a police vehicle! Isn't there a law against that?'

'If there is not, sir, then there ought to be,' said Zena.

'Right!'

William Ewart was the second richest man in the world, but it seemed that neither his wealth nor the law could protect him from this kind of treatment. He'd have to make sure the law was changed. After all, he had the best politicians money could buy. Or he thought he had, until now. They were all in his debt, because how else would they ever have been elected without Ewart Communications Corporation persuading the public to vote for them?

When he became the richest man in the world, he'd find out who had failed him, all those who were in Larnvik's pocket. Ewart had enough dirt on each of them. Today's audience for Sol Global Network would be nothing in comparison. Ewart Communications

Corporation's ratings would soar when all the misdeeds of those who had let him down were revealed. Revealed and exposed. Literally.

If he became the richest man in the world . . .

The SGN logo was on every wall. This was Larnvik's court, or as good as. Ewart looked around the courtroom to see if his rival was in the public gallery. There were always a few crazies who personally attended shows such as sports events, and a trial was just another type of entertainment.

There was no sign of him. Larnvik would be enjoying Ewart's ordeal from the comfort of his own satellite – just as millions, billions, of others throughout the solar system would be watching from their own homes. Sol Global Network had made sure of that, abandoning their usual schedules and devoting many of their prime stations to Ewart's court appearance.

'It's absurd expecting me to pay taxes like everyone else,' said Ewart. 'And it's not even the *same* tax as everyone else. They expect me to pay *more*. I should pay *less*. I should pay *nothing*.'

'You do pay nothing, sir,' said Zena. 'That is why you are here.'

'They don't realize I need all my income for reinvestment. I'm a wealth creator. I employ thousands and thousands and thousands of people. They get paid for their work, and they pass on part of their income as tax. The government only gets that money because of me. Right?'

'Pay?' asked Zena. 'People who work for you get paid?'

'I pay those whose contracts I don't own. I have to. And I've donated enough to politicians over the years. That's the same as paying tax. As for my wives, my wives! They've already had plenty from me, all they could ever need, while I was unlucky enough to be married to them.'

Ewart gazed impatiently around the court again.

'Is there nothing you can do, sir?' asked Zena.

'It's all up to Abdenga,' Ewart told her. 'He's with the judge, trying to make a deal with the prosecution.'

'I did not mean that, sir.' Zena nodded towards the datadek which Ewart clutched in his left hand. 'You say that wherever you are is the headquarters of Ewart Communications Corporation. I know, sir, you are concerned about whether today's commercial arrangements are proceeding according to schedule. Can you not find out what is happening?'

'If I could, I would, but the whole court is screened. I can't get any information in or out.'

Ewart stared over at where Candy, or perhaps Mandy, was standing on the judge's bench as she set the scene for the trial. Sol Global had no problem getting information out and sending it all across the solar system.

But where was Mandy, or perhaps Candy?

'She's in with the judge!' Ewart realized. Everyone in the world, in every world, could hear what was being said. Except him!

'Try to relax, sir,' Zena told him.

'Relax, relax! How can I relax?'

Zena took Ewart's right wrist, studying his biocount, then reached for the medpack. Although the fix improved the readings, he didn't feel as though it had.

Ewart was also screened. The court allowed him private discussion with his lawyer without it being picked up by the prosecution. Or by Candy and Mandy. So far, his only discussion had been with Zena.

Communications was Ewart's business, and it was so strange being unable to communicate, to know instantly what was happening anywhere, everywhere. With his datadek blank, he felt as if he'd been deprived of one of his senses.

It was impossible not to think about the financial conflict which was going on at this very moment, the battle between his corporate empire and Larnvik's. Without any doubt, Larnvik had arranged for Ewart to be dragged here, depriving the general of direct control over his troops. His campaign was already planned in every detail, however, with reinforcements standing by for every eventuality. For a while at least.

'Larnvik knew I'd make my move today,' said Ewart. 'I've been betrayed.'

'You said you had told no one, sir. No one except me.'

'You knew most of it, but lots of other people knew small pieces of what would happen. All Larnvik needed to do was add a few of those pieces together.' Ewart shook his head. 'I can't trust anyone.' He glanced around the court again. 'Bringing me here, that's a really dirty trick.'

Until now, there had always been a tacit truce between Ewart and Larnvik. Hostilities occasionally broke out, and every ECC salvo would be matched by a broadside from SGN. But they seldom resorted to direct personal attacks on each other, despite all the ammunition each of them had accumulated over the years. This was different. Larnvik had crossed the line, and Ewart would fight back. It was war, total war.

'I'll get him,' he muttered.

'You will, sir.'

When Ewart Communications wiped out Sol Global, he'd still go for Larnvik. Their professional rivalry would be over, but their personal hatred would continue.

But what if Sol Global fought off the assault, what if Ewart Communications were defeated?

'I'll still get him.'

'You will, sir.'

Ewart sighed and stretched. 'How long's this going to take?'

'The course of the law is never swift, sir,' Zena said. 'This was especially the case – no pun intended, sir – in earlier times, when proceedings could last for days and days, sometimes even weeks or months. The reason for this becomes evident – again no pun intended, sir – when one discovers that lawyers were paid by the hour.'

At least live transmission had dramatically – no pun intended, thought Ewart – cut the length of court cases. Trials were held in a series of brief segments timed to fit with the 'important messages' in between. Advertisers and audiences wanted a fast trial and a quick verdict, interspersed with interviews with the accused and witnesses, the lawyers and expert commentators, members of the jury and anyone else who happened to be around.

It wasn't only the lawyers who did the cross-examining. Viewer competitions were held to find more interesting questions, and these need have no particular relevance to the case. Even the prosecuting attorney could be summoned into the witness box and interrogated on any subject. Because they were on oath to answer correctly, perjury could lead to the judge administering summary punishment.

Once upon a time, a judge might have issued an order of forfeiture, the confiscation of the guilty party's goods and chattels. Now anyone in court might be punished by a forfeit: commanded to sing a song or perform a feat of acrobatics or discard a certain number of garments . . .

Allowing the entire audience to be the jury was a natural progression, Ewart supposed.

Serious crimes were never tried at the Central Law Court. They were dealt with in a more serious, and secret, fashion. But the real criminals were never tried at all. People like the government officials responsible for Ewart being here.

'Women,' he said.

'Sir?'

'Women have always been my downfall. Married women. The women I've married. Why do I have to spoil things by marrying them? It's always caused problems. Problems? An understatement. That's why I'm here now. Because I got married. If there had been no marriages, there would have been no divorces, no problems. I'm just an incurable romantic.'

'Yes, sir, you are.'

'If I'm ever about to make another marriage proposal, you must stop me. Right?'

'Yes, sir.'

'Four wives is enough. More than enough. I should have learned from my mistakes.'

'Five, sir. You have been married five times.'

'Right.' Ewart hadn't been at his latest wedding, so it was easy to forget. 'That was different, a business arrangement.'

'But your new bride is on her way here.'

At least she wasn't someone who used to work for him, which was how he'd met the other four. They were all parasites, only wanted him for his money.

That was the only reason Ewart had married again, he realized: for the assets which his new wife's father could put at the disposal of Ewart Communications Corporation. But it hadn't worked out like that, or so it seemed from the message he'd received earlier. He had a bride but not her dowry. Whatever happened, Ewart always lost out when it came to marriage.

'If she has to travel a hundred light years, when will she arrive?'

'The binary system of Algol is ninety-five light years away, sir. The timing of your new bride's arrival depends upon when she began her journey.'

'Right.'

Ewart couldn't remember her name, but he always had that problem with his wives. Perhaps he'd never known it. He knew why he had married her, but what was her reason for the nuptials? Or rather, what did her father get out of the deal? This was something he hadn't thought of until now.

It was a long time since he'd had nothing else to do except think, and he didn't like the direction his thoughts were taking him.

The door to the judge's chambers opened. Abdenga and the other attorney were visible within. They were shaking hands. That was a good sign. They must have negotiated a satisfactory agreement. Then Ewart realized they weren't shaking hands. They were holding hands.

He doubted that this was usual legal procedure, but perhaps Abdenga had applied unorthodox tactics in order to make a deal with the prosecution.

The two lawyers emerged into the courtroom, their fingers no longer intertwined. Ewart hadn't paid any attention to the other attorney until now, but he had to admit that she did look particularly attractive in her traditional black robes. Her cloak swirled around her body as she walked, first hiding and then revealing her long lithe limbs, and her hair was covered by a white wig. He wondered what she looked like without the robes, the cloak, the wig . . . and everything else.

Perhaps after this was all over, he should buy up her contract. That would be one way of finding out. What had made him take on someone like Abdenga when he could have employed a desirable young woman instead?

'Sir?' said Abdenga.

Then Ewart remembered where he was and why he was here. If it weren't for having a male lawyer working for him, he would probably have reached his sixth wife by now. And five of them would be against him today.

'You've fixed it?' Ewart rose to his feet. 'I can go?'

Abdenga shook his head. 'No, sir.'

Ewart hadn't really expected a postponement, or that he could walk away after paying a fine, but there was no harm in hoping.

'What's the deal?' he asked.

'A combined trial, sir. Your first four wives for alimony, the tax authorities for all their various claims against you.'

'What? But there's no connection between them.'

'There is, sir. Both sides want money from you.'

It didn't make sense, not from a judicial point of view, but Ewart recognized that it would make a good Sol Global Network Candy and Mandy 'Doubletime News Show'.

'That's the best you can get?'

'Yes, sir.'

'How long before I'm out of here?'

'The case will be concluded today, sir.'

'That's not what I asked, Joe. How long before I'm out of here?' He stared at Abdenga. 'I *do* get out of here, don't I?'

'The tax charges are very serious, sir.'

'I can pay,' said Ewart.

That wasn't true. Most of what Ewart intended to say today wouldn't be true. At one time, every word spoken in court was subject to verification, but the system was stopped. Some said it was because ensuring that witnesses were always honest was an infringement of their natural liberties; others claimed that trutests were

47

halted because they could be fixed. Ewart believed they'd been banned because lawyers would have become redundant.

All his wealth was tied up in his diverse enterprises. Even assuming his wives accepted that they could not claim more than he was worth, it would take some time to raise the minimum necessary to pay off all the various claims against him.

By the end of today, perhaps, time might be all that was left to him.

That was one small consolation. If Larnvik emerged victorious, then Ewart would never have to pay his grasping ex-wives or the tax vultures anything. Because he wouldn't have anything.

'Payment may not be enough, sir,' said Abdenga. 'The prosecution is demanding a custodial sentence.'

'Prison!'

'It would only be a nominal sentence, sir.'

Abdenga gazed across the court to where the prosecuting counsel was being interviewed by Candy or Mandy. In the years that he had worked for Ewart, Abdenga had never shown a trace of emotion and his expression had always remained impassive. There was only a subtle difference now, and Ewart couldn't make out exactly what it was, but Abdenga had changed.

Had he made a deal with Larnvik, agreed to provide a more dramatic court case for Sol Global? If Ewart couldn't trust his own lawyer, who could he trust?

'What if I plead guilty instead? If I do, there's no trial, no show. Tell them that, get a better deal. I'm not serving time! What have I done to deserve that?'

'William Ewart, you're finally in *court* where you *belong*. Have you any last *words*, any more *lies*, before you're sworn in and are legally *obliged* to speak the *truth*?'

After Candy and Mandy had been biotechnically altered for the 'Doubletime News Show', Ewart had never been able to tell them apart. Not even when they were both in bed with him.

He ignored her, but Zena stared at her so fiercely that she took a step backwards. Zena glanced at Ewart, silently repeating her earlier request to inflict severe pain.

The idea was tempting, because Candy and Mandy were also traitors. Ewart looked at all the surrounding cameras, then shook his head. Pounding half of the 'Doubletime News Show' to a pulp was likely to create a bad impression on the jury.

'All rise,' announced the court usher. 'The Central Law Court is now in session, his honour Judge Solomon presiding.'

Ewart stood up. This was the way it was going to be, he realized. They were all here. His four previous wives. The government and the Terrestrial Taxation Authority. Larnvik and Sol Global Network. Candy and Mandy. The prosecuting counsel and perhaps even Abdenga. And they were all against him.

He was used to it, because this was how it had always been. The whole world was against him. The whole galaxy.

They didn't stand a chance.

CHAPTER FOUR

'Let's go,' said Ewart.

'Sir?' said Abdenga.

'We're leaving.'

'We're leaving?'

'Is there an echo in here?'

'Sir?'

'Never mind. Come on.'

The court was in recess, and Ewart had requested a natural break of his own. Abdenga had been under great stress all morning, but at least now he could relieve the pressure on his bladder. Two guards made up their escort, guiding them deep beneath the court. Zena was also with them, and for a moment Abdenga thought she would remain on personal guard duty while he and Ewart availed themselves of the facilities. But after giving the place a security check, she'd returned to the corridor.

She was standing there when Ewart and Abdenga walked out. The two guards were also in the corridor, but they were no longer standing. They lay prone and motionless.

'That way, sir,' said Zena, nodding in the opposite direction from which they had first come.

'The other way, sir,' said Abdenga. 'Lunch is being served next to the courtroom.'

'You think I'm going to eat the kind of food they have here?' said Ewart, as he began walking in the direction Zena had indicated.

Was he intending to go out for a meal? He couldn't do that. And even if he wanted to, he was going the wrong way.

Then Abdenga suddenly realized what was happening: Ewart was escaping!

'You can't leave, sir,' he said. 'That's contempt of court.'

'Contempt of court!' Ewart didn't look back. 'What about contempt of me? I've been treated with nothing but contempt all morning.'

Zena hadn't moved. She was waiting for Abdenga to follow Ewart – and also blocking the lawyer's route back to court.

Abdenga watched Ewart getting further and further away. He couldn't go with him. That would mean breaking the law, aiding and abetting an attempted escape. It would only be attempted, he knew, because Ewart couldn't possibly get away.

There must have been spycams in the corridor. Zena's immobilization of the guards had been witnessed, and Ewart's escape attempt was being watched at this very moment.

'As your lawyer, sir,' Abdenga raised his voice for the benefit of the recording which was inevitably being made, 'I strongly advise against this course of action. It would be best for all concerned if you returned to court immediately.'

'As your employer, Joe, I strongly advise you to come with me.'

Zena had been staring at Abdenga all this time, and now she gestured for him to follow Ewart. Having seen what she was capable of, there seemed no alternative but to do as he was ordered. The evidence would clearly show that he was being forced to accompany his employer. He hurried to catch up, with Zena close behind.

'You should return now, sir,' he said, once he reached Ewart. It was obvious to anyone watching that he was trying to convince him to go back. 'You can testify that you took the wrong turning. It's not too late.'

'Left here, sir,' said Zena, from behind them.

'It is too late, Joe.'

Ewart's tone of voice and his expression made Abdenga realize that he wasn't referring to the court case. Something important had been happening today, something very important to both Ewart and Hiroshi Larnvik, which was why the latter must have wanted his rival kept incommunicado. The best place for that was the Central Law Court.

Abdenga didn't approve of the due processes of law being manipulated for the purpose of commercial gain, but in this case he was prepared to make an exception.

He and Miss Yasmerel had their own reason for

facilitating Ewart's court appearance: it seemed the only chance Abdenga would ever have of changing his employer. Although she sometimes worked as a public attorney, Miss Yasmerel was sponsored by Sol Global Network. After today's successful prosecution, she would ensure that Larnvik bid for Abdenga's contract. Ewart couldn't refuse to release him. He didn't own Abdenga, not totally; his terms of employment were supervised by his guild.

Abdenga and his true love would then be together. Always.

But things weren't going according to plan. It was Abdenga who was supposed to be escaping from Ewart, not Ewart escaping from court.

'It's never too late, sir.'

'I've been betrayed.'

'Who would do a thing like that?'

Ewart glanced at him. 'Everyone.'

'I'm sure you're wrong, sir,' said Abdenga, in what he hoped was the convincing manner which he'd spent years learning.

He thought of what Candy had said earlier, that joining Sol Global was a career move. She wanted a better opportunity, that it was nothing personal. But in Abdenga's case it was personal: he hated Ewart. He was sure he wasn't unique. Almost everyone who had dealings with Ewart came to hate him. As for his wives . . .

Abdenga almost shuddered as he remembered some of their testimony against their ex-husband. He felt guilty because of the part he had played in this. Almost his first task for Ewart was to handle the divorce of his fourth wife, Karis, and to persuade her lawyer to accept the unacceptable terms.

'Right here, sir,' said Zena.

Ewart turned. Abdenga turned. Zena followed.

Where were the other court security guards?

Because Miss Yasmerel had convinced Abdenga to help all of Ewart's unfortunate wives by bringing their plight to public attention, he'd finally been able to make up for the settlement imposed on Karis. He hadn't known about the equally imminent tax case, however, although Miss Yasmerel was fully briefed. It was odd that she'd neglected to tell him.

And what would Miss Yasmerel think if Abdenga were arrested for aiding Ewart's attempted escape? She wouldn't wish to be associated with him ever again. Why did this have to happen now? By the end of the day's proceedings, Abdenga had hoped that their relationship would have advanced towards its next stage of intimacy. Miss Yasmerel had been truly magnificent in court today. He was as awed by her commanding legal skills as he was overwhelmed by her total femininity.

'This morning's proceedings have all been one-sided, sir,' said Abdenga. 'Things may appear bad, but you haven't heard my defence yet.'

'And it's too late for that, Joe.'

'But my line of argument will be totally devastating. The jury will inevitably be swayed to your side. You'll be awarded costs and damages, I assure you.'

Ewart believed that he was the centre of the universe, and he never spared a thought for anyone else. He had done exactly what he wanted all his life. Because no one had ever stopped him, he assumed that he could get away with anything. This time, however, he would be stopped. He couldn't ignore the jurisdiction of the supreme court, and he deserved everything that was coming to him.

Abdenga glanced back along the corridor, but all he could see was Zena. Where did Ewart think he was going? There could be no exit down here, deep beneath the Central Law Court.

'Stop, sir,' said Zena. 'Stay where you are.'

Ewart halted, so did Abdenga. Zena walked past them, reaching out to touch the wall.

'Turn around, sir. And you, Mr Abdenga.'

They both turned, and a second later came what sounded like a handclap and a sudden gust of wind blew past them. But Abdenga knew no one had begun to applaud, and neither was there a fresh breeze down here. He looked around. There was a neat circular hole in the wall, approximately one metre across, through which he could see daylight.

To add to his current list of offences, Ewart had now added that of damaging government property. The Central Law Court was an important building. Defacing it was a serious felony. It must have been. No one had ever done it before. Nor had anyone ever escaped from here before.

Ewart moved towards the wall, then stopped, carefully studying the opening. While he paused, Zena brushed the dirt and dust from his shoulders. A hand reached through from the other side, beckoning, and

Ewart made his way out of the new exit.

'This way, Mr Abdenga,' said Zena.

Abdenga ducked through the hole in the wall. The spycams would show that he had no choice. If the cams were operating. The whole building was supposedly secure, but that hadn't deterred Ewart. If anyone could breach the court's comscreen, then it was the owner of a communications corporation, and his allies on the outside knew exactly where to locate him on the inside.

But it seemed that Grawl was the only one on the outside.

Abdenga stepped out into the open, joining Ewart and Grawl, and Zena followed him. He stared around. They were at the back of the Central Law Court. The building was relatively isolated from most others in the capital, partly because that gave it a more impressive appearance, partly because the government could only afford locations in the cheaper areas of the metropolis.

He felt very vulnerable. The four fugitives must have been the focus of countless official spycams and Sol Global Network autocams. The eyes of the whole galaxy were upon them.

There were a number of people crossing the open square, but they paid no attention to what was going on. Hadn't they seen the wall being breached? Where were the security squads from the court? Where were the city police?

And why was Grawl carrying an illegal weapon . . .?

Abdenga felt a sudden chill. He didn't know precisely what type of gun it was, or its exact lethal capabilities, but he didn't need to. It was enough to know that possession of such off-world armament was a very serious offence.

Grawl began walking across the square, not even trying to hide the weapon, and nobody seemed to notice.

'Come on, Joe,' said Ewart, as he followed his bodyguard.

Abdenga looked at Zena. Zena looked at Abdenga. Abdenga looked at the hole in the court wall. Zena shook her head. They kept looking at each other, then Abdenga turned and followed the other two. He didn't move as fast as they did, hoping to stay further back so that the police would know he wasn't really with them. Then he felt Zena's hand on his back, propelling him forward, and he increased his pace.

Grawl was moving rapidly across the open, his short legs taking long strides, and Ewart kept close behind. By the time he caught up with them, Abdenga was almost out of breath. Ewart was known as 'the fat man' by his enemies, which meant almost everyone. He was certainly overweight, but it seemed that he was also much fitter than a slimmer man less than half his age – a man such as Abdenga.

Abdenga kept gazing around, wondering when he would be rescued.

Or, he thought, would he also be arrested?

Then he realized that he didn't want an attempt to stop Ewart. Because if anyone tried to prevent the escape, Grawl would have no hesitation in using his weapon. Discharging such powerful armament could lead to only one thing: imprisonment. There would probably also be some casualties.

If Grawl killed anyone, Abdenga would become an accessory to murder. He'd end up on Arazon. As a lawyer stranded on a penal planet, he wouldn't last long.

He slowed down again, and Zena pushed him forward again.

Despite what the spycams might show, their evidence was not allowed in court. The camera could lie, and it often did.

Would he be allowed to defend himself? Or perhaps he could persuade Miss Yasmerel to be his defence counsel. But would she be willing to defend him – or would she prefer to be the prosecutor?

It probably wouldn't come to a trial. If Grawl started shooting, the authorities would respond with over-whelming firepower. In their case such armament was legal. Abdenga could get injured, seriously injured. Perhaps even fatally, which was the most serious injury of all.

Yesterday his life had been so simple. Today he might not even have a life.

He glanced up and all around, searching for armed police and security guards and space troops and combat mercenaries. But apart from the various passers-by, there was no sign of anyone.

'Sir,' he panted, as a terrible thought occurred to him, 'why has no one tried to stop you? Don't you think it's very strange?'

'That's all been taken care of, Joe.'

'But what if it's Larnvik, sir? This could be what he wants.'

Ewart glanced at him for the first time.

'A live court breakout!' said Abdenga.

Ewart's eyes widened and he smiled, instinctively looking around for the cameras. He thrived on publicity, and every day ECC transmitted news and features about its owner's activities, no matter how mundane. But the record for longest continuous appearance by a media magnate was now held by Sol Global Network: the trial of their rival, William Ewart.

'Right,' he said. 'This is far more dramatic than sitting in court answering stupid questions.'

'Being killed is very dramatic, sir,' Abdenga agreed.

'Killed?' Ewart frowned. It was as if he didn't understand the word. He shook his head.

'Think of it this way, sir: wouldn't you prefer a world without Larnvik?'

Ewart didn't answer.

'And wouldn't he prefer a world without you?'

Ewart still didn't answer, but he slowed his pace slightly, gazing around anxiously.

'As your lawyer, sir, I advise you to stop where you are, tell Grawl to put down the gun, and then we should all wait here until we are taken into custody. It's the only safe option.'

'I've never played safe in my life,' said Ewart. 'You expect me to surrender, to give up everything?'

Ewart had lost everything, but Abdenga didn't say so. He knew any advice would be ignored, although that wouldn't normally have stopped him offering it. It was his function to make recommendations. The only thing which did stop him was that he couldn't think of any

59

constructive suggestion. His mind was too busy considering other things. Trivial matters such as life and death. His own life and death.

What if he simply turned and ran away? Zena had better things to do than chase after him, even though she would inevitably catch him in a few strides. And Grawl wouldn't risk a charge of murder in order to stop him, stop him permanently. Would he . . .?

Logically, Abdenga knew he should make an escape bid of his own. But logic had nothing to do with what was happening. His limbs refused to obey. Breathing heavily, damp with sweat, he continued walking by Ewart's side. Grawl led the way. Zena followed.

They reached the far side of the square, Grawl leading them beneath a towering inverted silver pyramid. Abdenga felt slightly less exposed in the shadows, but he knew the feeling was illusory.

'Look,' said Ewart.

A Ewart Communications Corporation infocore was set into the side of the overhanging silver wall, and Ewart stopped in front of it.

'Let's read some honest, unbiased news,' he said, reaching into the pocket of his jacket.

Abdenga thought he was searching for a coin, but instead he produced a piece of twisted plastal. He glanced over his shoulder to make sure he wasn't being watched, but that was pointless: the entire solar system was probably watching.

'Let me pay, sir,' said Abdenga, anxiously hunting for a coin.

Coins were a recent reintroduction to the world.

Electronic payment, by whatever means of credit identification, was so easily nixed that a safer method had to
be found for minor purchases. But even that was too
simple for Ewart.

'I own this, Joe,' said Ewart, as he slid the plastal into
the coin slot. 'I'm not paying for it.'

At least being on the move had given the impression
that they were getting somewhere. Zena and Grawl
didn't seem bothered about the delay. They both
appeared as calm as ever, although their eyes were
never still.

'Sir,' said Abdenga, offering a coin.

'And I own you, Joe, which means that's my money.'

Abdenga was already constructing a defence – there
could be no crime if Ewart stole from himself – when he
realized that breaking into an infocore would come very
far down the list of Ewart's offences.

'I'm glad that some people still bother to read,' said
Ewart, carefully turning the plastal loop. 'These cores
run at a loss, but I don't mind. If I cater for enough
minorities, they add up to the majority.'

Ewart never subsidized any of his enterprises,
Abdenga was sure. If any division failed to make enough
money, it was ruthlessly sacrificed.

'There!' said Ewart, triumphantly, as the infocore spat
the thumbnail-sized newsbit into his palm.

Abdenga watched as he slipped the bit into his pocket
without even activating it. He hadn't wanted it at all, he
just wanted to prove that he could still tap into the core
without paying.

Grawl suddenly brought up the gun, aimed, fired.

There was a brief hiss, a flare of light a hundred metres away, and what must have been an autocam disintegrated.

'Time to go,' said Ewart.

Grawl fired again, again, again, each time shooting at different points around the pyramid. White light blazed, dimmed, blazed, dimmed, blazed, dimmed, and three spycams were no more.

Abdenga heard a noise to the right, and a security squad appeared around the angled side of the silver building. Grawl shot at them. They disappeared, retreating into the shadows. Grawl had aimed above their heads, otherwise their disappearance would have been permanent.

'This way, sir,' said Zena, pointing in the opposite direction.

She and Ewart headed towards the left. Grawl destroyed a few more cameras, aimed a few more bursts in the approximate direction of the guards. Abdenga started to raise his hands in surrender, then Grawl looked at him.

'Autocam!' Abdenga explained, raising his right hand even higher, lowering the left.

Grawl glanced up, fired in the direction Abdenga was pointing. Another hiss, another burst of white. Abdenga stared in astonishment: there *had* been another autocam.

The worst place he could possibly be was between Grawl and the security men, which was exactly where he was. He couldn't trust the former, and it probably wasn't such a good idea to rely on the latter. At least the bodyguard was a known risk, and so he hurried after Ewart and Zena.

Grawl shot down two other approaching autocams, sprayed the guards once more, then followed. They ran between buildings, down walkways, over bridges, under ramps. Grawl kept shooting, and Abdenga became even more out of breath. He was soaked·with sweat, his heart raced, his whole body ached. He felt as if his legs were about to give way beneath him, and he half hoped they would. Then Zena was behind him, pushing him on.

It seemed forever until they reached the skimmers, but was probably only a minute or two. Grawl shot out the spycams around the bay in which the three craft were hidden. Two of these were police vehicles, the other an ambulance. One of the former was decorated with the ECC logo, the other two were in SGN colours. Because they had their own motive units, these were almost the only kind of vehicles which couldn't be grounded if the capital's transport beams were cut.

Zena thumped her fist on the side of the SGN cop craft. The first decoy accelerated away, arrowing upwards. Grawl fired at the police squad which suddenly arrived on the opposite corner, then at the security crew who had been chasing them. They all vanished. Temporarily.

'Right,' someone shouted, 'I'll hold them!' A dark shape appeared from the shadows fifty metres away.

Abdenga knew the voice but couldn't place it.

'Get going, you fat bastard!' shouted the figure. He ran diagonally across to the opposite building, taking a line halfway between the encroaching pursuers.

That was when Abdenga recognized him. He was

thinner than ever before, but he was William Ewart.

Except that Ewart was standing next to Abdenga, looking very baffled as he watched himself dive out of sight. This was evidently another type of decoy. The real Ewart glanced towards Grawl, nodding his approval. Grawl looked at Zena. She shrugged, then sent the ambulance on its way. It zoomed up into the air.

The only escape vehicle left was the one with Ewart Communications Corporation identification marks. The only way it could have appeared more distinctive was if a picture of Ewart had been emblazoned on every surface.

Zena opened the rear door for Ewart, who climbed in as casually as if he were entering his own limousine. She raised the driver's hatch. Grawl backed towards the craft, slowly surveying the whole area as he did so. The ersatz Ewart seemed to have drawn all attention away from the escapees. Grawl reached the hatch and started to climb in. He paused, stared all around one final time, glanced at Zena, then threw her the gun. She caught it and smiled. The hatch retracted. Zena looked at Abdenga.

He shook his head. He wasn't going. He couldn't go. He couldn't leave Miss Yasmerel, not before extending their relationship beyond a professional handshake. It was the only physical contact they had ever shared, but her touch had promised so much.

Without Miss Yasmerel life was not worth living.

Zena nodded her head, then suddenly raised the weapon.

But without a life he could do no living.

Abdenga dived into the skimmer.

Zena fired, and another autocam erupted into a ball of white flame. She sprang into the skimmer, braced herself in the open doorway and continued shooting as the craft sped off.

Abdenga kept his eyes closed and remained motionless, waiting for his breathing and his pulse to return to normal. He tried to blank his mind, not to think about what had happened and what was happening and what would happen. It was impossible, because he could never stop thinking, but one question was paramount.

'Where are we going, sir?' he asked.

Ewart pointed upwards.

'The Moon?'

Abdenga had lived on the Moon when he was first employed by Ewart. Ewart would be safe there. The Moon had its own laws, and there was no extradition treaty.

'Further,' said Ewart.

'Further?' said Abdenga.

'Is there an echo in here, too?'

'Sir?'

'It's a joke, Joe. I know there's no echo. But when you repeated what I said, it was as if there was. Right?'

Something was seriously wrong with Ewart. He'd never been the kind of man who would make a humorous remark. Even if he were, circumstances such as these were entirely inappropriate. The events of the day must have seriously unbalanced him.

Abdenga had already suspected that, however,

because no one in his right mind would have attempted to escape.

'You said "Further", then I said "Further?". Yes, that was almost like an echo. I see what you mean, sir. Very amusing.'

But then Abdenga realized what Ewart meant by 'further' – and he wasn't at all amused.

PART TWO

Lunch

Space

CHAPTER FIVE

Ewart soon became so fed up with Father Ahmed Lamakinto that he had the missionary locked up.

'I'm a reasonable man, and I tried to be reasonable with him. That was my mistake. He doesn't know the meaning of the word "reason". How could he? What he does is based on the exact opposite. Superstition and irrationality, that's all religion is. Faith? Faith! That means believing in something which doesn't exist. Maybe he can't help being unreasonable, but at least he could have been polite. You think he'd be grateful for everything I've done for him. Instead, all I get is condemnation and abuse. Criticizing me for my wealth, but he wouldn't he here if it weren't for my money and influence. Wealth? Wealth! United Religions of Terra is probably the richest organization in the world. And they've been around long enough to own most of it, buying up the planet with all the donations they've received from gullible followers over the years. I've had plenty of dealings with URT. They were one of my biggest advertisers, always demanded a massive discount. Lamakinto thinks because I'm giving him a free ride that he can squeeze even more from me. That's all he does, all any of them ever do. Take, take, take. He's taken advantage of my generosity and good nature. But what did I expect?'

'You must relax, sir,' said Zena, as she checked his biocount and reached into her medpack. 'You need not see him again. You must forget him.'

'Right,' Ewart agreed, then he shook his head. 'No, I don't need a fix. I can handle this myself. Why did I bring him? I should have known, should have remembered. God! No, not God – forget I said that! And I don't want to hear any mention of United Religions of Terra again, right?'

'Yes, sir.'

'And you, stop that!' Ewart glared at the third occupant of his stateroom. 'I don't want you to record *everything* I say and do!'

'Total filming is essential,' said the auteur, 'otherwise something which is very important and significant may be missed.'

'If that happens,' said Ewart. 'I can repeat it for you, right?'

'That won't be one hundred per cent true.'

'Ninety-nine per cent will do,' said Ewart, who knew that the word 'true' was not an absolute. 'You can leave now.'

The man turned and left the room.

'What is "film"?' Ewart wondered. 'What does "auteur" mean?' Before Zena could answer, he added:

'No, I don't really want to know.'

He glanced at the door through which the man had gone. He'd already forgotten what he looked like; and even before that, he couldn't remember his name. His job was to be anonymous, Ewart supposed, to blend into the background so that no one was aware of his presence or what he was doing. He was making a film of the voyage on behalf of the Ewart Foundation, the charitable organization in whose ship Ewart was now travelling. Or escaping.

Ewart had made a fortune through the latest in communications technology, but he didn't want cams tracking him all the time. He preferred the human touch. Someone totally human, without even an opti-cam where one of their eyes should have been.

'You won't even know I'm here,' the man had said, and somehow it was true.

He had been present when Ewart first met Lamakinto, when Ewart expected to be thanked; but the priest had been far too arrogant for that.

'You can't stand it when you lose an argument,' he'd claimed, as Grawl hauled him away. 'You've surrounded yourself with sycophants for too long. None of them ever dares say "no" to you. You're a bad loser, Ewart.'

Ewart always thought that was an odd phrase. Of course he was a bad loser. What was the point of being a good loser? He hated losing, he wasn't used to it, and now he had made his biggest loss of all. He'd lost everything; he'd lost Ewart Communications Corporation.

Taking on Larnvik and Sol Global Network had been the greatest gamble of Ewart's career, but it was an essential risk. Ewart Communications Corporation was stretched to the very limit. It had substantial assets, but far more was owed in loans and debts, none of which could ever be repaid until new resources were acquired. That was why Ewart had needed extra capital to finance his latest venture – and why he'd married again.

And because there was a strong chance that his assault upon SGN would be repulsed, he'd made arrangements for a civilized retreat.

Ewart had a spaceship. This was a recent acquisition, although technically it was owned by the Ewart Foundation. He had called it the *Demon Star*, which was one of the old names for the Algol system. It was the least he could do, the ship having been paid for by his fifth wife's dowry. Or so he'd thought. Another ancient name for Beta Persei was *Winking Demon*, but he'd decided that might not be appropriate.

'Look at that,' said Ewart, gazing up at the huge screen and the spectacular view which it presented. 'We're out in deep space, heading for the stars. Isn't that amazing?'

'Yes, sir,' said Zena. 'It is amazing.'

Ewart looked at her, remembering what Lamakinto had said earlier. 'You don't have to agree with me.'

'Sir?'

'If I say something you disagree with, you can argue with me.'

'Why should I disagree with you?'

'Just because I say something, that doesn't mean it's right, does it?'

'No, sir.'

'You're just saying that because it's what you think I want you to say. Aren't you?'

Zena didn't reply. Because, thought Ewart, she didn't know how he wanted her to reply.

'If I say something wrong,' he told her, 'you should tell me.'

'How would I know if you are wrong, sir?'

'Because you know so much, that's how. If I say something that isn't right, you should say so. I don't want you to agree with me all the time. Say "no" sometimes. Understand?'

'No.'

'No?' He glanced at her.

Zena smiled. 'I am disagreeing with you, sir.'

He looked at the screen again, still very impressed even though it was a simulation. The only reason stars twinkled that way was because they were seen through a planetary atmosphere. Even so, the screen conveyed a truly magnificent vision of the infinite. It was far better than the real view: nothing could be seen beyond the *Demon Star*, in fact, because it was now travelling through falspace.

As he gazed at the galaxy, Ewart shivered for a moment.

'Do you ever get the feeling you've been here before?' he asked.

'You mean *déjà vu*, sir?'

'Do I?'

'If you mean you are in an unfamiliar situation but you sense you have previously experienced exactly that place and time, yes.'

73

'Right.'

'No, sir.'

The strange sensation faded away. He had felt it several times before, but this was unique. He knew he'd never been here, on this ship, embarking upon the experience of a lifetime.

William Ewart was on a leisurely expedition across the universe. And Hiroshi Larnvik had been left to pick up the bill.

He stared at the small sample of the galaxy's three hundred billion stars. Ten billion galaxies. Or was it the other way around?

'What's it all for, Zena? Why are we here? What's the purpose of life?'

Zena said nothing. She must have presumed the question was rhetorical. Although if there was a proven answer, she'd have been able to tell him.

'I know the purpose of my life. Lamakinto told me.'

'What did he tell you, sir?'

Because Zena had been carrying out a security check on the ship, Grawl was on guard duty when Ewart first met the priest. Hadn't there also been a fourth person in the stateroom? Who was it? Then Ewart remembered: it was the auteur.

'He told me,' said Ewart, 'that I was driven to make money because I was searching for something else. I thought he was going to tell me what it was, because I've always wondered. But apparently it was all God's idea, and I was part of his One Great Plan. I became rich so that I could buy a spaceship and take Lamakinto on his vital missionary work to a heathen world. If only I'd known! One minute he berates me for my wealth, the next he says that my whole purpose in life was to become wealthy and give him a free ride!'

Zena stepped closer to Ewart and checked his bio-count.

'Relax, right, I know,' said Ewart. 'It's impossible, it has to be, but ... what if he's right? What if this is my destiny?' He gazed at the star-speckled screen again. 'We must all have a purpose in life. That's why we exist.'

'The human race exists in order to procreate, sir, to produce the next generation which will then in turn reproduce itself.'

Ewart continued watching the viewscreen; he could have stared at it for hours.

'Like the lowest of the animals?' he said. 'Is that all we are? We have no other function apart from the biological one?'

'What function would you like, sir?'

'I don't know, but I wish I did. Birth, life, death. And that's it?'

'Is that not a theological question?'

'Oh God! No ... ahhhh! The only god I believe in is money. I wish that I still had some.'

But he did have some. Plenty, in fact.

Many years ago, Ewart had planned to reward his loyal employees for their faithful service to ECC. But as time went by, he'd come to realize there was no such thing as a loyal employee. Those who worked for him were just like his wives, their only interest in Ewart was financial. The last thing to give them was money.

Instead, the accumulated total became an insurance

policy. With himself as the sole beneficiary. These investments had been spread very wide, as wide as could be. Ewart could now travel to a score of planets, and he'd be a wealthy man on each of them. It was like having different pension funds throughout the galaxy.

'It could also be argued, sir,' added Zena, 'that the reason for Father Ahmed Lamakinto's existence is so that you could leave Earth.'

Ewart looked at her. 'Right!' He nodded, smiling. 'Maybe I should tell him.'

Lamakinto might have thought he was getting a free flight, but giving passage to a missionary entitled the Ewart Foundation to various financial benefits. These included certain tax advantages, although considering Ewart's recent dealings with the revenue authorities such allowances would probably no longer be applicable. Because the *Demon Star* was to carry a United Religions of Terra missionary, other church subsidiaries had carried out conversion work on the ship at reduced cost. Slipping away from Earth had also been far less of a problem, departure coinciding with the time that the crews of orbit patrol had devotedly paused for prayer.

'Or maybe not.' Ewart didn't want to have to talk to the priest again, and he felt sorry for the innocent savages on the planet where he was going. 'I don't even have to take him to GX486/33-C, I suppose.'

'33-D, sir. 33-C is the third planet, the one which is no longer inhabited.'

'Right. Our other mission.' He felt that the word 'mission' had become tainted after speaking with the missionary – or, rather, having the missionary speaking at him.

Ewart had been the second richest man on Earth. That was no longer true, and not only because he was no longer there. He had never acquired wealth for its own sake. He didn't own priceless works of art or famous antiquities or huge tracts of extra-terrestrial territory. Everything he ever earned had been reinvested in his various enterprises. Almost.

Larnvik was still the richest man on Earth, but what was that? He wasn't even the richest in the solar system. And even the sun was an insignificant star, a tiny speck of light lost in the grandeur of the universe.

All of it, or so Lamakinto claimed, created by God. No wonder he'd needed a few days off every month, he must have been shagged out.

Even so, there still weren't enough holidays. That was where the new religions were beginning to score, the off-world churches which had won more and more con-verts on Earth. These were the religions which said *Do* instead of *Don't*, which preached indulgence instead of abstinence, and hence offered paradise to the living instead of promising heaven to the dead.

'United Religions,' said Ewart, 'is just another business. What do the customers get for what they pay? Nothing. What a great product! All they have is the promise that their investment will be rewarded in the afterlife. But by the time they realize there is no heaven, it's too late to complain. They're dead. And even when they're dead, they're still customers. The church buries them, and they have to pay. Even the dead need money.'

Like any other business, there had been mergers and take-overs amongst the original Terran religions in order to benefit from the economies of scale. But the home market had continued to decline, unable to counter the temptations of the new alien creeds. A business must keep expanding, Ewart knew, which was another reason why Ewart Communications Corporation had to make a move against Sol Global Network. And that was why United Religions was going for the export market. There was a whole universe of potential converts out there.

'It must be time to eat,' said Ewart, putting his hand on his stomach. Escaping into space had disturbed his internal clock, but he always knew when it was meal time. 'What shall I have? Read me the menu. No. Have the steward bring me a menu.'

At an expensive restaurant, one paid more for the personal attention than for the meal itself. And this was what Ewart expected aboard the *Demon Star*, his very own trans-galactic restaurant: personal service.

'Yes, sir.' Zena sent the message.

Ewart was eagerly looking forward to his first meal in space. He'd been forced off his home planet, but that didn't mean he was leaving behind all of life's essential luxuries.

While making plans for his escape, he'd considered buying up the contract of one of the world's finest chefs, so that even out in the wilderness of space he would always be served the most exquisite of meals. Reluctantly, he had decided against the idea; the fewer in his entourage, the better.

Instead, one of his priorities had been to ensure that

the ship's larder was well stocked with sumptuous meals created by the world's greatest culinary masters. Ewart's gourmet palate would recognize the subtle differences which betrayed that such feasts were not as absolutely perfect as if they were freshly prepared, but that was a sacrifice which he had to make.

For a moment the alternative crossed his mind, the prospect which might have been facing him right now. He shuddered at the thought of prison food, and tried to forget by focusing his attention on the screen again.

'When I was a child, I used to dream – literally dream – of travelling into space. I was fascinated by all the strange new worlds which were being discovered and their even stranger inhabitants. So different from us, yet also so alike. Imagine meeting someone from another world. An alien . . .'

And now he was married to one of them.

'Not many people are fortunate enough to fulfil their dreams, sir.'

That was one way of looking at it. He would have preferred to travel at a time of his own choosing, however, instead of being forced into exile like this. When he was younger, he'd never been able to afford a space voyage; when he'd had the money, he was unable to spare the time.

That's what space travel took: time, and lots of it.

Another thing was money. Even more of it.

'Right,' said Ewart, nodding. He had to be positive about this.

Whatever had happened before was all in the past, far behind him now. Although he'd never be able to forget, or even want to, he had to concentrate on the future, on the rest of his life.

He was out in space, already beyond the solar system, starting a voyage he'd imagined all his life. Yet he would probably never have left Earth again if he hadn't been forced to.

He had lived on the Moon for a few weeks, which was as long as his fourth marriage had lasted. The only good thing about the Moon, apart from his wedding night, was that his weight had been dramatically reduced because of the low gravity – which had also contributed to the success of his wedding night, he remembered.

But the Moon was nothing. Nothing compared to the stars. The entire galaxy was his to explore. He would visit a whole spectrum of different worlds. See fantastic sights which he couldn't even begin to envisage. Meet bizarre new people. Eat their food.

'Where's the steward?' Ewart asked.

Zena thumbed her comset. Nothing happened.

It was easier, it seemed, to send data from one end of the solar system to the other than to talk to someone on board the same spaceship.

Ewart's whole life had been spent in the communications industry. Why travel when you could communicate? Perhaps that was another reason why he'd never gone to the stars before now: the galaxy had come to him. All the information he ever needed had been instantly available.

'It would probably be quicker if you went and found him.'

'Shall I do that, sir?'

'Ah . . .'

If she went, he'd be alone, unprotected. What did he need protecting from? He was safe here. Or he should have been. He was on board his own spaceship. There could be no danger. But Grawl and Zena hadn't yet given the ship a thorough security check. Because he had left Earth, that didn't mean he'd escaped from his enemies. Most of the crew were non-Terran, but one of them might have been in the pay of Larnvik.

The steward could arrive in Ewart's stateroom while Zena was searching for him. And acting as steward might be only one of his roles – he could also be an assassin.

'. . . no,' said Ewart.

A moment later, the door sounded. The comscreen showed someone standing in the corridor outside. He must have been the steward. And that was all he was. But if he wasn't, Zena was here. She opened the door. He was of Terran appearance. Tall, thin, middle-aged.

He looked at Ewart. Ewart looked at him.

They both stared at each other.

'You! No . . .!'

'No! Not you . . .!'

The steward wasn't an assassin.

He was worse, much worse.

'What are *you* doing here?'

'No, what are *you* doing here?'

'I work here.'

'It's my ship. I own it.'

'No! No, no, no, no, no . . .!'

They stood motionless for several seconds, glaring at one another. Then they both took a few steps towards each other, fists clenched, faces angry. Zena moved forward and stood between them, her gaze focused on the newcomer.

'You know this man, sir?'

'Right.'

'There seems some hostility between the two of you.'

'Hostility!' said the steward, and he forced a laugh. 'What makes you think that?'

'Do you want me to remove him, sir?'

If there had been any real danger, Zena wouldn't have needed to ask, but she was aware that the steward was no serious threat to Ewart. The steward, however, recognized that she could be a serious threat to him. He moved back to stand by the door.

'No,' said Ewart. 'Not yet.'

'I thought I was suffering from hyperlusions,' said the steward, 'that I'd seen the worst thing I could ever imagine. But I suppose that lusions don't ask for menus to be delivered by hand. Only greedy bastards like you. I wish it was a hyperlusion.'

He flicked the menu to the ground. Zena caught it before it landed, checked that it was harmless, and passed it to Ewart. Hungry as he was, he couldn't concentrate on food.

'It's been a long time,' he said.

'I wish it was longer. I wish it was never.'

'I thought you were dead.'

'Hoped I was dead, you mean.'

'That can be taken care of.'

'You'd do that to me, your oldest friend?'

'Oldest enemy.'

'And oldest partner.'

'Oldest rival.'

Ewart looked him up and down. 'But not any more.' He smiled. 'I always won, didn't I?'

'Did you? Hasn't done you much good, has it? You've ended up stuck on this old crate, just like me.'

'Except that it's mine. I own it. And now I own you.'

'That's why you bought the ship. So you could order me around, like you always tried to. But I'm not taking orders from you.'

'You're only here to spoil this for me, right?'

'Don't fool yourself. You think I'd be here if I'd known you were the new owner? I'd have jumped ship without a spacesuit.'

'Glad to hear it. Because that's exactly what you're going to do!'

'Good. I'll probably last longer than anyone who stays on board this wreck.'

'What? Why?'

'You always were tight with your money, weren't you?'

'I was careful with my investments. That's why I became so rich, while you . . .' Ewart gestured dismissively.

'Not any more. I know what's happened to you. And now we're both in the same boat! I bet you thought you'd got a real bargain with this ship. Why do you think it was so cheap?'

When the Ewart Foundation bought the spaceship it

hadn't seemed all that cheap, just comparatively inexpensive. At the time, there was only a small chance that Ewart would need to use the craft himself, or else he might have spent more. The refit had cost a fair amount, however, but that would have been recouped on resale.

'You're leaving,' said Ewart. 'I'm not having you on my ship.'

'OK, you want to turn back?'

'It's one of the lifeboats for you.'

'One of the lifeboats? Ha! You think this old tub has lifeboats?'

'You mean . . . it doesn't?'

'The escape capsules were sent for repair, but we had to leave orbit before they were ready. The new owner seemed to be in some kind of rush to get away.'

'You're lying. You always lied to me.'

'Me? Tell lies! This ship is brand new; it's packed with the absolute latest in interstellar technology; the captain is renowned as the best master in the whole galaxy; and no finer crew of skilled spacefarers can be found on ten thousand planets.'

'Are they all like you?'

'No, most of them are starbums or fugitives. You'll fit right in.'

'How come you're such an expert?'

'I'm a spacer. Where do you think I've been all these years? Remember when we were kids, when we talked about going to the stars?'

'No!' Ewart shook his head in denial. It had been *his* dream to soar through space, to see the galaxy.

'Yes, yes, yes! I did it first.' He gestured towards the viewscreen. 'I've been to the stars!'

'But as what? As a *waiter*!'

'So? I travelled when I was young enough to enjoy myself. Not like you. It's too late for you.'

'It's not!'

'I've been everywhere. Worlds without number. Stars, planets, aliens!'

Stars, planets, aliens . . .

Ewart had never felt so envious in his whole life. He'd have given a fortune to spend one day beneath a different star, on another planet, amongst an alien race. Except he no longer had a fortune.

'If it was that great, why did you come back to Earth?'

'Bad luck, the wrong ship going to the wrong planet. As soon as I found one that was leaving, I signed on. I didn't know that you'd bought it. More bad luck.'

'You make me sick.'

'Yes. But that was a long time ago.'

'Get him out of here, Zena. Lock him up with that missionary.'

Zena had been watching the steward all the time, and now she moved forward to take him into custody.

'Do what you want. You think I care? You can't wipe away what I've done. The Seven Wonders of the Galaxy? I've seen them all! But you never will.'

'I will!'

'Not in this ship.'

'Wait,' Ewart told Zena. 'What do you mean?'

'The Rollein-Twist, that's what I mean. You have heard of that?'

'Of course I have,' said Ewart; but of course he hadn't.

The steward laughed. 'You know nothing! You never have, you never will. You don't know what's happening on this old banger. You don't know who's on board. You might fool everyone else, and you did for nearly fifty years, but you could never fool me.'

'But I can still make you do what I want.'

'You never could.'

'I want you to do your job, which means I won't lock you up. As long as I'm on board, you'll be at my beck and call every hour of the day.'

'That's what you think.'

'And you'll be properly dressed, wear the uniform of a steward. I know there is one, because I paid for it.'

'I won't wear it.'

Ewart began to study the menu.

'You sure you trust me with your food?'

And Ewart realized he'd lost his appetite.

'You or Grawl,' he said to Zena, 'will always supervise the preparation of all my food.'

'Yes, sir.'

'Get out of here,' he told the steward. 'And don't you dare eat any of my gourmet meals.'

'You think I'd want any of the tripe you eat? Look what it's done to you.' The steward opened the door and stepped out of the stateroom.

'Tripe?' said Ewart.

'The stomach lining of a cow, sir.'

Ewart couldn't remember that being on the menu. He wondered what it tasted like.

He closed his eyes and shook his head. 'Give me a physcan.' After what had just happened, he knew he needed a fix. As Zena reached for the medpack, he asked, 'What was that he said about hyperlusions?'

'It is a subjective phenomenon associated with interstellar travel, sir, a condition whereby the human brain may become hyperactive and falsely interpret various sensory information.'

'So I might have imagined everything that happened in the last few minutes?'

'You did not imagine the steward, sir, because I also saw him.'

'But I might only think that you saw him. You could also be part of my hallucination, right?'

'It is possible, sir. There is no objective reality. Although we witnessed the same event, we may have had different experiences. If I told you what I saw and heard, even though my words might contradict your own memories, your brain would filter what I said so that you believed my version was in full correlation with your own.'

'So there's no way of telling?'

'All perception is subjective, sir, and hyperlusions are apparently very personal, often taking the form of repressed and forgotten images drawn up from the deepest recesses of the subject's mind.'

That was exactly right, but Ewart wondered if a hyperlusion would tell him about hyperlusions. Zena fixed the medpack back on her belt.

'Don't I get a fix?'

'You do not need one.'

'I do. I saw the readings.'

Even if he hadn't noticed the readings, he knew that his counts were too high. After such a shock, that was no surprise.

'No, sir, everything is fine.'

'Everything isn't fine, Zena. I need a biofix. And I think you need something. What's the matter with you?'

'Nothing, sir,' she said, reaching for the medpack again. 'I was only following your orders.'

'What orders?'

'You said you did not want me to agree with you all the time, that I should say "no" sometimes.'

Ewart nodded. 'Right. No.' He shook his head. 'Wrong. You can disagree, but not disobey. If I'm wrong, tell me. But you can't argue with a fact, and it's a fact that the readings said I needed a fix.'

'If you say so.'

'It's not what I say, it's what the physcan says.'

'Yes, sir,' said Zena, as she administered the dose.

'Forget what I said before. From now on, whatever I say, you do it. Right? Don't argue with me, don't disagree with me.'

'Even when you're wrong?'

'Especially when I'm wrong!'

'Yes, sir.'

Ewart closed his eyes and took a deep breath as he felt his body respond and relax. He knew he was fine again when he started to think about food.

'What was that other thing he said? About some kind of roll?'

'The Rollein-Twist, sir.'

'Right. What is it?'

'It is a method of interstellar propulsion, and this ship is unfortunately powered by engines based on the Rollein-Twist principle.'

'Unfortunately . . .?'

Then Zena explained – and Ewart needed another biofix.

The menu had slipped through his fingers, and as Zena picked it up she asked, 'The steward, sir, who is he?'

CHAPTER SIX

He called himself Rajic Jao Rajic.

That wasn't his original name, and he was probably the only person still alive who knew that William Ewart had also started life under a different name.

'You slime! You're the lowest of the low. You know that? You were always there, somewhere, near or far, all through my life. Until I left Earth. After so many years, I thought I was rid of you. But I make one mistake, just one, and I end up back in the solar system. I try to get away. And you buy the ship I'm on! You *total* . . . and *utter* . . . and *absolute* . . .'

He gazed at Ewart, at the familiar fat features which had haunted him for so long, and he swore. He swore as loud and as filthily, as long and as venomously as he knew, and all his years in space had taught him a whole lexicon of alien obscenities. But none of them made him feel any better.

Ewart stared back at him, his face frozen on the screen.

Rajic glanced around his tiny cabin, searching for something on which he could vent his anger, something which he could destroy in a suitably noisy and spectacular fashion. There was nothing.

He reached for the bottle he had been saving for today. There were other drinks which were far more potent to Terran physiology than Sadachbian vodsky, and there were much quicker ways of nixing the brain. Rajic had never used his favourite alien liquor simply to dull his senses, and it had been intended as a celebration for leaving the solar system for the second – and definitely final – time. There was little to celebrate now, and he needed the vodsky solely for its alcohol content. He tilted the bottle to his lips, taking a long swig.

'Of all people! Why? Why! Why . . .?'

There was only one way he knew of cheering himself up. He sat back, took another drink and said, 'Play.'

Ewart unfroze, looking very uncomfortable under cross-examination.

The prosecutor said, 'I believe you are one of the richest men on Earth, Mr Ewart.'

'The second richest.'

'So why haven't you paid your taxes for the last twenty-six years?'

'I'm sure I have.'

'If you had, Mr Ewart, you wouldn't be here.'

'Then it's a mistake.'

'What's a mistake? That you're here? Or that you didn't pay your taxes?'

'Right.'

'Right? What do you mean, Mr Ewart? That it's right

for you not to have paid your taxes?'

'No.'

'Then if it isn't right, why haven't you paid?'

'I'm sure I have.'

'You've already said that, Mr Ewart, to which I replied "If you had, you wouldn't be here" and you said "Then it's a mistake". Shall we carry on from there?'

'Right.'

'This is a court of law, Mr Ewart. You must reply in the affirmative or negative, not give directions. If you are unable to say the word "yes", you can nod, and we will all understand. Understand?'

'Right. Er . . . yes.'

'Good. That wasn't too difficult, was it? Let's go back to your last almost coherent remark: "Then it's a mistake." What, exactly, is a mistake?'

'It's something that's wrong!'

'Is that supposed to be a joke, Mr Ewart? A court of law is no place for levity. Your pathetic attempt at humour demonstrates your total disregard for judicial authority and complete lack of recognition of the severity of this case. I advise you to apologize to the judge.'

'I apologize.'

Judge Solomon was a very imposing figure. Sitting high above the rest of the court made him look even taller than he already was, and his black robes made him look even broader. Wearing a long wig and showing no expression, the judge surveyed the scene below him through his honorary spectacles. He nodded solemnly.

'And you should also apologize to the jury, to everyone who is watching these proceedings on the world's most magnificent comservice, Sol Global Network.'

Ewart said nothing.

'I didn't hear that, Mr Ewart, and neither did anyone else.'

'I ... I ... apologize.'

'Thank you. May we finally proceed? The court's time is valuable, even if your own is not. What is it that you claim is a mistake?'

'Everything. Why I'm here. It's all a mistake.'

'From the moment of your conception, Mr Ewart? You mean that was a mistake?'

'Are you accusing me of being a—'

'Be careful of your language, Mr Ewart. This is a court of law. We do not use that word, even where it may be true.'

'Your honour!' said Ewart's lawyer. 'Such slanderous remarks on my client's legitimacy have no bearing on this case.'

'I withdraw,' said the prosecutor.

'It is a pity that Ewart's father did not do the same,' said the judge.

The prosecutor laughed. The whole court laughed. Even the defence counsel laughed. Everyone except Ewart.

Although Rajic had watched this scene before, he also smiled. He had a professional interest in Judge Solomon; he had helped to create him.

Equal justice for all, that had been the original idea.

The only way such an ideal was possible was if everyone in the world could be tried by the same judge. That judge was Solomon: a whole legion of android magistrates, all centrally controlled and identically programmed. Solomon knew every law, every statute, every precedent, every punishment for every crime, every acceptable solution for every civil action.

Judge Solomon represented the sum total of judicial wisdom. Standing at the pinnacle of the legal system, his decisions were handed down without fear or favour. Solomon was the symbol of absolute jurisprudence, above bribery, beyond corruption. In theory.

The Solomon system had been built by one of Hiroshi Larnvik's subsidiaries, however, and so inevitably it was biased against Ewart. Whatever the evidence produced in court, he couldn't win.

'What is it that you claim is a mistake, Mr Ewart?' asked the prosecutor. 'That you're here or that you didn't pay your taxes?'

'Both.'

'So you admit you didn't pay your taxes?'

'Yes. No.'

'Which, Mr Ewart? "Yes" you're here, and "no" you didn't pay your taxes?'

'No.'

'No? You mean you're not here?'

'I am here. You can see I'm here. Are you talking to yourself?'

'I think I might be,' said the prosecuting attorney.

Rajic laughed and took another drink. The trial was still as enjoyable the second time. He'd seen the opening on SGN, picked up live on board the *Demon Star*, but had to stop watching because he'd only been on board his new ship a few hours and there was work to be done.

He'd saved every minute of the trial for later and kept wondering about the outcome. Although he could guess the result, it was like the replay of a sports game. It would be spoiled if he knew the final score before watching the whole thing.

Then he'd walked into the owner's suite and seen Ewart. Which had really spoiled the ending. And everything else.

Although knowing that the match had been abandoned after the losing side escaped into space did take away some of his pleasure as a spectator, Rajic admired the way that the prosecuting lawyer had Ewart tied up in knots. He was like a kid again, not knowing what to say.

Almost sixty years had passed since they'd first met. Rajic was five, Ewart two years older. It was tempting to say that Ewart had never changed, and to some extent it was true. As a child, he would never admit that he was wrong, always telling wilder and more improbable tales in order to protect himself.

But that was what always happened in court, Rajic supposed. No one ever told the truth.

Ewart, however, had probably changed more than most people. At one time, he had been very trusting and easy going, generous and willing to share what little he had. And then, then . . .

Rajic swallowed some more vodsky, remembering when Ewart had adopted his new name. In changing his identity, his personality had also changed: he became a real bastard.

'Over the past twenty-six years,' said the prosecutor, 'it seems you have not paid any personal tax. Is that correct?'

'I don't know,' said Ewart. 'My accountants take care of that kind of thing. I'm a busy man.'

'Don't you think it strange that a man as wealthy as yourself should pay no tax?'

'No. My income may seem high, but my expenses are even higher.'

'Expenses such as extravagant business lunches and dinners? And suppers and breakfasts, I suppose. I see you have a lot of those, Mr Ewart.'

'What do you mean you "see"?'

'I see from your last set of accounts,' said the prosecutor. She turned from Ewart, looked at the screen and rolled her eyes. 'But we are not merely talking about your personal accounts, Mr Ewart. Your company, Ewart Communications Corporation, also appears not to have paid any tax for twenty-six years. Have you an explanation?'

'My accountants deal with all that.'

'Shouldn't you be aware of your company's financial situation?'

'I'm a busy man.'

'Yes, so you claim. Companies pay tax on their profits, I believe. If no tax were paid for twenty-six years, what would that suggest to you?'

'You tell me.'

'I will. It suggests that either Ewart Communications

Corporation is a complete failure, having made no profit in quarter of a century, or else that there is some kind of serious deception involved in your company's accounting procedures.'

'ECC has been constantly expanding, becoming the best and most successful comservice in the solar system. All profits have been reinvested to provide this essential public service, and all of my own income has been returned to the business. I spend nothing on myself, because I don't have the time.'

'We're all so grateful to you, Mr Ewart.'

'Where would the world be without comservice? Because of such excellent communications, wars have stopped and the whole planet is united in peace. Now that talking is so easy, there's no more fighting.'

'I believe it's generally accepted that the banning of weapons stopped wars, and this happened quite some time ago. Despite your age, Mr Ewart, it seems unreasonable for you to take credit for establishing world peace.' The prosecutor paused. 'But doubtless ECC newsfacts include this as part of your biography.'

'Ewart Communications Corporation provides the most up to date and accurate—'

Ewart's voice was abruptly cut off, but the camera moved in closer and closer, until his face filled the screen.

'Do you trust a man like this?' said the voiceover. 'Do you trust a comservice which doesn't pay its taxes? Of course you don't. That's why you're watching Sol Global Network, the comservice you can trust. And which does pay its taxes.'

'—to provide essential services to the poor and the disadvantaged,' Ewart continued, 'to give people the best possible entertainment.'

'You're certainly giving them that today, Mr Ewart,' said the prosecutor, 'thanks to Sol Global Network, the comservice which serves you best.' She turned from the screen to face Ewart again. 'Your company, ECC, must be worth billions and billions.'

'Only on paper.'

'If you are a paper billionaire,' remarked Judge Solomon, 'then you really are rich!'

Over twenty years ago, Ewart had also bid to build the Solomon system, but he hadn't offered enough indirect financial inducements to win the contract. Whatever price he'd offered, however, it wouldn't have been sufficient for Rajic Jao Rajic.

Instead, it was Larnvik's payoff which had enabled Rajic to head for the stars.

Now he was on his way back towards the heart of the galaxy again. And this time Ewart was with him.

'The Seven Wonders of the Galaxy,' said Rajic, and he swallowed some more vodsky and rapidly scanned the court proceedings, advancing towards a scene he hadn't yet watched.

Rajic had never seen the Seven Wonders of the Galaxy; he didn't even know if there were Seven Wonders of the Galaxy. It was something he'd made up. Or, he wondered, was it something Ewart had made up? He could have invented the phrase when they were kids, planning on visiting the stars.

Although he'd spent twenty years roaming the galaxy, Rajic had hardly seen anything. He'd set foot on dozens of weird new worlds, with strangely coloured skies and strangely shaped constellations – and even more strangely coloured and strangely shaped people. But as soon as he made landfall he'd usually ended up in the nearest sex saloon. To an outsider, these may all have seemed very much the same, not much different from those on Earth. Over the years, however, Rajic had become an expert on such establishments. Every planet had its own unique pleasures, both physical and cerebral, and all had contributed to making each of his landing excursions memorably enjoyable.

The money he'd received from Larnvik had been enough to reach the stars, or the nearest ones: the double star, Centauri. To keep on travelling, he needed to work his passage on board ship, which was what he had been doing for the last two decades.

The distance from star to star, from inhabited world to inhabited world, was vast, but the gulf between one civilization and another was far greater than could be measured by mere distance. The rarest jewels found on one world would be as common as pebbles on the ocean shores of another; the finest of liqueurs, only one batch of which could be distilled in a generation, would be no different from tractor fuel in another solar system; a legendary spice, famed for its qualities as an aphrodisiac, a score of slaves having died to produce a single gram, would grow like a weed elsewhere; priceless antiquities became incomprehensible and worthless when carried across the universe.

The only thing worth transporting over such fantastic

distances was people, because they all believed they were of inestimable value. But the only people who did travel from star to star were those who had a lot of money, or who hoped to make a lot of money, or who owed a lot of money.

Ewart was all three.

There was one other group who travelled across the infinite distance from one infinitely distant world to another: the spacers who crewed the ships.

Rajic had checked out the *Demon Star* before signing on, but he hadn't bothered to find out who'd be travelling on board. He'd known it would be some rich bastard but had never imagined it would be Ewart. As the world's second richest man, Ewart had no reason to leave Earth. But now he had every reason.

Because Ewart was such a liar, he was always easily fooled. But that had never stopped Rajic's pleasure in deceiving him. The *Demon Star* was fully equipped with coffins, as lifeboats were known to spacers: if you had to climb into one, you were as good as dead.

The same thing was often said about ships powered by the Rollein-Twist.

And Rajic hadn't lied about that.

Neither had he lied about his uniform. All epaulettes and gold braid. He certainly wasn't going to wear that.

He took another drink of vodsky, then said, 'Play.'

'It's not only the Terrestrial Taxation Authority to whom you owe considerable sums, Mr Ewart,' said the prosecutor. 'You also owe each of your wives a great deal of money.'

'I don't owe those . . . those women a single rupan,' said Ewart. 'They all had plenty off me while we were married. If they wanted to continue sharing my wealth, they should never have divorced me.'

'You divorced them, Mr Ewart.'

'I did not. They married me for my money. And when they thought they could squeeze more out of me by divorcing me, that's what they did.'

'Why did you marry them, Mr Ewart?'

'Why does anyone get married?'

'You seem to misunderstand the situation, Mr Ewart. If you look around you will see that we are in a court of law, the Central Law Court to be precise. I ask the questions. You answer them. Understand?'

'Right. Yes.'

'Good. I'll repeat my question: Why did you marry them, Mr Ewart?'

Ewart looked embarrassed, and he said something in a very low voice.

'Louder, Mr Ewart, please.'

'Love,' muttered Ewart.

'Louder.'

'Love! I thought I was in love. They fooled me, all of them, fooled me into marrying them.'

'And you fooled them into divorcing them.'

'No!'

'Yes, Mr Ewart. By the letter of the law it might appear that they divorced you, but each time it was at your instigation. The prosecution will provide the court with evidence of how you *persuaded* your wives to end their marriages with you, and how each time you callously broke your agreement with them.'

'No! They broke their agreements with me.'

'That is for the court to decide, Mr Ewart, and each of your former wives will be here to testify against you. We will hear of all the cruelties and perversions which you inflicted upon these four unfortunate women, each of whom was unlucky enough to fall prey to your odious advances. They will testify that they were influenced by your wealth – because, let's face it, how else could you attract such young and lovely brides? Influenced by your wealth, each of them agreed to matrimony.'

The prosecutor gestured towards the witness stand, and a moment later a woman materialized there. She was only a simulation, a three-dimensional image, but she looked almost real.

Almost, thought Rajic, but almost wasn't good enough. 3V images were common enough in one-to-one communication, but holograms had never been success-fully adapted to the mass media. It was all a question of size and dimension: the size of people who were viewed in three dimensions. One person could be lifesize, but for a dramatic scene with numerous characters and lots of action, the size needed reducing to fit within the audience's perspective – and their viewing room.

Intimate, exotic entertainment might succeed in full-size 3V, but flat-screen SeeV, from wristsets upwards, was still the predominant format for popular media.

'Naheed,' said Ewart, as he looked at the witness stand, 'my darling.'

'No, Mr Ewart,' said the attorney, 'this is your first wife, Irina.'

'Irina, my darling.'

Irina deliberately avoided looking at Ewart, and she said nothing.

'We shall hear how Irina Ewart was married to Mr Ewart for almost ten years. She gave him everything, including three children. She cherished and cared for him, surrendered the best years of her life, then was cruelly cast aside. And how was her love and loyalty rewarded? Promised a meagre settlement, Mr Ewart even cheated her out of that paltry sum. Now, after all her selfless devotion, Irina Ewart finds herself destitute.'

'Zoom,' said Rajic, and the screen focused on the figure in the witness box.

Irina had always been very attractive, and she still was. She must have been sixty by now, but she looked less than half that age.

'Selfless devotion!' Rajic laughed, and he raised his bottle. 'Cheers, Irina.'

'Irina Ewart,' said the prosecutor, 'will testify that before her divorce from Mr Ewart became legally permanent, she was seduced by an associate of her husband. Thus, by a legal technicality, she lost her claim to alimony. But this seduction was arranged by Mr Ewart, and made public by him, in order to nullify the divorce settlement he had previously agreed with his wife.'

'I object,' said Ewart.

'Mr Ewart,' said the judge, 'it is the function of your lawyer to say "I object". However, as this is a preliminary statement made by the prosecution, objections are not permissible. Or did you mean to say something different? Perhaps, Mr Ewart, you meant "I am objectionable" – and we would all agree with you.'

Everyone laughed obsequiously. Except Ewart. And the defence attorney, who stood up and started to say, 'Your honour—'

'Sit down, Mr Abdenga,' Judge Solomon told him.

'You think I'd arrange for my ex-wife's seduction?' said Ewart. 'I've got better things to do. And a wife can't testify against her husband. Can she?'

'We all know you are not a lawyer, Mr Ewart,' said the prosecutor, 'but you don't have to prove your ignorance. Irina Ewart is no longer your wife.'

'Why has she kept my name? Why have they all kept my name?'

'I ask the questions, Mr Ewart. Remember?'

'It's all hearsay. Her word alone isn't enough evidence. You need to call the seducer as a witness. The *alleged* seducer. Where is he?'

'Right here,' said Rajic, as he watched the screen.

'Efforts to find your associate, one Rajic Jao Rajic, have been to no avail.'

'What did I tell you?' said Ewart. 'She's making it all up.'

'No, she isn't,' said Rajic.

He did have an affair with Irina, but it wasn't true that Ewart had arranged it all. Was it? No, it couldn't be, because Rajic and Irina had been involved with each other long before the divorce. If Ewart had known, his wife's adultery would have been the perfect excuse to get rid of her.

'We will, however,' said the prosecuting lawyer,

'produce another witness who will corroborate Irina Ewart's evidence: Angelique Jao Rajic.'

'Angelique!' Rajic hadn't seen his wife for thirty years. She was his first wife, his only wife, and he still felt very fond of her.

The prosecutor continued, 'She will also testify that she was seduced by Mr Ewart while he was still married to Irina Ewart, and while she was married to Rajic Jao Rajic.'

'What!' Rajic hadn't known about that. He took another drink, and suddenly he didn't feel as fond of his first and only wife as he had done. He stared at Ewart. 'You bastard,' he added.

His wedding, his divorce, they had happened so long ago, but Rajic could remember everything in between so well. Perhaps if he hadn't become entangled with Irina and, as he now knew, Angelique hadn't become similarly intertwined with Ewart, everything would have been different.

But Rajic would also have had to avoid his affair with Teresa, Ewart's second wife.

'My darling,' said Ewart, as she replaced Irina in the witness box. He was taking no chances on getting her name wrong.

Teresa also looked very good, thought Rajic, considering all the time which had passed. She also avoided looking at Ewart.

'Cheers, Teresa,' said Rajic. He raised the bottle, but this time he didn't take a swig.

'We will hear a similar story from Teresa Ewart,' said the prosecutor. 'She married Mr Ewart, bore him two fine children—'

'They weren't mine!' Ewart said. 'She claims they are, but they aren't.'

'And they aren't mine,' said Rajic. His score was better than Ewart's, he realized. He'd bedded two of Ewart's wives, but it had been mathematically impossible for Ewart to sleep with more than Rajic's one and only wife. This time he did take another drink. 'Or at least I don't think so.'

'Do not interrupt, Mr Ewart,' said the judge.

'Thank you, your honour. Teresa Ewart married the accused, bore him two fine children, and was also left without a single rupan to support herself.'

'What about her other husbands?' said Ewart. 'She got married again. And again.'

'She married against your wishes, Mr Ewart, is that not true?'

'I ... er ... I can't remember.'

'Then I will remind you. By the terms of your divorce settlement, you agreed to support your second wife and her two children – *your* two children – as long as she did not remarry. But Teresa Ewart married again within a month, a doomed marriage which lasted less than a week. Wasn't that very fortunate for you, Mr Ewart?'

'You're not suggesting I had anything to do with her getting married again?'

'Certainly not, Mr Ewart. I am not suggesting that at all.'

'Good.'

'Instead, I will *prove* that you arranged for Teresa Ewart to marry again, thus nullifying the terms of your divorce settlement with her.'

'But then she married again,' said Ewart. 'What about her third marriage?'

'Do you also wish to confess to arranging that?'

'No. I didn't. And I didn't arrange her second marriage.'

'That is up to the court to decide, Mr Ewart, a decision which will be made right here on Sol Global Network, the most trustworthy comservice in the solar system, but first—'

'Forward,' said Rajic. He took another mouthful, then said, 'Play.'

The hologram of Ewart's second wife was replaced by what Rajic presumed was that of his third.

'Zoom.'

Rajic had never had the chance of an intimate encounter with this one, because he had left Earth by the time Ewart met her. He wished he'd waited.

'Naheed, my darling.' This time Ewart seemed to get it right.

When Irina had first materialized in the witness stand, Ewart thought she was Naheed, and Rajic was struck by the close resemblance. Yet Naheed also appeared very similar to Teresa. All three were tall, slim, with delicate features.

Rajic wasn't surprised that Ewart should mix up his wives. If they looked so much alike, he should have made sure they had the same name. Perhaps it was because he had such a bad memory, for everything except money, that Ewart was such a liar. He couldn't remember the truth, so he had to invent it.

'Naheed Ewart,' said the prosecutor, 'will tell a

variation of a story which is becoming sadly familiar. She, too, married Mr Ewart, gave him a child—'

Ewart seemed about to speak, but thought better of it.

'—and was then ruthlessly cast aside. Her agreement with Mr Ewart was that he would continue to maintain her and her child – *his* child – on condition that she did not sell the story of her marriage. Because this was the kind of salacious material which he would have used on his own comservice, Mr Ewart seemed to believe that Sol Global Network was interested in his sordid private life and wished to purchase Naheed Ewart's intimate memoirs. SGN, as the court knows, would never stoop to the same despicably low level as ECC.'

Ewart was saying something, but his voice was censored. Presumably he was making some remark about Hiroshi Larnvik's sordid private life, attempting to make it public.

'We will hear,' continued the attorney, 'how Naheed Ewart, under the misapprehension that she was talking with a close personal friend, was tricked into revealing her nightmare life with Mr Ewart. Instead, this supposed trusted confidant paid Naheed Ewart a token sum of money that she neither expected nor wanted – and her story was transmitted, thus breaking the terms of her settlement with Mr Ewart. And who transmitted this story, albeit in a very edited form? Do you know, Mr Ewart?'

'How should I know?'

'Because it was a subsidiary of Ewart Communications Corporation, a company based on Phobos, one of the two moons of Mars. This comservice usually covers all of the red planet, but on this one occasion, and on this one occasion alone, Naheed Ewart's story was available only to the population of Phobos, a potential audience of less than a hundred. Can you explain that, Mr Ewart?'

'I don't know every detail of every one of my companies for every day of every year,' said Ewart.

'You'll be pleased, therefore, to know that you can find out full details of the Phobos transmission. Sol Global Network has obtained an unedited copy of Naheed Ewart's confessions. She has granted her permission, and the prosecution will offer this as evidence.'

'I can't wait,' said Rajic, as he smiled and swigged.

He didn't have to, because he had instant access to what happened later, right up until the recess. Which was when Ewart had decided not to wait. But Rajic wanted to see Ewart's fourth wife.

Karis Ewart was very similar to Naheed, which meant that she also resembled Teresa and Irina. It seemed that Ewart hadn't learned from his mistakes. Whether he'd been aware of it or not, he had tried to marry the same woman each time. Or same girl, because as he had grown older, each of his brides had become successively younger.

Both Irina and Teresa looked younger now than when they had married Ewart, which meant they must both have been rejuved. Ewart appeared to have prescribed his own anti-ageing treatment: taking a younger wife each time.

Or perhaps it was hereditary: his father had had several wives, most of them at different times.

'Karis Ewart was Mr Ewart's fourth wife,' said the prosecutor.

'She signed a pre-marital agreement,' said Ewart. 'I don't see what she has to complain about.'

'I presume that anyone married to you, Mr Ewart,' said Judge Solomon, 'would have plenty to complain about.'

Once again, the court laughed and laughed at such a fine example of judicial wit.

'When Karis Ewart gives evidence, Mr Ewart,' said the lawyer, 'we will discover that this case comes full circle, linking up with your unpaid taxes. You married your fourth wife, a citizen of the Moon, so that you could acquire lunar citizenship for yourself and avoid paying Terran taxes.'

'No,' said Ewart.

'You cannot deny that as soon as you married Karis Ewart, you went to live on the Moon.'

'Right. Yes. Karis was born there, she came to Earth, worked for Ewart Communications Corporation, which was how we met, and—'

'We don't want to hear the sordid details of how you seduced your innocent young bride, Mr Ewart.'

'But I do!' said Rajic.

'Karis was from the Moon,' said Ewart, 'and we decided to live there as soon as we were married.'

'*You* decided, because it was another way to avoid paying the legitimate taxes due on your personal and corporate income.'

'No. If that was so, I'd never have returned to Earth. I didn't go to the Moon for financial reasons.'

'Then what was the reason?'

'For my health. I'm no longer a young man, and I wanted to get away from the pressure of work for a while.'

'You heard that people live longer on the Moon?'

'People do not live longer on the Moon, Mr Ewart,' said the judge. 'Life there is so dull and boring that they only think they live longer.'

This was Judge Solomon's best line yet. The occupants of the court had never heard anything so funny in all of their lives.

Rajic didn't think it was very amusing, because he knew it was true. He'd been on worlds where a day lasted a month and felt like a year.

'Four wives, Mr Ewart,' said the prosecutor, 'each of whom you have treated in an abominable fashion. Four wives. Isn't that an excessive number?'

'Not at all,' said Ewart. 'There are religions which allow men to have four wives simultaneously, or a woman to have four husbands. We've all heard of people who have been married to ten or more partners. Over the years, I've only been married four times. For a man in my position, that's nothing. I'm practically a monk.'

'I said *four* wives, Mr Ewart. But it isn't four, is it? It's *five*. Would you care to tell the court about your latest wife?'

'I married again, not long ago.' Ewart shrugged. 'What's there to tell?'

'What's there to tell? There's everything to tell. You claim you married your four previous wives for "love".

What about your new wife? Did you also marry her for "love"?'

'Er . . .'

'Have you met your new wife, Mr Ewart?'

'Er . . .'

'Mr Ewart, you own the world's second largest comservice. I find this very difficult to believe as you appear to have great difficulty in communicating any information to me, to the judge, to the court, to the vast audience watching these proceedings on Sol Global Network – the world's largest and most informative comservice.'

'No, I haven't met my new wife.'

'Why haven't you met your new wife, Mr Ewart?'

'Because she lives almost one hundred light years away.'

'Where?'

'Algol.'

'Would I be correct in supposing, Mr Ewart, that your new bride is . . . an *alien*?'

'She is. Does that bother you? I'm proud of it.'

'Why have you married an alien you've never met?'

'It's personal. I don't want to tell you.'

'You may not want to tell the prosecuting attorney, Mr Ewart,' said Judge Solomon, 'but you have to tell the court.'

Ewart looked slowly around, at the judge, at the prosecutor, at the judge again. 'I wish to register the strongest protest at being forced to reveal this, but there seems no alternative. The prosecution claims that I've paid no taxes for twenty-six years. I don't know if this is true or not, but what I said earlier is true: I do have a lot of expenses, some of which are not strictly business expenses. These are the donations which I make through the charity which bears my name, the Ewart Foundation.'

'You mean, Mr Ewart,' said the lawyer, 'that the money which you should have paid in taxes has been given to charity?'

'As I said, I didn't want to have to reveal this. It's something I'd have preferred to keep private.'

'You expect us to believe you?'

'As with my charitable donations, I expect nothing. Even if you don't believe me, that doesn't affect the truth of what I say.'

Rajic smiled. Ewart was always good at inventing stories, but over the years he'd got better. The best lie to tell was a big lie.

For the first time, the prosecutor seemed unsure of how to proceed. 'What ... what's this got to do with a planet ninety-five light years away?' she asked.

'It's one of my projects,' Ewart told her. 'The galaxy is a big place, a very, very big place. Even a man of my wealth can't hope to make a useful contribution to every world which is in need of assistance. I chose to concentrate my efforts on a few planets, one of which is Algol.'

'You plan to start a comservice on this planet? That's why you've invested there?'

'Not at all. I haven't invested, I've donated. I've always been a businessman, but this is one time that I expect to reap no financial reward.'

'You are telling the court that you've suddenly become a philanthropist, Mr Ewart?'

'Not suddenly.'

'Was getting married part of your charity work?'

'The Algolans are an ancient people, very proud and very independent. Although they cannot reach their true potential without education and agricultural aid, and many of them die for lack of basic medicines, they refuse to accept gifts from outsiders. They have no concept of what charity is, and they will only take what is given by other members of their family. Understand?'

'Not really.'

'I'll speak slowly, so that you do,' said Ewart. 'In order for the people of Algol to accept the assistance they so urgently need, I had to become one of them. Understand so far?'

'Continue, Mr Ewart.'

'On Algol every gift must be repaid by another gift. Because I was giving them so much, Algolan honour demanded that I was also given a gift of great value. I was offered the daughter of one of their warlords, and I had no choice but to agree. If I'd refused, they wouldn't have accepted the aid which they so desperately needed. I insisted that we were legally married, of course.'

'Of course.'

'We were married by proxy. It's all symbolic, although I must admit that becoming an honorary Algolan warlord was one of the proudest moments of my successful life.'

'William Ewart, warlord of Algol!' Rajic laughed, and toasted Ewart in admiration. He was very convincing, probably because he believed it himself. He'd never quite understood the difference between the truth and a lie. If he said something, then it was true.

'I see,' said the lawyer. 'I think. So your wedding was purely symbolic? You have no intention of going on honeymoon with your new bride?'

'No!' Ewart laughed, looking relaxed for the first time. 'I'm a busy man.'

'I'm very glad to hear that, Mr Ewart, because your new wife is only four years old.'

'Four? No, she's nineteen.'

'Beta Persei, or Algol, has a single planet. This planet, also known as Algol, has a very slow orbit around its twin suns.'

The lawyer had got it wrong, thought Rajic. She was implying that a year on Algol lasted much longer than a Terran year. Therefore if Ewart thought his bride was nineteen years old, she must have been much older. How old? Sixty? Eighty? A hundred? More . . .? Rajic smiled at the thought.

'Because of this,' continued the prosecutor, 'the inhabitants of Algol divide their year into smaller sections, the same way we divide our year into months. You seem to have misunderstood this division, Mr Ewart. Perhaps the information was badly translated, but there was definitely a fault in your communications.'

The judge nodded his approval at a witticism almost as clever as one of his own.

'Believe me, Mr Ewart,' said the lawyer, 'your new wife is only four years old. Four Earth years.'

Ewart looked absolutely astonished. For one of the few times in his life, he was lost for words.

It was bound to happen sooner or later, thought Rajic. Ewart's wives had kept getting younger and younger. And now he'd married one he would have to play with.

Rajic took another mouthful of vodsky, remembering.

'Off,' he said, and the screen blanked.

The court had heard about Ewart's new wife, his fifth wife. But she wasn't the fifth: she was the sixth. Rajic Jao Rajic was probably the only other person still alive who knew that Ewart had first married when he was very young, when he had another name, when he was someone else.

CHAPTER SEVEN

'You have no right to take me away from my work and bring me here! Do you know who I am?'

'Tell him who he is,' said Ewart. 'He seems to have forgotten.'

'You are,' said Zena, 'Doctor Ling Gorf Carrillos, previously holder of the Murray chair of archaeology at Tarbert University.'

'Previously?' said Carrillos.

'You'll notice you're no longer there,' said Ewart. They were in his stateroom, and he gestured towards the viewscreen, towards the stars. 'I bought your contract.'

'You can't do that!'

'The university was happy to sell it to me.'

'My guild wouldn't allow it!'

'Your guild seemed equally happy.'

'Those dogs! It's jealousy, that's what it is. I'm the best there is, that's why they all wanted rid of me.' Carrillos looked at the screen. 'Where are you taking me? You shouldn't take me anywhere. I'm an old man. I shouldn't travel, not at my age. Do you know how old I am?'

He was almost bald, his long beard was grey; his face was gaunt, his hands trembled; his feeble body was bent, and he supported himself with a walking stick.

'Tell him how old he is,' said Ewart. 'That's another thing he's forgotten.'

'You are thirty-one years old, Mr Carrillos,' said Zena.

'*Doctor!* Doctor Carrillos. Thirty-one! You're mad. Do I look thirty-one?'

'No,' said Ewart. 'But isn't that the idea?'

Carrillos opened his mouth to speak, then closed it again. He looked from Ewart to the viewscreen, back to Ewart again, and he shrugged.

'It was the only way I'd ever be awarded the chair,' he said. 'Unless I wanted to wait another fifty or sixty years, I had to get myself fixed like this and pretend to be as old as I look. Universities seem to expect that archaeologists should be as old as the things they study.'

As he spoke, he straightened his back and stood upright, stretching out his arms. He glanced at his walking stick, then hung it over his left arm.

'I still think I should have been consulted first,' he added.

'I bought your contract, Carrillos, because—'

'Doctor Carrillos.'

'—because, Carrillos, I needed an archaeologist.'

'Who are you?'

Ewart didn't understand what the archaeologist really meant. Everyone knew who William Ewart was.

Carrillos must have recognized him.

'I'm William Ewart.'

'And . . .?'

'You've heard of me, of course.'

Carrillos shook his head. 'If you're not an archae-ologist, why should I have heard of you?'

'ECC,' said Ewart.

'What's that?'

'You must have heard of ECC: Ewart Communications Corporation. And I'm *the* Ewart. William Ewart of Ewart Communications Corporation.'

'Oh.'

It didn't seem that Carrillos was pretending. He really had never heard of Ewart or of ECC. Having spent so much of his life researching the past, it was as if that was where he lived. He knew far more about ancient history than he did about the real world.

A movement in the corner caught Ewart's eye, and he glanced around, remembering that there were four of them in the stateroom, not three. The auteur was the fourth, filming as Ewart met the archaeologist for the first time.

The sequence with Carrillos not knowing who Ewart was would, of course, have to be edited out.

'William Ewart?' Carrillos said slowly, as he studied his new employer. 'Was it you who bought Chichén Itzá?'

'Right.' Everyone had heard of William Ewart.

Carrillos stared at Ewart, his eyes wide, his teeth bared, and he lifted his walking stick.

'You—!'

He took a step forward, raising the stick like a club. Another step, with the walking stick even higher . . .

A moment later Carrillos lay flat on his back. Zena's left foot was on his chest, pressing him down, and she held the stick between her hands. She studied it closely, snapped it in two, then examined it again, crumbling one of the splintered ends. Made from real wood, the walking stick must have been an antique. Zena threw it aside.

'Do you want me to kill him, sir?' she asked.

Ewart shook his head. He'd paid good money for Carrillos's contract. Or at least his money had been good at the time. His financial position was somewhat different since his enforced exile. As the university had probably discovered to its cost.

'What's wrong?' he asked. 'I own Chichén Itzá, right. It's a great place.'

'It was,' said Carrillos. 'Before you got your hands on it.'

'Let him up,' Ewart told Zena.

Ewart didn't feel threatened by anyone who looked as ancient as Carrillos. And Zena could easily deal with anyone, no matter how young or old.

Carrillos slowly rose to his feet, rubbing at his chest, then backed as far away from Zena as possible.

'I spent my second honeymoon in Yucatán,' said Ewart. 'Or was it the third? I had a great time.' He'd always had a great time on his honeymoons, for the first few days – and nights. 'But I was disappointed by Chichén Itzá. The most famous Mayan site, and it was such a dump.'

'You ruined it!'

'But it was nothing but ruins!' Ewart laughed. 'And don't pretend that was how it was meant to be. It had all collapsed after centuries of tourism. I bought the place and restored it to its former glory.'

'Former glory! Did the Maya have a gravslide to the top of the *castillo*?'

'The pyramid, you mean? If they'd had the technology, they'd have built one. Who wants to climb a hundred steep steps?'

'Ninety-one. Each of the four sides has ninety-one steps, making a total of three hundred and sixty-four. Including the top level, that makes three hundred and sixty-five – the same number as days in the year.'

'Right. But the pyramid would have no steps if I hadn't rebuilt it.'

'You turned the sacred *cenote* into a swimming pool!'

'You should have seen it before. It was just a filthy pond. And it's more than a swimming pool. It's educational, it gives visitors a better insight into the true history of Chichén Itzá and Mayan civilization.'

'Splashing around in superfloat water, gazing down through a transparent floor at fake gold and phoney skeletons – cheap replicas of the fabulous treasures and sacrificial victims thrown into the sacred pool as offerings to the rain gods! That's educational?'

'Right. It's those touches of authenticity which make tourists realize the true significance of where they are, that it's a genuine historical site, not some dream park.'

'But that's where tourists should go – to dream parks!'

ECC had never operated any dream parks. Communications companies took the world to the people, instead of vice versa. There were too many people in the world, and travel had to be restricted to those who appreciated it – and were prepared to pay the appropriate price. Ewart did, however, own a few other famous sites apart from Chichén Itzá. Or had owned them, until very recently.

'You've got to give people the real thing,' he said. 'Like Stonehenge.'

'Stonehenge? Was that you? It was you who rebuilt Stonehenge!'

'I picked up the pieces, right, made the place look like it was when the druids originally built it.'

'Druids?' Carrillos shook his head and stared at the floor, his body becoming almost as bent as it had been when he was pretending to be as old as he appeared.

'You know about Stonehenge?' said Ewart.

'Stonehenge was built on astronomical principles, just like the buildings at Chichén Itzá – one of which was an observatory.'

'Right,' said Ewart. Did the archaeologist think he bought such places without knowing anything about them? 'And at dawn on midsummer's day, the sun always rose directly above the heelstone. But who wants to wait a whole year for that?'

'So you arranged for Stonehenge to revolve, and now the sun rises above the heelstone every day.'

'What's wrong with that? If the druids could have

122

figured it out, that's what they'd have done. It's a pity it always happens at dawn. Who wants to get up at that time?'

Ewart had tried to find a way of solving the problem of sunrise being so early, but he hadn't succeeded. It no longer mattered, he supposed. Who cared what happened on Earth, the insignificant third planet of an inconsequential star?

'You can't cheat the public,' said Ewart. 'Not for long. So if you can't give them the real thing, give them something better than the real thing.'

'Like android druids cutting out the hearts of their android victims?'

'It's entertainment.'

'What about Chichén Itzá? How about real human sacrifices in the sacred pool? Who'd miss a few tourists? That would be a really genuine experience for them! And educational!'

'What's wrong with education? Most people know nothing about the Mayans.' Ewart paused. Most people knew nothing about anything, he supposed. 'I like the Mayans, that's why I chose you.'

'You *like* the Mayans? What does that mean?' Carrillos shook his head in bewilderment. 'Firstly, you mean "Maya" not "Mayan". Chichén Itzá only became what it is – what it *was* – after it was taken over by the Toltecs in 987. For a real Maya site, you need somewhere like Uaxactún or Yaxchilán, Utatlán or Kaminaljuyú.'

'You're an expert, and—'

'I'm *the* expert,' Carrillos interrupted. 'I'm the leading authority on Maya civilization, the only person in the world who speaks classical Maya.'

'In the galaxy,' said Ewart. 'In the universe. So who can you talk to?'

'What do you mean?'

'If you're the only person who can speak a lost language, who can you talk to?'

Carrillos shook his head again, either in denial or because he didn't understand.

'Why waste time learning another language?' asked Ewart. 'That's what slates were invented for.'

'To understand, that's the reason. Language is more than just words. What's the use of translation without comprehension? I learned Maya in order to understand their culture, their civilization. That's all I know, all I do.' He stared at the viewscreen once more. 'You said you chose me. What for?'

'To do your job. To find out about a lost civilization, a forgotten world. You've concentrated on one small part of Earth, but I'm offering you a whole new world!'

'But . . .' Carrillos shook his head. '. . . why?'

'Because I say so.'

'We're going on a ... a dig ... a field trip?' asked Carrillos.

'Right.'

'I've never done that before.'

'You must have done.'

'No. Archaeology is more than digging up ancient ruins.'

'But that's what you did in Yucatán,' said Ewart. 'Isn't it?'

'No. I've never been there.'

'You're the world's greatest expert on Mayan—'

'Maya.'

'—civilization?'

'Yes.'

'And you've never been to Yucatán?'

'Never.' Carrillos shook his head. 'But the Maya weren't restricted to the Yucatán peninsula. Their civilization stretched south to the Pacific coast.'

'Right. You almost had me worried for a moment. That's where you've been, to the coast?'

'No.'

'So where have you been?'

'Nowhere.'

'You must have been somewhere.'

'I've never been anywhere.' Carrillos looked at the stars again. 'Until now. You think there's anywhere left on Earth to excavate? All my work has been done at university, either as a student or fellow or professor.'

'Get Abdenga,' Ewart said to Zena. 'Now.'

She thumbed her comset.

'I'm no use to you,' said Carrillos, 'so you'll have to take me back.'

Carrillos was beginning to irritate Ewart. Perhaps he should be locked up with Lamakinto, then they could annoy each other.

'We're not going back,' said Ewart. 'So you'd better learn how to dig before we get to GX486/33-D.'

'D? Don't you mean C? GX486/33-C?'

Ewart glanced at Zena, and she nodded.

'How do you know?' he asked.

'I like to keep up to date,' Carrillos replied. 'C and D are the third and fourth planets of Galentic Xplorations's star system 486, discovered and explored by the company's thirty-third ship. D is inhabited – and C used to be.'

'Right,' said Ewart. 'And it's our mission, your mission, the Ewart Foundation's mission, to investigate the lost civilization of the third planet.'

'But . . . *why?*'

Ewart wasn't answerable to Carrillos, so he didn't answer.

'The 486 system has just been discovered,' said Carrillos. 'Every spacefaring world in the galaxy will be sending expeditions there, to steal whatever they can. Anything that could have been learned will be totally destroyed in the rush. Archaeology is a slow process, not a race. And what do you expect me to do all by myself? It's a dead planet, which means the people who once lived there are the lucky ones – compared to those who live on the fourth planet. The people of 33-D will be robbed and cheated and corrupted. Just like the people of Earth.' He gestured towards the viewscreen. 'You abducted me from my university, dragged me away from my work, from all my vital researches, for *this?*'

He spoke as if the magnificent stellar display before him were as insignificant as the sawdust beneath his feet.

'Right,' said Ewart. 'That's where we're going and that's what you'll be doing.'

'You can't make me.'

Ewart laughed. 'I can.'

'But I was happy where I was. I liked what I did. I enjoyed my work.'

Ewart couldn't imagine Carrillos ever being happy or enjoying himself. He had the kind of face which made Abdenga seem ebullient.

'It's a unique opportunity,' Ewart said. 'You've never done any field work on Earth, and I'm offering you a whole new planet to dig up! This is a great challenge, something new and different.'

'I don't want something new and different.'

Ewart was more excited about exploring the planet than the archaeologist. Carrillos had made himself look almost senile in order to secure his professorship, and the role had taken him over.

'What do you hope to get out of it?' Carrillos demanded.

'Nothing. Much.'

That was true, although Carrillos probably didn't believe it. But Ewart didn't care whether he believed it or not.

'Are you hoping to find some buried treasure? Is that it? The GX486/33-C equivalent of Tutankhamen's tomb?'

'Who?'

'Pirates were the ones who buried treasure. But that was only a myth. Like space pirates.'

What was Carrillos talking about? There was no doubt now; he'd turned into the old fool that he appeared to be.

'You mean space pirates might have buried treasure on 33-C?' asked Ewart.

'No! Buried treasure is a myth. Space pirates are a myth.'

'Are they?' said Ewart. Carrillos was an unlikely specialist in interstellar crime.

Zena opened the door, and Abdenga entered the stateroom. Ewart was glad to have someone else to talk to.

'Read up the latest info on the planet,' he said, pointing Carrillos towards the dataset. 'You know how to use one of those?'

Carrillos gave him a disdainful glance, then sat down at the console.

'Coffee,' Ewart told Zena, and she thumbed her comset again.

Ewart's antique porcelain cup and matching saucer stood on the silver tray, with the silver jug of cream and the silver spoon, both embossed with the monogram *E*, and the cafetiere of freshly ground coffee. The beans had not been freshly roasted, however, and this was the last of the fresh cream. Because Ewart refused to accept any substitute, from now on he would have to do without. Many years ago he had given up sugar, but that had been a voluntary sacrifice.

Although Grawl had used his own initiative to bring Ewart's coffee paraphernalia on board the *Demon Star*, he'd allowed Zena to take turns in serving it. He remained in the stateroom, and Ewart noticed that he stood closer to her than he had ever done on Earth.

Ewart pushed down on the plunger and poured the coffee into his cup, then stirred it. He slowly added the cream, which spiralled around and around on the surface before sinking into the coffee, lightening the blackness. It reminded him of something, and he glanced at the viewscreen, at the distant galaxy which could be seen far beyond the closer stars, white upon black, spinning with infinite slowness.

'Is that coffee?' asked Carrillos, raising his head from the dataset and sniffing at the aroma. 'May I have some?'

'No,' said Ewart. What little coffee Grawl had brought had to last him . . . well, for ever.

Ewart also noticed Abdenga looking at his cup. 'I suppose you'd like coffee, too?'

'If you have some to spare, sir, yes, thank you, I would,' said the lawyer.

'I haven't,' said Ewart. 'But there must be something similar on board. Zena, order some coffee. Get the steward to bring it.'

'Yes, sir.'

'What am I going to do with him, Joe?' asked Ewart, nodding towards Carrillos. 'He's never been on an archaeological expedition in his life.'

'Is that relevant, sir? He's already served his purpose.'

'Right. Like Lamakinto.'

United Religions of Terra had paid the Ewart Foundation to take one of their missionaries to the stars, and Ewart had also been paid to carry Carrillos into space. And, not entirely coincidentally, they were bound for adjacent planets.

Carrillos was right. Because GX486/33 had only been discovered recently, everyone wanted a piece of the action. Its inhabitants hadn't yet discovered spaceflight, and so Galentic Xploration was able to divide the whole system, selling off various rights and franchises and options on each planet to the highest bidders.

It was different when it came to the religious rights of any inhabited world. Galentic and its rivals were unwilling to offend any beliefs, even those minor creeds from some one-spaceship planet which couldn't afford to make an offer. The method they had adopted was that any religion which set up a missionary church on a newly discovered world could claim all the converts it could find – which was why Father Ahmed Lamakinto was on his way to GX486/33-D.

When it came to exploring pre-used worlds, the inhabitants of which had either annihilated themselves or become extinct through natural causes, Galentic would admit genuine archaeological expeditions for a short time, before selling off the commercial rights. To prove that such an expedition was not there merely to investigate potential mineral sources, a genuine archaeologist was essential.

That was why Carrillos was heading for GX486/33-C, although he didn't know it. But he didn't know anything, thought Ewart.

His mission was to set up base and act as front man for MMM, a mining company owned by one of those asteroid belt crazies who was even richer than Ewart had been.

Lamakinto and Carrillos had aided Ewart's escape from Earth. But he was away now, and so there was no reason to fulfil his obligations. Who would know? And even if they knew, what could they do about it? United Religions of Terra and Mac's Mineral Moons were far, far behind.

'You're right,' said Ewart. 'I don't need either of them.'

As he looked at Abdenga, he realized that neither did he need his lawyer. Who did Ewart have to sue here, out in the galaxy? What injunctions did he have to avoid, what lawsuits to evade?

'Perhaps they could simply be jettisoned,' said Ewart.

'As your lawyer, sir, I would advise against committing premeditated homicide.'

'There aren't any laws here, Joe. Who's going to arrest me?'

'A crime such as murder is an absolute, sir. The fact that there's no law, no police, no courts, makes no difference.'

Ewart thought it made a lot of difference, but he shrugged. He had no real intention of dumping anyone into the vacuum of infinite space, although he might make an exception if he ever had to listen to Lamakinto again. And Abdenga still owed him eighty-seven years.

The *Demon Star* was heading for GX486/33, and so he might as well deliver the archaeologist and the missionary to their destinations.

But the only reason the ship was aiming for GX486/33 was to deliver its two passengers – so if Ewart didn't go there, where would he go?

He'd avoided considering this, and as long as the ship was en route to somewhere or other he wouldn't need to think about it. Only when he left GX486/33 would he have to wonder about where he was going, where he would spend the rest of his life.

Always assuming the Rollein-Twist allowed the

Demon Star to reach GX486/33 . . .

'I know,' said Ewart, and he smiled. 'We'll drop Lamakinto off on the dead planet, where he can do the least harm; and we'll leave Carrillos on the other one, where he can meet up with some real live people.'

'If you can call them "people", sir,' said Abdenga.

'Aliens are people, Joe.'

'But they aren't human.'

'Some are,' said Ewart. 'Some are very human. But speaking of non-humans . . .'

Grawl went to open the door, and Rajic came into the room. He was carrying a tray laden with cups and jugs. He was naked. And Father Ahmed Lamakinto was with him.

'Wait,' said Ewart, as Grawl stepped towards the missionary. 'How did you get free?'

'It was God's will,' said Lamakinto, glancing around the stateroom.

One more person made little difference, Ewart supposed. The word 'spaceship' was completely wrong, because there was so little space on board. He signalled for Grawl to close the door.

'You took your time,' he said to the steward.

'Is that Earth time – or Algol time?'

Ewart didn't bother asking why he was naked. Rajic had previously said he wouldn't wear his uniform, and he'd always gone to extremes whenever he wanted to make a point.

'Serve the coffee,' Ewart told him.

'This is better than coffee, it comes from the fifth planet of—'

132

'Shut your mouth and do your job.'

'Whatever you say, old chap.'

'I forgive you for your mistake,' Lamakinto said to Ewart.

'What mistake?'

'Locking me up.' Lamakinto accepted a cup, which Rajic then filled with whatever it was from the fifth planet of wherever.

'That was no mistake.'

'More importantly, God forgives you.'

Ewart ignored the priest, instead watching as Rajic served the drinks to all the others. Grawl refused, and so did Zena.

'Are you sure?' asked Rajic.

'Yes.'

Rajic stood in front of her, naked, one hand holding the jug, the other hand holding the tray. Sensing he was being watched, he glanced over his shoulder. Grawl was staring at him, and he took a step away from Zena.

'Don't you notice the resemblance?' he said.

Zena looked him up and down. 'What resemblance?'

'The family resemblance.'

'What family?'

'Me and your boss.'

'You are related to Mr Ewart?'

'I'm his brother,' said Rajic as he poured himself a non-coffee.

'William Ewart.'

'What?'

Ewart turned and saw someone he'd never seen

before. A man who held a cup in one hand and a document in the other.

'I'm here on behalf of Solar Transit Leasing,' he said, 'to take possession of the vessel known as *Demon Star*.'

Solar Transit Leasing was one of Larnvik's companies. He hadn't bought the ship from his hated rival. Had he?

'You've broken the terms of your agreement with STL, and the ship must be returned to Earth immediately.'

'Who are you?' Ewart stared at the man, half recognizing him.

'My name is Timo Jarker.'

Ewart looked around the stateroom, at Lamakinto and Carrillos, at Zena and Grawl, at Abdenga and Rajic. Only Zena and Carrillos had been with him to start with. Then he remembered there had been someone else, someone who'd been there all the time.

The auteur. That was who Jarker was, he realized, the man he'd hired to film the expedition.

'I advise you,' said Jarker, 'to call the master and instruct him to turn back.'

'Sir,' said Zena, listening to her comset, 'there's a message from one of your wives.'

Ewart shuddered at the thought. 'No,' he said, and he shook his head. 'There's no communication across falspace.'

'I can hear her, sir. In translation.'

'Translation?'

'It's your fifth wife, the one from Algol.'

Ewart looked from Zena to Jarker. This couldn't be happening. He was suffering from hyperlusions, imagining the impossible. Larnvik. His wives. They were all in the past. He was so far from Earth that he was free from all of them. For ever.

There was no one here to repossess the ship. There was no message from his latest wife.

'She's on board the *Demon Star*, sir,' said Zena.

CHAPTER EIGHT

Ewart couldn't lock everyone up, so he'd locked himself away; and he was still there, in his suite on board the *Demon Star*.

'Will he leave us here?' asked Abdenga, glancing up into the alien sky as if checking that the ship were still in synchronous orbit directly above them.

'It's not up to him,' said Rajic. 'The ship won't leave, not with some of the crew on the planet.'

Unless, he thought, Ewart made the captain an offer which was too good to refuse. But that was unlikely, because it seemed Ewart didn't have anything to offer – and the master knew better than to rely on promises.

'There are a lot worse planets than this,' he added, as he looked around at GX486/33-D.

'I don't want to be stranded here,' said Abdenga.

'Why not? Wouldn't it be better than working for Ewart?'

Careful not to commit himself, Abdenga said nothing.

'Is he really your brother?' asked Carrillos.

'All men are brothers,' said Lamakinto. 'Whatever planet they are from, we are all God's children.'

'Half-brother,' said Rajic. 'Same father, different mothers. He's two years older than me. We grew up together. There's no reason to be stranded here. A new world like this means plenty of visitors, plenty of ships to get a ride on.'

'Not for me,' said Jarker. 'I'm responsible for the *Demon Star*. Where it goes, I go. And I've got to make sure it goes back to Earth.'

'God's children!' sneered Carrillos. 'Why don't you leave them alone? They don't need your religion.'

'So what are you doing down here?' asked Rajic. 'Shouldn't you have remained on board?'

'They have their own gods,' said Lamakinto, 'which they worship in their own primitive way, but such deities are only different aspects of the one true God who created the universe and all of its inhabitants.'

'I'm doing my other job,' said Jarker, gesturing to the autocams which were exploring the landscape. 'I'm still working for Ewart.'

Rajic knew that Jarker was on the planet for the same reason as the rest of them. After being cooped up on board the *Demon Star* for so long, he wanted to stretch his legs, to breathe fresh air. And while Ewart remained on the ship, they were all as far away from him as possible.

'Is Ewart really going to take me to GX486/33-C?' asked Carrillos.

'What kind of ships?' asked Abdenga, as he gazed into the sky once again.

'He expects me to pay for my flight!' said Jarker. 'Solar Transit Leasing owns that ship, not Ewart. I'm their agent, so he should be paying *me* the cost of *his* passage.'

'How should I know?' Rajic was surprised that Ewart had even brought the missionary here. 'Why would he want to do that?'

'You were on board the *Demon Star* under false pretences,' said Abdenga.

'Because I'm Doctor Ling Carrillos, that's why.'

'Let us give thanks to God for our safe arrival,' said Lamakinto, 'and for this magnificent food which He has granted to us.'

'I didn't know you were a quack,' said Rajic. 'Take a look at my knee, will you? I've had a lot of trouble with it lately, and alien medics are useless with Terran anatomy.'

'Who was it who bought a spaceship but didn't have the finance to pay for it?' said Jarker. 'That's false pretences!'

'I'm not that kind of doctor. I'm a doctor of archaeology, and that's why Ewart wants me to scrabble around amongst the ruins of the third planet. The whole idea is preposterous!'

'It's very sad about that world,' said Lamakinto. 'All of its people destroyed before they ever learned the truth about their creator.'

'Doctor of archaeology?' said Rajic. 'My knee's quite old.'

He continued serving food to the other four Terrans. Apart from Lamakinto, they hardly noticed, and even he seemed to think that God had done the catering for their galactic picnic.

Originally, Rajic had become a steward because that was the only way he could continue travelling across the galaxy, but he'd discovered that he really enjoyed his work. It was the steward's job to look after a ship's passengers, and over the years he had served all kinds of nutrients to all kinds of aliens on all kinds of ships.

There had been many times when he'd been required to perform some particularly repulsive service, times when he wished he were somewhere else and definitely doing something else. But every job had its drawbacks, and the positive aspects of his chosen occupation had more than outweighed the negative.

Rajic had always found it very creative and satisfying to prepare a meal, inventing it as he went along. When he and Ewart were kids, they used to raid the kitchen for midnight feasts. He enjoyed finding the food, devising some bizarre culinary concoction. And Ewart enjoyed eating it.

It was unlike his brother to miss a good meal, but perhaps not very surprising as Rajic hadn't invited him. He was beginning to wish that he had, because Ewart would definitely have appreciated the banquet he'd prepared so the other Terrans could celebrate their first landing upon an alien world. But the site was too dramatic and overwhelmed the menu, and so the food was only secondary.

While the others ate the finest fare which the galaxy had to offer – or the best that the *Demon Star* had on board, which wasn't quite the same thing – and were not even aware of it, Rajic surveyed the planet and wondered about his chances of finding another vessel.

The fourth world of the GX486/33 system was relatively primitive, and so any ship which landed here wouldn't be much of an improvement on the *Demon Star*. But any vessel which didn't have William Ewart on board would be an improvement, he supposed.

The best kind of spaceship to work on was a diplomatic vessel, because no expense was spared when it came to transporting ambassadors. Most such craft carried their own chefs, and Rajic wouldn't need to flasheat even a single plate of food. Diplomatic postings were a reward given to favoured politicians and businessmen, an extended vacation on some sophisticated and exotic world. It would take a long time until GX486/33-D reached that category, if at all. Having now been 'discovered', it would become no different from thousands of other exploitable planets.

'You belong in the dark ages,' said Carrillos.

'I seem to sense some hostility,' said Lamakinto.

'Seem to? Religion is totally based on fear of the unknown!'

'Not at all. You are the one who is in fear. The knowledge of God would lift that fear from you. There is nothing to fear, believe me.'

'I wouldn't believe you if you said the sky was green!'

Lamakinto looked up; the sky was green.

Rajic walked away from the argument and stood watching the aliens. They weren't watching him. None of them seemed to have paid any attention to their off-world visitors.

'Religion is the most dangerous weapon in the universe,' said Carrillos. 'More people have been killed by religious wars and persecution than anything else. Than everything else! That's what happened on Earth, and that's what you want to bring here. Admit it! Bigotry, ignorance, intolerance.'

'You're the intolerant one,' said Lamakinto. 'Do I complain about your work, tell you to get another job?'

'You've seen this all before, I suppose,' said Jarker, as he joined Rajic.

Rajic shrugged. Every inhabited world was so alike yet so dissimilar, and the same was true of its people. Perhaps what was wrong with being on an alien planet was that it wasn't alien enough.

But if GX486/33-D were totally hostile, a boiling mass of liquid lava, or a desolate wilderness with a poisonous atmosphere, they wouldn't be here. And any creatures which could survive on such a world would be so absolutely alien as to be unrecognizable.

'What will happen to them now?' asked Jarker, as he also looked at the natives down in the valley. 'Will they become corrupted or civilized?'

'Civilized?' said Rajic. 'What does that mean? Living in cities, that's all. An ancient Terran philosopher once said: "Civilization is the distance between society and its excreta." And that's our idea of civilization, isn't it?'

'I suppose so.'

'But not elsewhere. I've been on planets where the sanitary arrangements are, to say the least, less than satisfactory. The inhabitants can have no sense of smell, because they couldn't tolerate the stink if they did.' Rajic wrinkled his nose at the foul memories. 'Aliens are alien, never forget that. They have their own worlds, and they can do whatever they want. But when they travel into space . . .' He shook his head, not wanting to continue, not wanting to remember.

'Clearing up after is part of your job?'

Rajic nodded. 'Even that's not the worst. If you ever hear that a male Rigelan is nearby, get out. Fast. They spray everything, marking out their territory, claiming it as their own. I was once on a ship that had carried a couple of Rigelans thirty years earlier, and the stench still lingered.'

'When there's a war,' said Carrillos, 'it's always fought in the name of God.'

'When was the last war on Earth?' asked Lamakinto. 'God gave peace to the world.'

'It took long enough!'

'Time is infinite to the infinite one.'

'And every army always claimed that God was with them. How could God be on both sides?'

'He can. God doesn't choose sides. God has no favourites.'

'Not even those who pray, those who go to church? Not even priests? Not even missionaries? Then why bother?'

'God is everywhere. God is with everyone. God is with the people of this planet. God is with you.'

'No! There is no God!'

'How can you deny God's existence when all around you is the evidence of his creation?'

Abdenga came to stand with Rajic and Jarker, also

driven away by the argument at the table.

'Could he be right about God?' he said. 'That he created the universe, all its different people. Is that why they all look so much like us?'

'Or do we look like them?' said Rajic.

'What?' said Abdenga.

'Wasn't there some old idea about God making mankind in his own image?' said Jarker.

'It's the other way around,' said Rajic.

'If you think about it,' said Abdenga, 'there isn't really that much difference between them—' He gestured towards the natives in the distance. '—and us. They look far more like us than any other Earth creature does.'

'The ones which aren't extinct,' said Jarker.

'Yes. So perhaps the superior form of life on each world really was created by God.'

'What about the inferior forms of life?' asked Jarker.

'And those.' Abdenga nodded. 'I suppose.'

'God used the same pattern each time?' said Rajic. 'The same way he made planets? He found that the best shape was round, so all planets are round.'

'Spheres,' said Jarker. 'And I'm not being rude.'

'OK, the best shape for a planet is spherical. And the best shape for – what did you say? – the superior form of life is humanoid: two legs, two arms, two eyes, two ears, two heads.'

'One head,' said Abdenga.

'Two heads are better than one,' said Jarker.

'I'm serious,' said Abdenga, as he looked from Jarker to Rajic.

'So am I,' said Jarker. 'But I don't think God used the

same pattern. He'd have kept experimenting.'

'Trying to improve the basic design with every new world He made, you mean?' said Rajic.

'Yes. On one planet the people would be covered with fur, on another they'd have scales.'

'That's not experimenting, because exterior design depends on the environment.'

'Everything depends on the environment. It's survival of the fittest design. If the design is unsuitable, the animal can't survive.'

'We're not animals,' said Abdenga.

'What are we?' asked Rajic.

'We're people. We're human.' He looked from Rajic to Jarker. 'Or I am.'

Jarker held the autocam control in his right hand, but he raised his left for inspection. 'God gave us four fingers and one thumb, but he'd have kept trying to improve the design each time. On different worlds, people might be given an extra finger, or perhaps another thumb, as an experiment to see if that was any better.'

Abdenga held out his own hands and looked at them. 'No,' he said, and he shook his head for emphasis.

'You really think God couldn't improve on us?' said Jarker, and Rajic said, 'You really think God couldn't improve on *you*?'

'Why aren't you preaching to the locals,' said Carrillos, 'instead of wasting time with me?'

'You must not think of yourself as a waste of time,' said Lamakinto. 'God created you, and you are as important to me as any other of God's children.'

'There's only one of me, but there are thousands of

them over there, millions of them on the planet. That's why you're here. Because of them, not because of me. Go do your job, get them to join United Religions of Terra, threaten them with eternal damnation if they don't sign up!'

'I'm not here to threaten anyone. I'm an observer, that's all.'

'Ha!'

'We all worship the same God, although in different ways. URT doesn't force its ideas upon anyone.'

'You do on Earth! When does the inquisition start here?'

'You spoke of the dark ages, and I see why. Your idea of religious conversion is medieval. You think I intend to torture every alien unbeliever and burn every heretic at the stake? Of course not. I am a lone messenger from God, and I'm here to look and listen and learn, to discover what beliefs we have in common.'

By now, Lamakinto was talking to himself. Carrillos had walked over to join Rajic and Jarker and Abdenga.

'We all look the same, more or less,' said Rajic, 'because all the inhabited worlds are the same, more or less. Or the ones which humans can recognize as being inhabited, which means the ones which we can inhabit. We need a certain range of gravity, a climate which isn't too extreme, an oxygen/nitrogen atmosphere.'

'That's why no underwater aliens have been found,' said Jarker. 'Or found us. Fish seem to have had trouble discovering fire, for some reason. and they'd need spaceships full of water.'

'The same kind of conditions produce the same kind

of creatures. Parallel evolution means that as human-oids from the rim of the galaxy travel towards the centre, they meet more humanoids venturing out from the heart of the milky way.'

'If everyone's the same,' said Abdenga, 'why bother going into space?'

'Everyone isn't the same,' said Rajic. 'Two arms, two legs, one head – but the number of variations in shape and size and proportion is infinite. And that's only the way they *look*. The really alien part is how they *think*.'

'What about them?' asked Carrillos, looking towards the natives of GX486/33-D. 'How alien are they?'

'Eighty, eighty-five per cent, I'd say,' said Rajic.

'Eighty, eighty-five per cent of what?'

'Earth norm. When you get to under fifty per cent correlation, that's what you call really *alien*. Twenty-five per cent, and it's like talking to a brick wall – and having the brick wall talk back to you. Nothing makes any sense because you're on totally different levels of com-prehension. You know that one of you is a stupid ugly alien, but you begin to realize that it could be you.'

Before landing, Rajic had run a datascan on GX486/33-D. Compared to Earth, the gravity was low, the temperature high, the atmosphere thin. The natives were tall and slender; their thick skins were ochre coloured; they were long-limbed, with broad chests to encompass their enlarged lungs.

The planet was hot and dry, its villages far apart and clustered around isolated oases, and the natives lived in the cliffs around these waterholes. What appeared to be stone houses built on top of each other were in fact carved out of the sheer rockface, enlarged from the caves where their ancestors must have sheltered from the fierce heat of the midday sun.

'They look more human than a lot of Earth people I've known!' laughed Jarker.

Perhaps it was because he'd grown up with Ewart, which inevitably affected his perception, but Rajic was always very suspicious of his fellow Terrans. Even after all his experiences in space, humans still seemed the most untrustworthy of all races.

He was fairly certain that Lamakinto and Carrillos were what they appeared to be: a missionary and an archaeologist, setting foot on an alien world for the first time. They were only here because Ewart had used them to aid his escape from Earth, while Abdenga was here because he had the misfortune to be Ewart's lawyer. There was less to Abdenga than met the eye – or even two eyes.

But the opposite was true of the man who called himself Timo Jarker. He had joined the *Demon Star* to make a complete record of the expedition, but he'd already proved that he was more than an auteur. Although employed by Ewart, his latent function was to act on behalf of Solar Transit Leasing, which meant he also worked for Hiroshi Larnvik.

This wasn't the first time Jarker had been into space, Rajic knew.

'Do you think there are any archaeological sites nearby?' asked Carrillos.

Rajic glanced back and noticed that Lamakinto had finished eating and was about to join them.

'Let's go for a stroll,' he said, 'before the ruddy sky pilot gets here.'

'Is it safe?' asked Abdenga.

'Safe enough,' Rajic told him, as he began moving down the shaded slope on which they stood. 'We'd know if anything had happened to the crew. Don't worry, you've got Galentic Xploration's full guarantee. If you're injured by hostile natives, they'll fix you up. If you're killed, you get a funeral on the planet of your choice, and your nearest and dearest – or furthest and dearest – gets full compensation. In either case, all the locals get wiped out.'

The crew and the natives weren't the only aliens around, however. William Ewart's four-year-old bride was also on the surface of GX486/33-D, along with her chaperone. The two of them had been in space longer than anyone else, having arrived from Algol and transferred to the *Demon Star* shortly before Ewart boarded the ship.

At first Rajic didn't know who the aliens were, although he assumed that Ewart was aware they were on board. That turned out to be incorrect, but letting Ewart know wasn't amongst Rajic's duties. Because the Algolans were very spaced out by the long journey from their native world, the *Demon Star* had been underway for quite a while before Ewart's new bride announced herself.

'You're on shore leave,' said Rajic to the others. That probably didn't apply to Lamakinto, but he wasn't talking to him. 'So do what you want to.'

He made his way down the incline towards the two

Algolans. They had remained in their cabin throughout the voyage. Although Rajic had delivered their meals, he hadn't yet spoken to them. It was time that one of the family did.

There ought to be some way of screwing up things between his half-brother and his alien wife.

CHAPTER NINE

'Look at the screen!' said Ewart. 'Look at them!'

Zena looked at the screen, looked at them: Joseph Abdenga, Father Ahmed Lamakinto, Doctor Ling Gorf Carrillos, Timo Jarker, Rajic Jao Rajic.

'I bring them all this way, out to an alien planet, and what thanks do I get?'

'None, sir.'

'None, right! It was the same on Earth. I provided people with power, with all the energy they needed to survive and thrive, but did they appreciate it?'

'No, sir.'

'No, right! Ewart Communications Corporation gave them the best information and entertainment system in history. But did anyone ever thank me?'

'No, sir.'

'I might have expected that kind of behaviour from the others, but Abdenga's with them! Am I being old-fashioned to expect loyalty from my employees?'

'No, sir, not at all. May I take your biocount?'

'I don't need a fix.' Ewart closed his eyes, took several deep breaths, then looked at the viewscreen again. 'Rajic's holding a party down there! Why? What's he got to celebrate? Nothing. It's deliberate provocation. He's planning a mutiny, that's what it is. He wants to take over the ship! It's a conspiracy. He knows I can see him but not hear him.'

There was a privacy screen around Rajic, and the *Demon Star* didn't even have the simple surveillance equipment required to penetrate it. The screen not only absorbed every word, it blanked out the features of whoever was talking, which meant that Zena couldn't lip-read what was said or even interpret its meaning from the speaker's expression.

'And he's taunting me,' Ewart continued, no longer referring to what he couldn't hear – but to what he was being forced to watch.

He looked on in frustration as Rajic served the other four the most intriguing meal he'd ever seen: strange and enticing food the like of which he had never encountered, in such lavish profusion and extreme variety, all of it in tantalizing shapes and alluring colours. He wanted to turn away, but the viewscreen held him transfixed. His mouth watered as he watched and imagined all the exotic aromas, the delicious flavours, the succulent textures of the magnificent feast that Rajic had prepared.

He hadn't arranged this banquet for the benefit of the other Terrans, because it was obvious they didn't appreciate the culinary delights spread before them. The whole gastronomic extravaganza was Rajic's revenge, designed to show Ewart what he was missing.

'It's as if they don't have a care in the world. Any world. Do they know how lucky they are to be there? That the *Demon Star* could so easily have ... what? Exploded? Imploded? Or just ploded! Who knows what happens when the Rollein-Twist rolls and twists the wrong way?'

'Mr Rajic is one of the crew, sir,' said Zena. 'He must have been aware of the danger.'

'So why was he on board? To annoy me, that's why. That's how crazy he is. He'd risk his life just for the opportunity of irritating me.'

'I must emphasize that the probability of anything happening to the ship on any one voyage is statistically very small, and I am sure Mr Rajic is aware of that. His presence on board should reassure you, sir.'

'Nothing he's done in his whole life has ever reassured me! It's always had the opposite effect.'

Ever since Zena told him about the Rollein-Twist, Ewart had been worried that the *Demon Star* would never make the GX486/33 system. Now that the ship had arrived safely, he had to worry about whether it would reach its next destination.

The *Demon Star* was an old craft, but old could mean reliable. It was powered by an old method of propulsion, but old did not mean slow. Unfortunately, in this case, old meant Rollein-Twist.

And more ships propelled by such engines went missing than any other. A lot more. Even on the most remote world, the Rollein-Twist had not been installed on any vessel for several decades, and there were very few such ships left in commission. Most of the others had been dismantled. Or vanished.

No one knew what had happened to any of them. Each vessel had set off to travel from one star to another, slipped into falspace. And never reappeared.

'There ought to be a law,' said Ewart. 'Ships like this shouldn't be allowed to fly.'

'You have always said, sir, that business works best when unfettered by petty bureaucratic rules and regulations.'

'I believe in regulation, but it has to be self-regulation. The people who operate a business are the ones who know best how to manage it. It isn't the job of government to control the free market.'

When it came to interstellar travel, no single government, no single planet, could enforce restrictive legislation. This might mean there were a few unsafe ships still in operation, but freedom had its price. It was unfortunate that Ewart might have to pay it.

'That bastard Larnvik!' he said. 'He owned the *Demon Star* and he knew it was me who was buying it. That's why it was such a good deal. Because of the Rollein-Twist. He hoped I'd be dragged through a wormhole or sucked into a black hole or drawn through a spangle-hole or end up in the arsehole of the universe. But at least the bastard didn't get a single rupan.'

The father of Ewart's Algolan bride had reneged on the promised dowry, which meant that Larnvik hadn't been paid for the *Demon Star*. That was why Jarker was trying to reclaim the ship. But he wasn't going to get it. He wasn't going to get anything. Jarker would end up stranded on GX486/33-D. Like all the others who were down there, enjoying themselves at Ewart's expense.

'Could it all be a hyperlusion?' said Ewart, gesturing towards the screen. 'I can see this fantastic meal, but I can't eat it.'

Throughout his life, Ewart had always slept soundly, dreamed only pleasant dreams. But being denied such a wonderful banquet was a true nightmare, the worst thing his subconscious could imagine.

'I can see the meal, sir,' said Zena. 'I do not believe I could share the same delusion as you.'

'But I might only think you say you can see it. There's no objective reality, isn't that what you told me? You could be part of my illusion, right?'

'It is possible.'

Ewart looked at Grawl. 'Can you see those five down there, all stuffing themselves?' But even as he asked, he knew it could prove nothing.

Grawl nodded. And it proved nothing.

The Rollein-Twist could have trapped them all in falspace. A split second was stretched to infinity. Ewart was imagining everything, unable ever to escape. He might never eat again.

'I suggest you relax, sir.'

'How would you suggest I do that?'

'By watching something else.'

'Is there anything interesting, anything I haven't already sampled?'

'There are lots of things which you have not seen, sir.'

'I don't have to see them. They're all as bad.'

154

Ewart owned Ewart Communications Corporation, but he was a busy man. He'd seldom had time to watch any of his comservice's output. His only regular viewing had been the Candy and Mandy show. Traitors . . .

It seemed that everyone he knew was a traitor. There was nobody he could trust. Even his new wife had tricked him by finding her way on board the *Demon Star* while it was still in orbit.

Before leaving Earth, the ship's library had been stocked with a full selection of ECC product. Ewart had chosen the first show at random and couldn't believe how mind-numbingly moronic it was. He'd then scanned the catalogue, looking for some quality programming, and realized this was as good as it was ever going to get.

'Grawl and I have been watching a very entertaining drama about space pirates, sir, which we both recommend.'

Ewart kept hearing about pirates.

'Both?' He glanced from Zena to Grawl.

'Yes, sir,' said Zena, and Grawl nodded, once.

'I don't think so.'

'You could try some sim/stim, sir.'

'No.'

Ewart had never understood the attraction of abandoning his mind to simulated actuality, of surrendering his body to artificial stimulation. He'd tried it several times, with the very best equipment, but he soon grew bored and always felt very disappointed afterwards.

It was claimed that people using sim/stim could actually control what was going on around them, choose what would happen within whatever nexus they had entered. But that was what they were meant to believe. Being the focus of a neuroscape was as passive as watching the same thing on a two-dimensional viewscreen, because every possible alternate choice had been calculated and computed to produce the images and sensations with which the person was infused.

Most people preferred to relax while being entertained, to let events happen. They didn't want to work for what they experienced, which was why the majority audience selected a format which had already been devised by an expert.

It was like cooking, Ewart supposed. The same ingredients were available to anyone who could afford them, but they could produce very different results. It took time and skill to prepare a meal properly, which was why Ewart always employed master chefs, while most people consumed pre-prepared meals.

Most of ECC's general output was already personalized. Shows were not designed for individuals, naturally, but to match different categories of viewer. The precise details of what was transmitted to each SeeV depended upon their occupation and income and location.

Demographic direction meant that product projection could be totally targeted at the correct consumer. Or so the advertising jargon claimed. Ewart had never believed it, but he was glad that ECC's sponsors did.

As an ex-tycoon, totally broke, in orbit around an alien world, Ewart's purchasing profile didn't fit into any of the commercial categories.

During his brief survey of ECC output, however, he

had seen a number of edible items worth trying. But he'd never have the chance now.

'Is there any Sol Global output in the library?' he asked.

'No, sir!'

'Only for comparison.' Ewart turned away from the screen. 'Call the captain.'

Zena thumbed her comset. There was no reply. There was never any reply.

'Why won't he answer?' Ewart muttered.

'Or she. The captain could be female, sir.'

'Right.'

'Or it. The captain might be neither male nor female. It could be an inanimate entity, sir. The ship and the captain could be part of each other, just as the ship and the Rollein-Twist are one and the same thing.'

'What?'

'I have discovered that the *Demon Star* does not have engines as such. The ship is also the engines, sir. That is why it has never been refitted with a new propulsion unit.'

'What else did you find out?'

'Very little, because all the primary data has been deleted. It seems that the ship was originally a military vessel, built approximately three hundred of our years ago.'

'Three hundred!' He'd known it was old, but not that old. No wonder it was so cheap. 'Where was it built?'

'A planet called Earth, sir.'

'Earth? Impossible. We weren't building spaceships three hundred years ago.'

'Lots of planets are called Earth.'

Ewart thought about that. 'Right. And lots of stars are called the sun?'

'Yes, sir.'

Ewart glanced around his stateroom. Three hundred years was a long time, and he wondered how far the ship had travelled over the centuries, how many worlds it had orbited, how many voyages it had made – and how many it had left.

Once a military vessel, it was now an old wreck, crewed by galactic derelicts like his brother. If the *Demon Star* had any class, then Rajic certainly wouldn't have worked here. He might not have needed any qualifications to be a steward, but what bothered Ewart was that this level of experience and skill and competence was probably matched by the rest of the crew.

He'd invited the captain to dine in his suite, but there had been no reply. It didn't really matter, because after all the captain was only another employee. He was little more than a chauffeur, hired to take Ewart from one planet to another instead of from one city to another.

The main reason for the invitation was so that he could ask the captain various questions. Rajic would probably have been able to supply the answers, but Ewart was determined not to ask him.

It was also likely that Jarker could have told him some of what he wanted to know, but Ewart refused to talk to him again despite his constant requests.

'We must talk, Mr Ewart,' Jarker had said, the only time when Ewart allowed him on screen.

'There's nothing to talk about. The *Demon Star* isn't going back to Earth.'

'That's fine by me.'

'You said you wanted the ship to go back.'

'That was by way of opening negotiations, Mr Ewart. Solar Transit Leasing wants the ship to go back to Earth. I don't. Not necessarily.'

'But you work for STL.'

'I'm a free agent and I work for anyone who will pay me. That includes you, Mr Ewart. You are employing me to make a film of this voyage.'

'Not any more. You're a traitor. You're working for Larnvik.'

'Not necessarily. If you make me a better offer, you can have my exclusive services. I'm sure we can come to some mutually satisfactory agreement.'

'Why should I make an agreement with you?'

'Because I can give you full legal title to the *Demon Star*, Mr Ewart.'

'Why do I need legal title? There's no law here. The only law that matters is possession. We're out in space. Possession is nine-tenths of the law. And repossession is impossible.'

'Once you reach a planet, Mr Ewart, you need proof of ownership. If STL has reported the ship as missing and you're found in possession, you could be arrested for piracy. On most worlds, the penalty is death. On some, it's worse.'

'I have proper title to the *Demon Star*. I bought it.'

'You bought it, Mr Ewart, but you didn't pay for it.'

'There was a slight financial hitch. It's a technicality.

If there are any problems when we get to another planet, my lawyer will handle them.'

By now Hiroshi Larnvik would have more to worry about than how much Ewart owed for the *Demon Star*. The sum was infinitesimal compared to the debts of Ewart Communications Corporation, which with luck would totally destroy Solar Global Network.

At first, Larnvik probably hadn't cared about being paid for the ship. It was a small debit on the balance sheet, and the account would be more than balanced by getting rid of Ewart. That was why he must have ordered Jarker not to make a move until the *Demon Star* was already in falspace. He'd hoped that the Rollein-Twist would do the rest.

'Not necessarily,' Jarker had said.

'How do I get proper legal title?'

'We make a deal, Mr Ewart. I'm a businessman like you.'

'You're a crook.'

'What's the difference?'

'If I refuse to make a deal ...?'

'I'm still working for Solar Transit Leasing, and I'm empowered to take control of this ship on their behalf.'

Or maybe it had been Jarker's own idea to wait until the *Demon Star* had entered falspace. Because the ship was further away from Earth, he could charge more for its return.

'Firstly,' Ewart had said, 'I doubt if Solar Transit Leasing is still in business. Secondly, I'm sure there are other ways of acquiring the proper documentation. Thirdly, you are a stowaway. You add extra mass to the ship, which could endanger the safety of the passengers and crew. You will therefore be jettisoned. Forthwith.'

'No! Wait! Listen! I can give you the genuine title.'

'Right. Give it to me.'

'No, not give. Sell, I mean, sell. We can make a deal, Mr Ewart. You can't jettison me. I'm not a stowaway. I'm supposed to be on board. I'm working for you, Mr Ewart. I'm your auteur.'

'I told you: not any more. That means you're an unauthorized person. And you know what happens to those.'

'What?'

Ewart had waited several seconds, watching the anxious look on Jarker's face, until he said, 'They have to pay their fare.'

'Thank you, Mr Ewart, thank you. And what you said about jettisoning me . . .?'

'That was by way of opening negotiations.'

They had reached an agreement, but any contract made under duress was not legally binding and so its terms were irrelevant. Ewart was a businessman, and he would have full and proper title to the *Demon Star*. Jarker was a crook, and he would have nothing. That was the difference.

Jarker's plan was that the ship would be sold, and he would take a share of the proceeds. The former was a good idea, the latter was not.

When he'd recovered from the shock of hearing what the Rollein-Twist might do to the *Demon Star* and its occupants, Ewart had planned a refit with more reliable engines; but from what Zena had now told him, this appeared to be impossible. The ship would have to be sold. Because of the Rollein-Twist, he wouldn't get a very good price. Except from someone who was unaware of the inherent eccentricities of such a method of propulsion.

Ewart couldn't risk travelling in the *Demon Star* again. Trapped in orbit around GX486/33-D, the sales prospects weren't very good. He'd have to accept whatever was offered, because he needed to pay for passage to another star system.

It was a pity. He liked the idea of owning a spaceship, of always moving from world to world. This was what he and Rajic had dreamed of when they were kids, he remembered.

There was a lot of potential in such a business. If a ship kept travelling to different star systems, how could any one planet impose tax claims? Taxation inevitably reduced incentive and enterprise. Without it, profit and prosperity were inevitable.

He still had his pension fund. He could buy another ship, one that was more reliable – perhaps even discover the unknown planet that he and Rajic had always imagined they would.

Ewart's World! That was a far better name than GX486/33-A or B or C or D.

Why not? Everything else he had ever done was so ephemeral. He'd built up Ewart Communications Corporation from nothing, but it was all gone, lost as though it had never existed. To have a planet named after him would be a real achievement, almost like being immortal. Centuries from now, he would be dust but his name would still be known.

Ewart's World . . .

He thought of what Zena had said about the purpose of life: 'The human race exists in order to procreate, sir, to produce the next generation which will then in turn reproduce itself.'

If that were true, Ewart had fulfilled his role in life. Having ensured the continuation of his genetic line, he might as well stop breathing. It was a pity about his offspring, and he wished he'd never inflicted them on the world. With luck, that was where they'd stay, never venturing out into the galaxy.

He shook his head, trying not to remember what might have been, what should have been.

There was more to life than reproduction. There had to be. He was convinced he had another reason for existing. He didn't know what it was, not yet. Until then, he'd just have to stay alive.

Ewart had undergone his first rejuve several years ago. His body could take one more treatment, although that would only be half as effective as the original. A third rejuve, and he risked dramatically speeding up the final countdown on his biological clock. Midnight was inevitable, but he wanted to postpone it as long as possible.

And out here, where there were worlds so much more advanced than Terra, there surely must be one planet on which they had perfected a technique which guaranteed the longest of longevity.

Why become immortal by discovering a new world, when there was an even better way: by living for ever . . .?

CHAPTER TEN

'Genitals your us show,' Ewart's wife's chaperone said to Rajic.

The original protocol when testing the accuracy of translation between alien languages was that first exchange of phrases would be repeated to check whether the same words came back.

Both sides had to be extremely careful with their opening remarks, because if something went wrong it could lead to the death of either or both of them. Spaceships had been destroyed because of a simple misunderstanding, planets annihilated, solar systems wiped out, galactic wars started . . .

Rajic wondered if the Algolan knew of the old procedure and was deliberately misusing it. In either case, although certain subtleties and emphasis may have been lost in the translation, such first words weren't all that unusual. During his years as a spacer, he'd heard much stranger introductions.

He knew better than to say: 'Show me yours and I'll show you mine.' Instead, he replied, 'I'd prefer to leave that until we're better acquainted.'

'Male are you?'

'Yes.'

'Female are we.'

Sometimes appearances could be deceptive, very deceptive, but Rajic was prepared to accept the Algolan's word. Or her translated word.

'You with sex have can we that so own our with compatible are genitals your if discover to wish we,' she said.

And sometimes translations needed translating.

A slate was a highly sophisticated and sensitive piece of equipment which required expert tuning. Rajic glanced down at his unit. It had been made by ECC, he noticed, which probably explained the fault. He thumped it with his fist.

The slate screeched in protest, then recited, 'We wish to discover if your genitals are compatible with our own so that we can have sex with you.'

We? Did the she mean that they both wanted to have sex with him? Some aliens matured very quickly, but Ewart's four-year-old bride looked like a four-year-old Terran child. More or less.

While he was repairing the slate, the alien had reached out towards Rajic. If her hand had been directed towards his crotch, he'd have moved back. Instead, she stroked his left elbow. Which seemed an odd place for any race to keep their genitals.

Her caution was well advised, however. Just as aliens came in a wide variety of shape, size and proportion, so did the more private parts of their anatomy. Although to many of them, nothing was private.

'Your invitation is very much appreciated,' said Rajic, 'but I won't have sex with you.'

'You will do as we command.' She leaned down and rubbed his right knee. 'We are Princess Janesmith, and to disobey means death.'

Princess Janesmith? Slates could handle most things, but they weren't so good when it came to translating names. A princess wouldn't be a chaperone, and an alien wouldn't be plain Jane. As for 'we', that must have been a linguistic peculiarity. She was using the first person plural instead of first person singular.

Those who didn't know always presumed that 'slate' was short for 'translator'; those who knew even less thought it was short for 'translater'; but it was an acronym for Simultaneous Linguistic And Tonal Equalizer.

'Death?' said Ewart.

He looked at Princess Janesmith, and Princess Janesmith looked at him.

'It was worth a try,' she said, and she rocked her head from side to side – which must have been the equivalent of a shrug.

Ewart's new bride was kneeling a few metres away, throwing crumbs towards a small hole in the rocks. A tiny lizard-like creature darted out, snatched up the food, then sprang back into its lair. The girl bounced with excitement, just as any other four-year-old would do. She was small, her blonde hair plaited and tied with a ribbon which matched the colour of her skin. They were both blue.

'That's Princess Marysmith,' said Janesmith. 'Our sister. It's because we're ugly, that's why you won't have sex with us.'

'No,' said Rajic, which was true.

Janesmith was an eighty-five per cent, and he'd had sex with aliens whose correlation was far lower than that. All in the line of duty, of course. Or mostly. Rajic had checked up on Algolans, and he hadn't expected them to rate more than seventy per cent, perhaps seventy-five at maximum.

The physical appearance of a race was a reflection of the planet on which it originated. Algol had a high gravity, and its inhabitants were supposed to be small and squat. Although she was only a child, it seemed that Marysmith fitted those specifications. Janesmith was tall and slender, however, and Rajic found himself staring at her bare breasts. They were pale blue, but there were only two of them, nicely shaped with purple nipples. Perhaps she was nearer to ninety per cent.

She was wearing skin-tight shorts, and ankle boots, both made of the same scaled animal hide, zig-zagged in black and white. Her arms and legs were bare, although her elbows and knees were covered. These must have been Algolan erogenous zones, which explained why she had stroked Rajic's left elbow and right knee.

Comparisons were always difficult, but she seemed young and could easily be taken for the nineteen year old that Ewart thought he'd married – nineteen Earth years, that was. Her hair was white, cropped short to reveal her pointed ears; her features were almost feline, her oval face dominated by her huge sloping eyes.

Although Rajic had always liked cats, he'd never fancied them.

'We are ugly,' she said, hiding her breasts with her hands. Each hand had three fingers and one thumb, all of them tipped with sharp claws. 'If we weren't a princess, we'd have been destroyed at birth like any unwanted male.'

'You are a princess? She is your sister?'

'Yes. And we hate her.'

'I know the feeling.' Rajic gazed up into the green sky.

'You hate your sister?'

'My brother.'

'We have never had a brother, or not one who survived. They were all killed at birth, of course.'

'Of course,' said Rajic, being polite. That was another part of his job, to be polite.

'Where is William Ewart?'

Rajic pointed upwards.

'You know him?'

Rajic nodded.

'What does that mean?'

'Yes, I know him. He's my brother.'

'Your brother? Then we're related! You're our brother! It's fortunate we didn't have sex, because we would have been dishonoured.'

'Very lucky,' Rajic agreed. 'And would I have been dishonoured?'

'No. You would have been dead. We are a princess. After sex, we would have killed and eaten you.'

Janesmith made a low sound, almost like a growl. No,

168

it *was* a growl. She opened her mouth, and for the first time Rajic saw her teeth. They were sharp, like fangs. No, they *were* fangs . . .

He backed away, and the Algolan growled even louder. She stood watching him, her blue arms akimbo.

'That was a joke,' said Janesmith, and she growled again. 'Do aliens like you not have a sense of humour?'

'Sometimes.'

'We don't eat our males after sex! If we did, there would soon be none left, and what fun would that be?'

This time, Rajic presumed that by 'we' she meant all Algolan females.

'What's your name, our brother?'

'Rajic Jao Rajic. Call me Rajic.'

'We are Princess Janesmith. Call us Princess.'

She growled again, which Rajic guessed was the sound of Algolan laughter.

'Ewart is only my half-brother,' he told her.

'Half-brother? What's the other half? Your sister? You are bisexual on your planet?'

'We are half-brothers because we have the same father, different mothers.'

'How odd. Marysmith and us have the same mother, different fathers. You would call her our half-sister?'

'Yes.'

Janesmith turned her head, watching as the other Terrans made their way down the valley.

'We want to have sex with one of you aliens,' she said. 'We've been celibate for too long, and we want some fun on this voyage. Those four, are they all male?'

'Yes.'

'That one. What is his status?' Her clawed left thumb was aimed at Carrillos.

'He's an archaeologist.'

'No.' Janesmith rocked her head in what Rajic had thought was the equivalent of a shrug. 'We're not having sex with someone who digs up graves. What about him?'

'He's a lawyer.'

'What's a lawyer?'

'It's hard to explain.'

'Never mind. If they don't exist on Algol, they aren't important. That one?'

She indicated Lamakinto. Rajic wondered what tempting profession he could invent for the missionary, because he wanted to see Lamakinto's reaction when the Algolan princess demanded sex.

'Is he a priest?' said Janesmith, as she continued studying Lamakinto.

'How can you tell?'

'His clothing is so different from the rest of you, and he has a talisman around his neck. He's like our priests, except he's male. You have male priests on your world?' She paused. 'Is yours a male-dominated society?'

Rajic shrugged.

'What does that mean?'

'It means—' He shrugged again. '— I don't know. But I suppose the answer is "yes".'

'How strange. Earth must be a very odd place.' She rocked her head again. 'Do you only have sex for reproduction?'

'No. We also have sex for, ah, recreation.'

170

'Good. But not him. Sex and religion don't mix. And him?'

The only one left was Jarker, and Rajic said, 'He controls those autocams, and—'

'One of them? No! They are the ones who tell lies to the people, those who try to undermine the authority of the monarchy, those who would replace it with the ignorant rule of the masses. They should all be killed!'

'Eaten?' suggested Rajic.

'Yes,' agreed Janesmith, and she growled with laughter.

More than ninety per cent, he thought, and he asked, 'Did you know William Ewart owned and operated a media empire?'

'Media!' Janesmith hissed and flexed her claws. 'Empire?' Her eyes flared with anger. 'Algol is an empire. Our mother is the Empress, and we should have been her successor. Instead, we have to babysit for ... for that!' She spun around, her left arm arced out, claws aimed towards her sister, missing her by a fraction.

Marysmith was totally oblivious to everything, all her attention concentrated on the reptile she was trying to lure from its refuge with a trail of food.

'If the others didn't meet your sexual standards,' said Rajic, trying to change the subject, 'why did you ask me?'

'We can only have sex with someone of high status. You provide the food by which we all survive, which means you're a very important person.'

'That's right,' he agreed, impressed by her perception. 'That's right.'

'It's such a pity you're our brother and we can't have sex.' Janesmith glanced at Marysmith. 'Will you kill our sister for us?'

'Kill her? Why? So that we aren't related? So we can have sex? I can't do that.'

'Why not?'

'Because ... because she's also my sister,' said Rajic. Or according to Algolan reasoning she was. 'I can't kill my sister.'

'You can. That's the only honourable way. Death must be kept within the family. We've already killed three of our sisters.'

Rajic looked at her, but she didn't laugh. It seemed she meant what she said, and he asked, 'Why?'

'To become Empress. That was why our elder sister tried to kill us, but we killed her first. Then we killed the two younger ones, and we've tried to kill Marysmith several times.'

Rajic said nothing. There seemed nothing to say. He glanced up at the green sky, thinking of how he was on the surface of an alien world, with a strange female who came from a different alien planet. The gulf between their societies and cultures was beyond all calculation, but they were able to converse together without apparent difficulty.

And what did they talk about? Murdering her sister, who was his brother's four-year-old bride.

The galaxy was a weird and wonderful place.

'No,' said Janesmith, after a few more seconds, 'we're not going to kill her. Not yet. That's what Annsmith's father wants us to do.'

Rajic waited, then prompted, 'Who's Annsmith?'

'Our youngest sister, the heir to the throne. But we intend to be Empress, so we'll have to return to Algol and kill her. And if any more sisters are born, although that's doubtful because of our mother's age, we'll kill them.'

'What does your mother think when you kill her other daughters? Doesn't she mind?'

'That's the way it is. Our mother killed six of her own sisters to become Empress.'

'It's the youngest daughter who becomes Empress?'

'The youngest who survives.'

There would never be an Emperor, Rajic realized, because Algolan society was run by its women. Janesmith had already said that her brothers were killed at birth.

'What happened to your brothers?' he asked. 'Were they eaten?'

'Yes.'

Rajic laughed out loud, and Janesmith quickly sprang back. She raised her arms, claws aimed at him, and bared her teeth. Marysmith also retreated, striking the same defensive pose as her sister. Rajic became silent, realizing that the sudden unfamiliar sound of his laughter must have seemed like a threat. The fact that Janesmith could be so scared, however, made her even more human. Close to ninety-five per cent.

'The Empress eats her sons,' she said. 'What's wrong with that?'

The habits of one race couldn't be compared with the standards of another. It was impossible to translate 'morality' – either as a word or a concept. In any case, devouring one's offspring was tame compared to many other things Rajic had encountered.

'Isn't cannibalism a bit . . . anachronistic?'

'Traditional, you mean. The Empress is the head of the royal family, of the whole family of Algol, and she represents all our traditional family values.'

Janesmith lowered her arms as she relaxed, and she moved back to where she had been standing. Marysmith laid another line of crumbs.

'Tradition is one of the many benefits of a monarchy,' Janesmith continued. 'Hereditary rule offers political stability, an unbroken line of government going back for millennia, and there are plenty of colourful historic ceremonies to remind the lower orders of our divine right to rule. And of their own subservience.'

'How many brothers have you had?' Rajic asked.

'Who's counting? If there's a boy, he dies, his father dies.'

'You must be able to choose the sex of your children.'

'The common people can do that, but not the royal family. Choosing a child's sex spoils all the fun!'

'Your mother has sons, then eats them, and that's fun?'

'It's royal etiquette.' Janesmith rocked her head from side to side. 'And a baby is full of vitamins.'

Rajic stared at her, and Janesmith laughed her growling laugh. He had no way of telling how much, if any, of what she'd told him was the truth. It was easy to believe that slates provided accurate translation, but the misinterpretation of a single syllable could render a whole conversation meaningless, although neither party was aware of it. Sex and eating seemed almost inseparable to the Algolan, so perhaps there was some confusion between the words 'consume' and 'consummate'.

Then he heard another growl, and he glanced around to see Marysmith with the tiny lizard in her hand. She raised it to her mouth. Then bit off its head.

As she chewed and swallowed, Rajic realized that probably most of what he'd heard was true.

'Kids!' said Janesmith. 'She'll pick up anything and gobble it down, but she won't eat her vegetables.'

'If you're that worried about her diet,' said Rajic, 'you should have told me. I can prepare anything, disguise it as—' He glanced at Marysmith. The reptile had almost vanished, and she sucked its still-wriggling tail into her mouth. '—something she finds delicious.'

He wondered if Janesmith had thought her other three sisters were delicious. Would Marysmith also become part of her diet?

'When you ... er ... killed your sisters, did you ... er ... eat them?'

'Of course not.'

Rajic was glad to hear it.

'They were too big,' Janesmith added. 'We only ate their vital organs, so their souls would live on within us. They were our sisters, so it was the least we could do. When the Empress killed our father, she shared his heart with us. Is it like that on Earth, except that the father kills each of his wives?'

'Not exactly. When we're in love, we "give our hearts" – but not literally.'

'Love? You marry for love? On Algol, only the poor people do that.'

Rajic nodded, remembering when he'd been young and poor and in love. Then, like so many other times, Ewart had stolen away what had been his. It was Rajic who should have married Myiko, but it was Ewart who had.

'In the royal family,' said Janesmith, 'duty takes precedence over affection. The purpose of marriage is to produce daughters. Every male on Algol dreams of being chosen as the world's most handsome virgin, loved and respected by everyone on the planet. Brother will kill brother for the chance of catching the eye of the Empress, of fathering the next Empress.'

The way that Janesmith had spoken so casually of killing her sisters, Rajic supposed that fratricide was no big deal.

But marrying the Empress didn't seem much of a career move. The prospects weren't very good, and there was probably no pension. Not that they lived long enough to retire. If a son was born, the father died. If a daughter was born, the father died – although maybe not as soon.

'And there are always plenty of applicants for the job?' he said.

'Only the elite are considered, of course, males from one of Algol's top hundred families. Even if a male isn't chosen, he may soon have another chance. There are lots of royal weddings on Algol. The lower orders love them.'

'Have you had a royal wedding?'

Janesmith growled with laughter. 'Only the Empress has weddings. When we become Empress, we will have many consorts, many weddings. Until then, we can choose those males who were not chosen by our mother. We have spent our life studying all the arts and sciences of sex. Because we're so deformed, we trained very hard so that our partners wouldn't notice our ugliness. We practised and practised until we became an expert in eroticism.'

She stared at Rajic, then added: 'But perhaps there are new things to learn. We wish to make the lives of our consorts as ecstatic as possible.'

'Until you kill them,' said Rajic.

'We all must die.'

For an awful moment Rajic thought he was about to be treated to a lecture on Algolan religion and the afterlife.

Instead, Janesmith glanced at her sister and said, 'Some sooner than others than sooner some.'

Rajic hit his slate again, but Janesmith's words kept coming out backwards. She gazed up into the green sky, as if she could see her native planet, and said she would become Empress, perhaps after killing her mother, kill Annsmith and Annsmith's father, return to Algol and kill Marysmith.

Or, in non-reverse order, she'd kill Marysmith, return to Algol, kill Annsmith's father and Annsmith, perhaps also kill her mother, and then become Empress.

From what Rajic could make out, it seemed that Annsmith's father had wanted the two rival sisters off planet so that his own daughter could become Empress.

He'd pretended to be Marysmith's father and promised her to Ewart by offering a huge dowry. Ewart had only married her because of the money, but there hadn't been any.

Janesmith had been forced to accompany Marysmith in the hope that she would follow family tradition and kill her sister. So far from home, it was highly unlikely that she would ever return, and so Annsmith would ascend to the throne.

'Crown the inherit will we but we will inherit the crown,' said Janesmith.

Rajic stopped vigorously adjusting his slate.

'So it was Annsmith's father who arranged for Marysmith to marry Ewart?' he said, making sure he'd understood.

'They are betrothed, that's all. A princess cannot marry a commoner. An Algolan cannot marry an alien. The marriage will never take place. Even if Marysmith lives long enough.'

'Then we're not related,' said Rajic.

Janesmith had been lying to him, and lying was so very human – and she was more than ninety-five per cent human.

'You are the half-brother of our half-sister's husband-to-be. We are related.'

'Don't tell Ewart he isn't married.'

'Why?'

Because he should have as many problems as possible, thought Rajic, but instead he said, 'Because a male from our world isn't allowed to travel with a female unless she's his wife or a relative. If Ewart knew he wasn't really married to Marysmith, he'd leave you both on this primitive planet. You'd be trapped here and never get back to Algol.'

Janesmith looked at her sister, who had fallen asleep after her snack, at Rajic, at GX486/33–D, at the sky, and she said, 'We understand.'

But there was something Rajic didn't understand.

'After you travelled from Algol to Earth,' he said, 'how did you know you had to board the *Demon Star*?'

Janesmith gazed skywards again. 'We are a princess,' she said. 'We don't make travel arrangements, that was all done for us. What's that?' Her left thumb gestured upwards.

Rajic looked up. 'The lander,' he said. 'Someone else is coming down from the *Demon Star*.'

They watched in silence as the lander settled in the same place it had done earlier, some two hundred metres away from where the Algolan and the Terran stood. The door slid open and Grawl sprang out, gun in hand, surveying the landscape. Zena followed, also armed, also checking the area for any potential threat. There was none.

The natives must have been used to this by now, because few of them took any notice of the craft which had descended into the valley.

The third newcomer finally appeared, slowly stepping on to the surface of the alien planet. Protected by an envirosuit, it could have been anyone.

Not anyone, thought Rajic, it had to be some paranoid megalomaniac. As there was only one of those on board the *Demon Star*, it had to be Ewart.

There was absolutely no need for an envirosuit. They were clumsy and uncomfortable at the best of times, and those from the *Demon Star* were also unreliable. The last time Rajic had used one, he'd almost melted. And because Ewart was inside, the suit would fill with hot air much faster than usual.

'Who's that?' asked Janesmith.

'Your sister's husband.'

'Your brother?'

'Yes,' said Rajic.

It was the first time they had been on the same planet for twenty years, but if he wasn't careful he might be trapped on this one for a similar duration. Abdenga had asked about being stranded, but there was only one person that Ewart would want to abandon here. Although he was a member of the crew, Rajic was expendable, and the master might be persuaded to leave him behind as a favour to the *Demon Star*'s new owner.

Rajic had to convince Ewart that he needed his advice and experience, and they ought to be able to reach a tacit understanding. They hadn't exchanged a fraternal word for over two decades, but compared to what Algolan siblings did to one another they were on the very best of terms.

Ewart had landed on his first alien planet, having arrived on board his own spaceship. He hadn't paid for the ship, but that was a minor detail.

Apart from people, there was one other thing which was worth transporting between the stars: wealth.

Wealth was the whole motive for space travel: it was why companies searched for undeveloped worlds, to make money from their development; and it was why ships carried passengers, to make money from them.

Although Ewart might have lost everything he'd owned on Earth, that wasn't everything he owned in the galaxy.

And the day he was reunited with his fortune, Rajic intended to be with him – and reclaim what he'd been cheated out of all those years ago.

Rajic had to go and talk to Ewart; but he found it very difficult to leave Janesmith. It was a long time since he'd had sex with any kind of female; but that wasn't the reason he felt so drawn to her. She was dangerous, a killer; but that only added to her attraction.

'Who's that?' asked Janesmith again.

'Zena.'

'Who's she?'

'Ewart's sister.'

'And your sister?'

'Yes, our half-sister.'

'She's even uglier than we are.'

Neither of them were ugly, but beauty was more than skin deep. Janesmith was female and exotic, feral and erotic. What more could any man desire?

There seemed two ways of getting around the Algolan sex-with-relatives taboo. The first was to kill Marysmith, the second was to kill Ewart. They both seemed somewhat extreme.

'Who's that?' asked Janesmith again, again.

'Grawl.'

'A relative?'

'No.'

'Male?'

'Yes.'

'He's so handsome.'

Rajic looked at Janesmith, but she was still looking at Grawl. Handsome? He was as deformed as Janesmith thought she was, but his physique must have fitted the Algolan ideal.

'He has no status,' said Rajic. 'He's only a body-guard.'

'That's all we are,' said Janesmith, gesturing towards her sleeping sister.

She was one hundred per cent, and Rajic desperately wanted to give her a small percentage of himself. But with Grawl here, it was too late.

Why did the lander have to arrive now?

Once again, Ewart had screwed up Rajic's chances.

CHAPTER ELEVEN

It was one small step for Ewart, because if he took a larger step he'd fall over. That had already happened once. The envirosuit was very heavy, but it responded perfectly to the movements of his limbs. Too perfectly, in fact. When he first tried to walk, he'd lost his balance. Fortunately, he was still on board the *Demon Star* and there had been no one watching (except for Zena and Grawl, who always watched), no one laughing. (Zena didn't laugh and Grawl couldn't.)

Now that Jarker and his autocams were recording his arrival on the alien world, Ewart had to be very careful that his strides were neither too far nor too fast. The auteur was continuing his duties as Ewart's official biographer, which was part of their agreement, although Ewart had denied him access to his state-room.

Ewart moved slowly away from the lander, then paused, turning his head with equal slowness. The image would be very impressive: the brave explorer surveying the hostile planet he had conquered. Silhouetted against the alien sky, the figure inside the suit was indistinguishable; but as the autocam moved closer, Ewart's face would be revealed within the helmet.

What spoiled the effect was the arrival of Abdenga, who came up to him and said something – and who wasn't wearing an envirosuit.

'What?' said Ewart.

Abdenga spoke again, but Ewart couldn't hear. It probably wasn't important. Since leaving Earth, whatever Abdenga said was less and less significant.

It bothered Ewart that he couldn't hear properly, and neither was his vision very good. Everything was too dark. He'd expected that the envirosuit would enhance his senses, not diminish them.

He caught sight of Rajic. By now, he'd finished conspiring with the Algolans and was walking towards him. There was no sign of Lamakinto, and Ewart was glad of that, although his suit would have prevented him hearing the priest. Lamakinto was probably busy signing up the locals as members of the GX486/33–D subsidiary of United Religions of Terra.

Neither was Carrillos around. Although the archaeologist claimed he'd never been on a dig before, Ewart could imagine that he was digging right now, excavating a hideout for himself so he didn't have to go to the third planet.

'What?' said Ewart, this time to Rajic.

Rajic shook his head, then looked away and said something to Zena. Zena glanced at Grawl, and Grawl nodded. By the time Ewart had turned to see all this, Rajic had vanished.

Ewart felt something touch the back of his helmet, and he tried to twist around. But he couldn't move. It was Rajic, he realized. He'd immobilized the envirosuit.

'Grawl!' yelled Ewart. 'Zena!'

They did nothing because they couldn't hear him. A moment later, Ewart lost all vision. His helmet became opaque. His bodyguards could no longer see him within the suit. And couldn't see that Rajic was killing him!

The envirosuit was built to isolate the inside from the outside. When there was danger outside, it couldn't get in; but when the danger was inside, the occupant couldn't get out . . .

He was totally trapped, held immobile by the suit, hardly able to move a finger. It was suddenly very hot, and Ewart opened his mouth wide, gasping for air. Air! There wasn't any. He was suffocating. Rajic had cut off his supply.

How long before Zena and Grawl realized that something was wrong?

Too long.

How long did he have?

Not long.

He'd come all this way, so far from home, had finally achieved his lifetime ambition of setting foot on an alien world, but now his life was over.

And it was Rajic who had chosen this as the time of Ewart's death.

But why? They'd cheated and lied and robbed and deceived one another all their lives, but they'd never hated enough to want each other dead. Had they?

Zena and Grawl weren't going to save him, Ewart realized, even if they could. They were all part of the conspiracy, already enlisted by Rajic and promised their freedom. Ewart should have known. There was nobody he could trust, nobody. Not his bodyguards. Not even his own brother. Especially not his own brother.

In his last few seconds, Ewart felt strangely calm. The worst of it was the sense of betrayal that he felt. As a child, he'd imagined this moment so many times. Not how he would die, but how Rajic would be with him when he first set foot on an alien world. It had happened almost the way he'd hoped.

The difference was that they should have landed side by side. And as allies, not enemies.

He could have forgiven Rajic anything, perhaps even for killing him, but he couldn't forgive him for not waiting. They should have arrived together, the brave space adventurers they had dreamed of becoming.

Ewart would never forget gazing at the *Demon Star*'s viewscreen, the cold sense of loss and emptiness he'd felt seeing his brother already down on the surface. But he wouldn't have much time for forgetting, he supposed. He opened his mouth wide, trying to draw in the last of the hot fetid air within the envirosuit.

Rajic must also have remembered that childhood dream, which was why he'd chosen to kill Ewart at this precise moment.

The world suddenly exploded into a rainbow of colour, a roaring cacophony of sound, and the temperature within the suit dropped dramatically.

'No!' screamed Ewart, no longer calm.

His heart stopped.

He didn't want to die.

And he didn't.

Because he could see and hear and breathe and move.

Having missed but one beat, his heart resumed its function.

The envirosuit started to fall, taking Ewart with it.

'No!' he screamed again, because for a moment he'd imagined he was alive, but now knew that he was dead and dropping to his doom.

Then Zena and Grawl caught the suit, lifted him back into a vertical position.

'Is everything all right, sir?' asked Zena.

Ewart heard her. He could breathe. His heart was still beating. He could see and move. When he nodded, so did the helmet.

'Don't you think you're a bit overdressed, old boy?' said Rajic.

'What about you?' whispered Ewart. He breathed in deeply. 'You're wearing a lot more than last time.'

'Luckily.' Rajic looked towards the Algolans. 'It gave her a reason to speak to me.'

Ewart started to glance in the same direction. His helmet turned and the suit immediately responded to the focus of his gaze, projecting a closeup of the two aliens on to the inside of the visor. He was able to see them in as much detail as from the *Demon Star*. The chaperone. His new wife. Four years old . . .

'What did you do to the envirosuit?' he asked, quickly looking back at Rajic. The helmet spun back, with equal speed, and he felt dizzy for a moment.

'Adjusted it. The settings were all wrong for a Terran.'

'It can be altered from the outside?'

'If you know how. I sometimes repair suits, and that's one I fixed.'

Ewart took another deep breath. There was still air. Knowing that Rajic had repaired the envirosuit, he felt almost as vulnerable as when it had blanked during reset.

'You're wearing a bugbelt?' asked Rajic.

'Right.'

All the available readings said that the planet was safe, but Ewart had operated long enough in the communications industry not to trust any infodata. He was taking every precaution he could.

'Then you don't need a suit,' said Rajic. 'Take it off.'

He wanted to, but he didn't want Rajic to think he was doing as he suggested.

'This is all you need,' Rajic added. He patted the bugbelt around his waist, then waved his arm, the gesture encompassing everyone in the area: Zena and Grawl, Abdenga and Jarker, the two Algolans. They were all wearing belts.

Although Ewart was very reluctant to believe anything Rajic told him, surely he wouldn't risk his own life if it were safer to wear an envirosuit. Would he? He worked on board the *Demon Star*, despite the constant threat of the Rollein-Twist.

'From microbes to missiles?' Ewart said, quoting the slogan.

A bugbelt offered a shield against most of the dangers encountered on an alien world: protection against viruses, shelter from the rain, defence against hostile natives.

'It depends on size and velocity,' said Rajic. 'If the missile's a stone, you'll be OK. If it's a planetbuster, there won't be much left of you, the belt or the planet. At a guess, I'd say this world's military capabilities tend towards the former end of the scale.'

'You haven't been bitten by insects?'

'Bugs get blasted. Which could be why it's called a bugbelt. GX486/33–D is almost standard, so most of the other functions are used to a minimum, if at all. Climate control. Radiation filter. Gravity assist. If you're staying, a belt's all you need.'

'Staying? Why shouldn't I be staying?'

'You've delivered the missionary, almost delivered the archaeologist. I thought you might want to head somewhere else.'

'Where?'

'Algol. To meet your new in-laws.'

Ewart looked over at the Algolans again, careful not to turn his head too quickly.

'What were you doing over there?' he asked.

'I went to meet your wife.'

'That was all a mistake. We aren't married. Not really. She shouldn't be here.'

'Is that what you're going to tell her?'

'I'm not going to tell her anything. I'm not going to talk to her. Why should I?'

'Because she's your wife. But I suppose you didn't talk

to your other wives, did you?'

'I saw you talking to the chaperone. What did you find out?'

'She's your wife's sister. You new sister-in-law. They're half-sisters, really, like we're half-brothers.'

'Did you tell them we're brothers?'

'Yes. Because we are. You don't want to start your latest marriage with a lie, do you?'

Ewart said nothing. That was always the best thing to say, and it was what Rajic should have said. It wasn't good policy to volunteer information to anyone, especially to a wife. Knowing they were brothers was of little importance, but what else had Rajic revealed?

'When dealing with aliens,' said Rajic, 'it's always best to tell the truth. Some of them are telepathic, they know when you're lying. If they believe you can't be trusted, you could be gone for a burton.'

'For a what?'

Rajic ran a finger across his throat.

Ewart had always hated that gesture, which was probably why Rajic had made it. The image made him think of a person who kept eating and eating, but whatever food was swallowed oozed out of his severed throat, and the victim starved to death.

Automatically, he raised his right hand to his throat. His arm slammed into the neck of the envirosuit, knocking him back. He thought he was going to fall, but the suit suddenly bent forward at the waist to maintain his centre of gravity.

Rajic smiled as the suit righted itself, then said,

'Your wife is called Marysmith.'

'Marysmith? I can't call her that.'

'You ought to. It's her name. Or you could call her "my darling" like you did all the others.'

Ewart noticed Rajic looking at Zena, but he was sure he'd never called her 'my darling'.

'Zena,' he said, 'help me off with my suit.'

Enough time had passed, and it would no longer seem that he was following Rajic's advice.

'That's one of her duties, is it?' said Rajic. 'Helping you off with your clothes?'

Ewart thought of asking Grawl instead, but that would look as if he were giving in to Rajic. He said nothing, and Zena removed the helmet. Grawl continued surveying the sky and the landscape, his weapon poised. Abdenga stood patiently by, and Jarker kept filming. Rajic yawned and scratched his stomach. His flat stomach. He'd always been thinner than Ewart. His metabolism was so much faster, that was why.

'The other one's called Janesmith,' he said, 'and I told her that Zena is your sister.'

Ewart took a small breath of alien air and was slightly reassured not to be immediately poisoned. The atmosphere could still prove to be lethal, he supposed, but he wouldn't know until later.

'Any particular reason why?' he asked, as Zena continued dismantling the envirosuit. 'Or just to cause trouble?'

'Because as a married man, under Algolan law, you're not permitted to travel with any female who isn't a relative.'

'So?' Ewart shrugged. 'Why should I care about Algolan law?'

'If she finds out that Zena isn't your sister, your new wife will be dishonoured.'

'So?'

'She'll kill herself. Or her sister will do it for her.'

That would solve one problem, thought Ewart. 'So?' he said.

'You want the death of a four-year-old child on your conscience?'

'Conscience? What's that?'

Ewart and Rajic looked at one another, and they almost smiled.

What was Rajic up to? Why did he really want Zena to masquerade as Ewart's sister? But Ewart was prepared to go along with this and see where it led. Although he knew he might never find out.

'Right,' he agreed. 'Until we get rid of my new wife, Zena, you're my sister.'

'Yes, sir.'

'And mine,' said Rajic.

'Yes, Mr Rajic.'

'Call me Rajic.'

'But it's a lie,' said Ewart.

'So?' said Rajic, repeating what Ewart had said before.

That was something else he always used to do when they were kids: copy what Ewart said, repeating whole sentences just to annoy him. And he was a good mimic, able to catch the right tone and inflection so that every word sounded exactly the same as the original.

'You said it's always best to tell the truth when dealing with aliens,' said Ewart.

'Algolans aren't telepathic, I discovered. In any case, Zena and Grawl can protect you from any physical danger.'

'What other type is there?'

'As I said, some aliens can read emotions, know if you're telling the truth or not.'

'That must be useful,' said Ewart, adding silently, when dealing with you . . .

'Other alien races have developed their mental powers as a weapon. They can alter your thought processes, change your memories. Less subtly, they can dissolve your brain so it drips out of your nose like snot.'

Ewart shuddered at the thought, and glanced at the two Algolans. Without the envirosuit's visor, he couldn't see them as well as before.

'But the only one in danger is your new wife,' said Rajic. 'Janesmith plans to kill her and blame you.'

'Why?'

'They're sisters, both princesses of Algol, rival heirs to the throne. With Marysmith dead, Janesmith becomes Empress.'

'How do you know?'

'It's a process called conversation. You talk to someone. They say something, then you say something. You ask a question, they give an answer. You should try it. You *are* trying it! We're having a conversation, you realize?' Rajic looked at the autocams. 'Can't you get rid of those?'

'No.' If Rajic wanted to talk privately, then Ewart was

determined that it would all be recorded. 'Maybe Jarker should also cover the Algolans.'

'As a deterrent?' Rajic shook his head. 'Marysmith needs a bodyguard, not an autocam. Janesmith would probably consider a recording an ideal souvenir of the murder, proof that her sister was dead and she should inherit the crown.'

'She said she was going to kill her?'

'Yes. Go and ask her.'

'No,' said Ewart, and it was a relief to shake his head without worrying that it would dislocate his neck. 'I'm not having anything to do with them.'

'The least you can do is send Zena to protect your wife.'

'Why should I do anything for her? There was no dowry. Her father cheated me. He won't get away with it.'

'He hasn't. He's dead.'

'That's no excuse.' Ewart paused. 'How do you know he's dead? It came up in the conversation, I suppose.'

'Yes. With her father dead, she's no one to protect her.'

'She—' Ewart couldn't bring himself to call her his wife, or even to call her Marysmith. '—really is in danger from her sister?'

'Yes,' said Rajic.

And, as always, Ewart had no idea whether to believe him or not.

Rajic had always been a liar, but he didn't always lie. When he was telling the truth, it often sounded like a lie – sometimes deliberately, so that the truth would be disbelieved. Probably half of what he said was untrue. The difficulty came in trying to decide which half.

It was Rajic who had been the first to change his name and identity, reinventing himself. Always willing to adopt a good idea, Ewart had done the same.

'Send Zena over,' said Rajic. 'You don't need two bodyguards. You don't even need one. What enemies have you got here?'

Although Ewart was reluctant to admit it, Rajic was probably right. He was far safer on GX486/33–D than he had been on his native world.

'Only you,' he said.

Rajic smiled. 'What about Jarker?' He looked at the auteur. 'Would you call yourself a friend of Ewart's?'

Jarker said nothing.

'No?' said Rajic. 'If you're not his friend, you're his enemy.'

'Mr Ewart is my employer,' said Jarker.

'What's the difference?' said Rajic. 'You don't like Ewart, do you?'

'So?' said Ewart. 'I don't like him.'

'What about you?' Rajic looked at Abdenga. 'Ewart's your employer and therefore your enemy.'

'The words "employer" and "enemy" are not synonymous,' said Abdenga. 'Mr Ewart and I have a professional relationship.'

'You don't like him.'

'As a lawyer, I have no personal feelings.'

'But you hate him for bringing you here.'

Abdenga must have advised himself to remain silent, because that was what he did. But Ewart couldn't understand what Rajic was driving at. Likes and dislikes were irrelevant. Ewart owned Abdenga's contract, and Abdenga did what Ewart told him.

'Carrillos also hates you for bringing him here,' Rajic said to Ewart. 'In fact, the only person who's glad to be here is Father Lamakinto. He claims he doesn't hate anyone.'

'I hate him,' said Ewart.

'And there's your wife,' said Rajic, 'which in your case is synonymous with "enemy".'

'A four-year-old can't be much of a threat. Even less of a threat if her sister kills her.'

'Don't you think it's odd that almost everyone here hates you? Given enough time, the whole planet will hate you. It'll be just like Earth.'

Rajic was up to his old tricks, trying to provoke Ewart into an angry reaction. Ewart ignored him and looked around. No one here was a real enemy, any danger to his wealth or his life. If people didn't like him, it was because they were jealous. So? He hadn't got where he was by being popular.

And where had he got? To an alien planet.

'An alien planet,' he said, softly, as he stared around.

He was here, really here, on an alien world. Only now did he fully comprehend what had happened. He'd left Earth by spaceship, his own spaceship, voyaged across the interstellar wilderness and landed upon another planet.

Then he noticed a shadow on the ground, and that made him feel very strange – because it was his own shadow. It only existed because of the alien sun, but he felt almost as if a part of himself had become alien. He gazed all around again.

'It's . . .'

Ewart tried to think of a word or phrase which was appropriate, but the significance of the event overwhelmed every thought. His childhood dream had been fulfilled, and it felt . . .

'Wonderful.'

Wonderful and awesome and magnificent and every other superlative.

Ewart turned from the alien landscape and looked at Rajic, who had provided the adjective.

'Right,' he agreed.

He should have prepared a speech commemorating the momentous occasion when he first set foot on GX486/33–D, for Jarker to record. It wasn't too late. These things didn't have to be filmed in sequence.

'You don't feel strange?' said Rajic. 'Stranger than usual, that is.'

'Should I?'

'Some people can't take it, being on another world. And when I say "people", that includes aliens. Being away from your native planet can lead to all kinds of trauma and psychosis.'

'Really?' said Ewart, which was never the right word to use when speaking to Rajic. Something was real only if it was to his advantage.

'Absolutely,' said Rajic, which was a word that became less than absolute when he used it. 'That's where the word "lunatic" comes from, because of the influence of the Moon. Leaving the world where you

197

were born, crossing space, landing on another planet. Some people go crazy. Others become catatonic or suicidal. Or it could be that it isn't leaving your native planet which leads to insanity. Going to the Moon or out to the asteroid belt doesn't seem to cause mental problems. Perhaps it's to do with leaving the sun, going to another solar system, coming under the influence of an alien star.'

Why was Rajic saying this? To give Ewart something else to worry about?

'Without the sun,' Rajic continued. 'we wouldn't exist. It's the source of all life. And, in your case, the source of all wealth.'

That was true. Ewart's primary business had been the supply of energy, and that energy came from the sun. Without it, life on Earth could not have existed. And what was his reward? He'd been forced into exile.

Would Earth survive without him? Probably.

Would he survive without Earth? Definitely.

He gazed up at the alien sun high in the green sky, then surveyed the planet on which he stood.

'Nice little place,' said Rajic.

Ewart nodded, then said, 'It's OK for a visit. I suppose. But who'd want to live here? All this empty real estate. What a waste of space.' He didn't want Rajic to think he'd grown soft and sentimental.

'The technical term is "an unspoiled paradise",' said Rajic.

'Paradise?' Ewart sneered. 'I bet there isn't a decent restaurant on the whole planet.'

'Why don't you open one? That used to be your plan.'

Ewart was about to deny it, but then he remembered. 'You were going to be the chef?' he said.

'I'd do the cooking, you'd do the eating.'

'Right.'

'We could still do it. Start up here.'

'With the natives as customers?'

'First thing you do is establish a power net and start an industrial revolution. The locals begin making things, which they then have to sell to each other. They do that by advertising on the comservice you've launched. That way they earn enough money to pay for the meals at our restaurant. Easy.'

'It would be easier get customers from other worlds, to turn this planet into the gastronomic centre of the galaxy.'

Did Rajic seriously think Ewart would go into partnership with him? It wasn't a share in a restaurant that he was after, but a share of Ewart's money, and that was why he was being so friendly.

All Ewart wanted was to leave GX486/33–D as soon as possible and reach the funds he'd hidden away, but he didn't intend to travel in the *Demon Star* again. He'd need Rajic's spacer skills to find another ship, a safe ship, and that might mean having to take Rajic with him when he left the planet.

One thing was certain: whatever star system Rajic advised they should head for, they'd go in the opposite direction.

'Talking of restaurants,' said Ewart, 'I noticed that you provided a few snacks earlier.'

Rajic said nothing, waiting for him to continue.

Ewart took a deep breath of alien air and asked, 'Is there anything left for me?'

'You said you didn't want me to touch your food.'

'Bastard.'

'No. Father was married to my mother. Was he married to yours?'

'You want to be left on this planet?'

'No. And you don't want to leave me.'

'Why not?'

'You'd miss my cooking. Give it a try. It's been a long time. I put a few things aside for you.'

'Did you?'

'Would I lie to you?'

Their eyes had been locked together as they stared at one another, neither wanting to be the first to blink. Exactly as they'd done when they were kids.

'Three,' said Ewart.

'Two,' said Rajic.

'One,' they said together, and they blinked together.

'When do we start looking for Kosmos?' said Rajic.

And lost memories from more than half a century ago suddenly filled Ewart's mind. He shook his head, remembering what he'd never really forgotten.

'Kosmos,' he whispered, still shaking his head in amazement.

'He's why we're here, isn't he?'

Ewart thought about it for a few seconds. 'I suppose he is.'

When he'd been a kid, Ewart had never really known who Kosmos was. He was just some adult, a friend of the family who visited every now and again and told them about his fantastic adventures in space.

'Remember the stories?' said Rajic.

'I remember.'

'Travelling between the stars . . .'

'. . . discovering new planets . . .'

'. . . meeting mysterious aliens . . .'

'. . . eating their meals . . .'

'. . . what . . .'

'. . . battling against their starfleets, I mean . . .'

'. . . fighting space pirates.'

It seemed that everyone was referring to space pirates.

But Kosmos could only have been a dozen years older than Ewart. Although that wasn't too young to have gone to the stars, it was too young to have come back.

Then he didn't come back, and it was only later that Ewart realized Kosmos was another of his half-brothers, the offspring of one of his father's previous marriages.

'Kosmos couldn't return because he must have been held captive by evil aliens or bloodthirsty pirates, and we were going to search the stars and rescue him.'

'And here we are,' said Rajic.

'Right.'

Ewart again gazed around at the alien world upon which he and his brother stood. Could it really be true? Were they here because of Kosmos, because he had fired their childhood ambition of becoming starfarers? It seemed so.

'He probably only got as far as the Moon or the asteroid belt,' said Rajic.

'He might not even have got that far. He might have

lied. He might have stayed on Earth.'

'What? Our brother? A liar? Never!'

Ewart smiled. 'Is that something you inherited from father?'

'A predisposition to mendacity? Not in my case.' Rajic also smiled. 'When did we work out that he'd changed his name?'

Now, thought Ewart, as he realized that Rajic hadn't been his first brother to give himself another identity. Kosmos. The name was so obviously a fabrication, but he'd never considered it before.

'Did you ever count all the half-brothers and sisters, all the step-mothers and fathers we must have had?' Rajic added.

'No,' said Ewart, and he shrugged. 'It was all a long time ago. I never think about the past.'

'Never?'

Ewart thought about the past, then said, 'I try not to.'

'You didn't have any of it deleted?'

'No.'

'Would you remember if you had? You know who I'm talking about?'

'I know,' said Ewart, as he remembered his first wife, his true first wife.

He'd often considered implanting false memories to replace the painful parts of his past. He didn't want to remember, but neither did he want to forget. Although it had been the worst time of his life, it had also been the best. Deleting the former would have meant wiping out the latter, obliterating all that he had left of Myiko and their daughter.

Ewart and Rajic stood in silence for several seconds, and Ewart knew they were both remembering, both wishing they could forget, both glad that they couldn't.

'What about your new wife?' said Rajic. 'Will you send Zena to protect her?'

Why was he so insistent that it should be Zena?

'No,' said Ewart. 'I'll send Grawl.'

Rajic shrugged. 'If that's what you want. Shall I take him over and make up some story? Or do you want to do it?'

'Grawl, you go with Rajic. You're assigned to the Algolans. Make sure the older one doesn't kill the younger one. Or vice versa.'

Ewart suspected that what Rajic had told him was a lie, but he didn't want the Algolan girl to be harmed. The best thing would be to leave the aliens behind when he quit the planet. Whatever happened after that would be no concern of his.

As Rajic and Grawl walked away, Ewart noticed Zena from the corner of his eye. Her gun was cradled in her right arm, and she raised her left hand and waved. She took things too literally sometimes, or maybe she was trying to be as realistic as possible. Rajic had become her brother, and so she was waving him goodbye.

Rajic didn't notice, however, although Grawl glanced back. No matter what his orders, his first priority was always to defend his employer. While he was with the Algolans, Grawl would also be keeping a professional eye upon Ewart.

'Do you ever get a feeling of *déjà vu*, Joe?' asked Ewart, as he watched his brother and bodyguard leave.

'I have done, sir,' said Abdenga, 'but very rarely. Are you experiencing the sensation now, sir?'

'I'm not sure.' Ewart looked all around once again, then shook his head. It all seemed very familiar.

He started to make his way towards the shaded slope where Rajic had presented his banquet. Zena followed, as did Jarker and Abdenga.

'Do you ever get a feeling of *déjà vu*, Joe?' said Ewart.

'You just asked me that, sir,' said Abdenga.

'Did I?'

'Yes, sir, a few seconds ago.'

'You're imagining things. This planet is driving you crazy. You're Earthsick.'

CHAPTER TWELVE

'Let me do the talking,' Rajic said to Grawl.

Grawl remained as expressionless as ever. Whatever had happened to deprive him of his voice, or even if he'd never had one, it could have been fixed either biologically or electronically. But Ewart was too mean to pay. He must have liked having someone around who could never reply, and he probably wished that nobody would ever talk back to him. On Earth, it had almost been like that.

'You heard what I told Ewart,' Rajic continued. 'Janesmith plans to murder her sister, and sooner or later she'll try it. When she does, it's your job to stop her. Got that?'

Rajic looked at Grawl. Grawl looked at Rajic.

Did he understand? He must have done, although he refused to acknowledge the obvious.

'But we don't want her to know you're a bodyguard, OK? Because she might see that as a challenge. If you're there to stop her killing her sister, it could provoke her

205

into making the attempt. Got that?'

Grawl didn't even blink.

'Good. Whatever she tries, I know she can't succeed because you'll be there to prevent it, but there's no point letting her think we don't trust her.'

As they kept walking towards the Algolans, Grawl glanced back for a moment. He must have been checking that Ewart was safe. Perhaps he thought this was all a pretext to draw him away, that the only murder attempt would be against Ewart.

'Zena can protect Ewart. Not as well as you can, of course, but at the moment he's in far less danger than his wife.'

One of the differences between himself and Ewart was that he believed there was no point fighting on when he was beaten, whereas Ewart would always continue the battle whatever the price. And whoever had to pay it. Rajic thought it was the best policy to concede an early defeat, because that increased the chances of turning it to his own advantage. He wasn't going to get anywhere with Janesmith, for example, not while they were related.

Another difference was that if Rajic couldn't help himself, he was willing to help others. His new sister-in-law was attracted to Grawl, and so he would be happy to introduce them. He'd advised Ewart that Zena should look after his new bride, but instead Grawl had been sent, and so whatever happened between him and Janesmith wasn't Rajic's fault.

And it was highly likely that something would happen. Janesmith lusted after Grawl. Grawl had never shown a single sign of ... of anything, in fact, but how could he resist?

'Give me a minute or two with the Algolans, and I'll come up with a good reason why you're here. You should go along with whatever happens. If Janesmith asks you for something, then do it. Because if she's happy, then Ewart's happy. Understand?'

Grawl remained as impassive as ever.

'Wait here. I'll go talk to them.'

Grawl kept walking towards the Algolans.

'Or I'll wait here. You go talk to them.'

Grawl slowed down. He looked over to Ewart and the others, stared at Janesmith and Marysmith, then glanced at Rajic, his cold eyes seeming to bore right through him. He halted.

'This planet is driving you crazy. You're Earthsick.'

If anyone was Earthsick, it was Ewart. And he was already crazy. That had begun before he'd even left Earth, and he was still attempting 'jokes' instead of confronting his predicament.

Abdenga wasn't Earthsick. For him, the word was 'spacesick'. Or, right now, 'GX486/33–D-sick'.

It wasn't Earth that he missed, but who he had left behind. He would never see Miss Yasmerel again. All he had were memories, and not many of those. The longest time he and his true love had spent together was those few glorious hours in court. Their shared life would have been in the future, but now Abdenga had no future. Only an eternity of loneliness. He was doomed to wander the galaxy for ever, the rest of his life an infinity of emptiness.

Throughout the voyage, he'd wished that the Rollein-Twist would end his misery, destroying the *Demon Star* and annihilating everyone on board. Instead, the ship had survived and now he found himself on a world inhabited by savages.

'What did you say, Joe?' asked Ewart.

'Nothing, sir,' said Abdenga, wondering if this was going to be another 'joke'.

'Zena?'

'He said "savages", sir.'

'Talking to yourself is another sign of madness, Joe.'

Abdenga hadn't realized he'd spoken, but he knew he was the only sane one here. Talking to himself was the sole source of intelligent conversation on the planet.

'What's your definition of "savages"?' Ewart continued. 'If they don't have lawyers?'

Lawyers and the law were always targets for derision. It was so easy to mock the dignity and formality of any revered and honourable institution. Society's bulwarks against the dangerous tide of barbarism had always stood firm, however, rising above all ephemeral criticism. Man or woman, lawyer or not, had but a short time upon Earth (or any other world) while ancient laws lived on. And lawyers, whether man or woman, were fortunate to serve a master (or mistress, for the symbol of justice was female) who was eternal.

'The rule of law is the basis of a civilized society,' said Abdenga. 'An independent judicial system. Representation by an attorney. A jury of one's peers. The right to a fair trial. A recognized appeal system.'

'A fair trial!' said Ewart. 'Is that what I had? You know it wasn't. I'd have stood a better chance of a fair trial here on Ewart's World.'

'Where?'

Ewart gestured dismissively. 'Anywhere. Anywhere in the galaxy. Anywhere where everyone wasn't against me.' He glanced around. 'They've got laws here, Joe. Just because it's a different system to the one on Earth, that doesn't mean it's inferior.'

'No, sir,' said Abdenga.

What was the point of arguing? Abdenga had spent all of his life studying law, but Ewart considered himself the absolute expert on every subject.

He wiped sweat from his face with the back of his hand. None of the others seemed to have any problem with the heat. Perhaps the temperature level on his bugbelt was wrongly adjusted. If so, it must have been Rajic's doing. As a 'joke', presumably.

'They might have something else instead of courts,' said Ewart. 'Trial by combat, for example. Maybe that's what we should have on Earth. When I went to court, who was I up against? My ex-wives? The Terrestrial Taxation Authority? So it seemed, but who was behind them? Hiroshi Larnvik, that's who.'

'Are you saying, sir, that instead of going to court you and Larnvik should have fought each other?'

'No.'

Abdenga was relieved to hear that. For an awful moment he'd imagined the two tycoons facing up to one another, spitting insults and grappling in hand to hand combat. It was a very unsavoury thought.

'We'd have champions to fight for us,' said Ewart.

'Like a duel, you mean? Grawl against Larnvik's nominee?'

'No. You're my lawyer, Joe, so you'd have fought for me. Using your muscles instead of words. A wrestling bout against the prosecutor. Remember her? She'd have looked good stripped and oiled, although I don't know about you.'

Abdenga stared at Ewart in bewilderment. He really was crazy. But, even as he thought this, Abdenga wondered how Miss Yasmerel would look without her legal robes. He tried to push the image from his mind, because thinking of her like that was a betrayal of their love. And because he'd never find out.

'So where's this food?' said Ewart.

'What?' Abdenga was still dreaming of Miss Yasmerel, of slowly disrobing her.

'Where were you eating?'

Abdenga looked around. With bare rock instead of buildings, there was no point of reference, and everywhere on this terrible world was the same.

'I don't know, sir.'

'Zena?'

'Another forty-six metres, sir.'

She must have had Abdenga and the others under observation from the *Demon Star*, studying them while they'd been eating. That meant Ewart had probably also been watching, listening. Because of the stress he was still suffering, Abdenga might have spoken too freely. He hoped he hadn't said something he'd regret – and which Ewart already had.

'There's nothing there,' said Ewart.

That was exactly what Abdenga had expected, because Lamakinto would have made certain there was nothing left over. He had a big mouth, which he used for two purposes: to talk a lot and to eat a lot. Perhaps that was one reason why Ewart hated the missionary, because they were so alike.

Abdenga gazed at where Zena had indicated. As Ewart said, there was nothing there. Nothing at all. The table was missing, the chairs, the dishes, the containers.

'Where's everything gone?' said Ewart. 'Did Rajic clear it all away?'

'I don't know, sir,' said Abdenga.

'Zena?'

'It happened while we were on board the lander, sir. Perhaps one of the others saw what happened. Mr Jarker?'

'The locals did it,' said Jarker. 'I've got the evidence. It's all recorded.'

'Evidence?' said Ewart. 'Where do you think this is? Why didn't you stop them?'

'Ah ... there were a lot of them,' said Jarker. 'And it didn't seem a very good idea to ... ah ... to interfere with the native customs.'

'Customs?' said Abdenga. 'You mean it was all confiscated in lieu of import duty?' Here was a legal problem at last, something for him to do.

'They stole everything,' muttered Ewart. 'They're all ...' He shook his head in disbelief.

'... savages, sir?' suggested Abdenga, as he realized

the type of customs that Jarker had meant. 'Do we apply for a felony summons?'

Ewart laughed. 'Good one, Joe.'

'Good what, sir?'

'Good joke.'

'Sir,' said Zena, 'some of the indigenous inhabitants are about to carry your envirosuit away. Are they the same ones, Mr Jarker, who took Mr Rajic's catering utensils?'

Abdenga, Ewart and Jarker all turned and watched the group of natives gathered around the suit. One of them was wearing the helmet, staggering around as if unable to see, while the others made what could have been appreciative noises.

'I don't know,' said Jarker. 'They all look the same.'

'Shall I kill them, sir?' asked Zena, as she prepared her weapon.

'No, don't.'

'I could kill one or two of them, sir. That should dissuade them from taking your envirosuit.'

'No. If they want the suit, let them have it. It's nothing.'

'It is nothing this time, sir, but they need to be deterred from further hostile action.'

'Forget it, Zena.'

'Very well, sir.'

Although he heard what was said and watched as the aliens took away their prize, Abdenga's attention was elsewhere. He was still thinking of Ewart's last words to him. Had he made a joke? Perhaps he really was becoming Earthsick.

And what about Ewart? Something very strange had happened to him. His property was being stolen, but he didn't care. Was he also Earthsick?

If there were such a thing. During the voyage, Abdenga had soon learned to trust Rajic's word as much as Ewart's. They probably were brothers, although the fact that they both admitted it was no reason to believe them. Their variations on objective truth were always very convincing, which Abdenga regarded as a great asset. Ewart had performed very well in court, and Rajic's similar talent would also have made him an ideal witness.

Rajic hadn't set any of the banquet aside for Ewart, but he must have known he was safe because he'd already seen the savages stealing everything he'd brought down from the *Demon Star*.

Perhaps Ewart realized the same thing, or maybe he wondered why Grawl hadn't responded to the theft of the envirosuit, because he looked over to where the other two stood with the Algolans.

Janesmith. Marysmith. Did they think those names would fool anyone? They were so obviously alien, but under Terran law they would have been treated as equals. Just as if they were human.

It was only because aliens were so similar to people that this happened. Whatever world they came from, they had two arms, two legs – and one head. Although Abdenga was prepared to admit that some aliens were more than animals, they were always less than humans.

The real danger came from those who looked almost

identical to the true-born. Who knew how many had infiltrated Earth, masquerading as real people? They were the ones responsible for giving aliens the same rights as humans. This couldn't have been done unaided, they'd been helped by their treacherous allies; so-called Terrans who had sold their birthright.

Aliens had achieved equality under the law. The next step would be the importation of unhuman laws to Earth. Aliens would then become lawyers, preventing pure-blooded Terran attorneys from making an honest living.

Ewart was one of many people to have been deceived. He had married an alien for an honourable reason, to make money, and never believed that he'd meet his new wife. But the marriage had been a pretext for two Algolans to reach Earth. One was alleged to be his bride, the other her sister, but what proof was there? It was only by good fortune that Ewart was leaving his native planet at the time of their arrival, thus depriving the two aliens of their opportunity to undermine humanity.

The lower races should be confined to their own worlds, forced to recognize the inherent superiority of mankind. Abdenga was also inclined to believe that humans should remain on Earth, because that was the only way to maintain the purity of the race.

There were always those who would surrender to the lure of forbidden desire. Such weaklings had to be protected from their primitive lusts. If there were no temptation, they would not be forever tainted.

Ewart was still watching the Algolans. Although she was scanning the whole area, most of Zena's attention seemed focused in their direction. One of Jarker's autocams hovered above them. And Abdenga realized that he was also gazing at the two aliens. Even he was fascinated by them, and so anyone with a lesser mind could easily fall under their unhuman spell.

He was pleased that Ewart was staying far away from the Algolans, and he must also keep his distance. Who knew what evil influences they could exert?

'Would you like me to initiate annulment proceedings, sir?'

Such a matter ought to be complex enough to occupy Abdenga's time, and it could all be handled under Earth law.

Ewart shook his head. Abdenga recognized the gesture, which wasn't a negative. He was thinking of other things and might give an answer later. Or he might not.

Abdenga knew he must keep his thoughts to himself. Although everyone lived in fear of alien domination, few dared to speak openly of the threat to human survival. No one could be trusted. Anyone could be an alien agent, could have become corrupted and betrayed their human heritage.

But Abdenga had always kept his thoughts to himself. He'd had no one to talk to since his mother died. Even then, it was she who had done most of the talking. Perhaps he'd have been able to talk with Miss Yasmerel. No: that was over before it had even begun, and he must not torture himself by considering what could have been.

'Sir,' said Zena, 'we have an intruder.'

They all turned. An alien, one of the natives of

GX486/33–D, was walking up the incline, heading directly towards them.

Until now, the savages appeared to have taken no notice of the visitors. Except to steal from them. The planet had been discovered during Galentic Xploration's first mission to this solar system, an undisclosed number of years ago. By now, the natives must have become used to off-worlders, and they continued about their daily routine. Some of them worked beyond the valley, in the fields irrigated by the canals fed from the oasis; some tended their animals, bizarre creatures that could only have developed on an alien planet; some seemed to do absolutely nothing.

'Shall I kill him or her, sir?' asked Zena, as she stroked her gun.

'That probably won't be necessary, Zena. Go and talk to him, Joe.'

'Me, sir?'

'Right. You're my lawyer. Deal with it.'

Abdenga failed to see that this was a legal problem. It was more of a security matter, which meant it was Zena's duty to make sure the alien wasn't carrying a hidden weapon and intent on homicide.

If an alien killed a human, would it be homicide? What if a human killed an alien? Was there a word for that? As far as Abdenga was concerned, it shouldn't be a criminal offence.

Ever since leaving Earth, or at least since recovering from the preliminary shock of doing so, Abdenga had wondered if he were still legally in Ewart's employ. His contract had another eighty-seven years to run, but was it valid off-Earth? Any agreement was worthless if it couldn't be enforced, and they were far beyond Terran jurisdiction.

This probably wasn't the time to query the technicalities of his contract, however. Zena was the only enforcement that Ewart needed, although her own contract would be as invalid as Abdenga's. He needed to talk to her about this, which was difficult because she was seldom away from Ewart's side.

Grawl was in a similar position, but there was no point trying to talk to him. He was unable to speak, but he also pretended he was unable to hear anyone except Ewart.

'Go on,' Ewart prompted.

'Yes, sir,' said Abdenga. He wiped the sweat from his face, his eyes switching from Zena and her gun to the approaching alien.

'Now.'

Abdenga nodded and began walking, slowly, reluctantly, towards the savage. Ewart must have known how much he hated non-humans, which was why he'd ordered him to talk to it.

Rajic had briefed him about the translator, but Abdenga hadn't taken much notice because he'd no intention of conversing with the savages. He wasn't even going to get near them.

But now one of them was getting nearer and nearer to him.

'Hey, man,' said the alien, 'what's happening?'

'Excuse me?' said Abdenga, as he halted, after only a few paces.

'Let it all hang out,' said the savage, who also stopped.

Although they were only a few metres apart, he couldn't see the creature in any detail, for which he was grateful. It was tall, but how broad was difficult to make out because of the thick robes. To protect them from the heat, they all wore hooded garments so dark that they appeared black. There was a hint of green to this one's robes.

Zena had said 'him or her' and the alien could have been of either sex. But its sex was of no consequence – except to another alien.

Its voice, even though the slate was on Abdenga's belt, seemed to come from the direction of its mouth; but its face was in shadow, hidden by its hood. All Abdenga could make out was the glint of inhuman red eyes.

He was too nervous to remain silent. 'Let what hang out?' he said.

'Crazy, man!'

Abdenga agreed. Everything was crazy.

And it became totally insane when the alien said, 'Which one of you freaks is William Ewart?'

Janesmith stood with her arms folded, watching as Rajic approached. She looked magnificent, and he sighed. Marysmith still lay curled up on the ground. Sleeping, Rajic hoped, rather than dead.

He activated the privacy screen again. Although Grawl couldn't speak, his other senses must have been enhanced. Also, one of Jarker's autocams was hovering too close.

'I've been talking to our brother,' Rajic said.

'Why won't he talk to us?' asked Janesmith.

'He will, but first we have to go exchange gifts. As the sister of the bride, William Ewart is pleased to give you . . .' Rajic gestured towards Grawl.

'For us?' Janesmith growled with pleasure. 'How lovely.' Her forked tongue flickered out from her lips. 'He shouldn't have.'

'You only have this gift because Ewart believes he really is married to Marysmith, you realize? He mustn't know.'

'He won't, not from us. We've already told you that.'

'And your sister?'

'She doesn't know anything. And she isn't going to live long enough to find out.'

'I think it would be best if you didn't kill her. Not yet. Because if she dies, you won't be related to Ewart. As an unrelated female, you won't be allowed to travel with him. You'll be trapped on this planet.'

Janesmith rocked her head from side to side, her eyes focused on Grawl.

'Alone,' added Rajic. 'If the bride should die, all gifts to the relatives are taken back.'

'Marysmith must die.'

'I understand, but you have to choose the right place and the right time.'

'Where and when would that be?'

'You're the expert. How many sisters have you killed?'

'Three.'

'You don't really need me to advise you, although perhaps you shouldn't kill Marysmith while she's under Ewart's protection.'

'He might disapprove?'

'He might. But if you wait a while, he'll soon get fed up with her. That's what Terran husbands are like. Then you can do what you want.'

Janesmith was still gazing at Grawl, but Grawl was staring behind him. Rajic also looked in that direction, watching as a group of locals picked up Ewart's enviro-suit and carried it away.

It wouldn't do them any good, not without the right coding. And what did they want it for? This was their world, their environment. They didn't need suits.

Grawl glanced towards Ewart, who could be seen in the distance also watching the natives. Ewart gave no order, and so Grawl relaxed one per cent.

'What about my gift?' said Rajic. 'As the groom's brother, I bring you a present. As the bride's sister, you give me a present.'

'That isn't our custom,' said Janesmith.

'Then I'll take your gift back.'

'No, no. We must keep up the pretence.' For the first time she looked away from Grawl, watching as Ewart made his way up the slope. 'If it's your custom, then it's our custom. We must find a suitable gift for you, our brother.'

'You don't have to give me anything now. I happened to be there when you saw something you wanted, so I arranged it as your gift. When there's something I want, I'll let you know, and then you can give it to me.'

Janesmith was in his debt. It was always useful to have favours owing.

'Yes,' she agreed.

'This is another thing you must never mention to Ewart,' added Rajic, 'although for a different reason. You mustn't even thank him, because it's against protocol to refer to gifts.'

'We understand.' She was staring at her present again.

'His name is Grawl, and he's unable to speak.'

'We like a male who can't say "no",' growled Janesmith, and she started walking towards him.

Grawl's eyes were again on his employer, and Rajic looked up the incline towards Ewart and Abdenga and Jarker and Zena – and the alien who was approaching them.

This shouldn't be happening. But if one of the locals wanted to talk with Ewart, then Rajic needed to be there. He must continue to be indispensable.

'I must go,' he said.

As he hurried towards where Ewart was making first contact, Rajic heard Princess Janesmith, daughter of the Empress of Algol, say, 'Show us your genitals.'

And, for what must have been the first time in his life, Grawl backed away.

CHAPTER THIRTEEN

'Which one of you freaks is William Ewart?'

When Ewart heard the alien, he was very surprised and very suspicious – and also very pleased.

Even on a remote and backward world like GX486/33–D, they'd heard of William Ewart. It was what he'd always expected.

Freaks? To an alien, that was what the Terrans must have looked like. But they couldn't see the alien, who was completely covered by dark robes.

'As your lawyer, sir, I advise you not to acknowledge your identity,' said Abdenga.

Abdenga was also suspicious, as he was paid to be, and probably surprised. He didn't seem pleased, of course, but he never seemed pleased.

He'd as good as admitted he wasn't Ewart, and Zena obviously wasn't. There should have been someone else with them, Ewart realized. Who was it? He glanced around and saw the auteur, who couldn't possibly be mistaken for a famous, wealthy, influential tycoon. That meant only Ewart could be Ewart, as the alien evidently knew, because the hooded head was turned towards him.

'You must recognize me,' said Ewart.

'No way,' said the alien.

'No way to where?'

'No way anywhere, man. This is nowheresville. You dig?'

The translator didn't seem to be working properly. Was there a replay function?

'Right,' said Ewart, which seemed safe enough.

'Right on,' the alien said, which could have meant anything.

'How did you know I was here?'

'The cool cat laid it on me.'

What cat? Did the alien mean Janesmith? From what Ewart had seen of her, there was something very feline about the Algolan. Had she been telling the native about him? What had she said?

'I believe that I should conduct initial discussions, sir,' said Abdenga.

Ewart was standing on an alien planet, a few metres from one of its inhabitants. He was actually talking to an alien! But it all seemed so ordinary, so was he really an alien? He appeared tall, but beneath those robes he could have been anyone. He could even be Rajic. He probably was Rajic.

Then Rajic was suddenly by Ewart's side.

'What's going on?' he asked.

'Don't ask me. Ask the alien. What he says doesn't make any sense.'

'You don't understand a word?'

'I understand the words. But not the sentences.'

'Who's "the cool cat"?' asked Abdenga.

'You tell me, man,' the alien told him.

'No, you tell me who informed you of Mr Ewart's presence.'

'The god squad fingered the main man.'

'Father Ahmed Lamakinto? Is that the person in question?'

'No label on his way-out gear, so you go figure.'

Ewart stared at Abdenga, whose cross-examination skills seemed to be producing results.

'It seems, sir, it was Lamakinto who identified you to the alien.'

What was Lamakinto up to? Ewart glanced at his companions. Zena's gun was at the ready, although not pointed directly at the alien because that would have been too provocative.

The autocams, however, were focused directly upon the native. Ewart tried to remember the auteur's name. Since reverting to his primary function, he seemed to have become as invisible as before, remaining unnoticed unless he spoke.

'Let's take a proper look at you,' said Rajic. He must also have doubted the alienness of the newcomer.

The alien took a step forward, and Abdenga took a step backwards.

'No,' said Ewart. 'We want to see your face. Take off the hood.'

The alien didn't move, either forward or backwards. Neither did he remove his hood. His hands were hidden by his long sleeves, and his robes brushed the ground, covering his feet.

Zena raised her gun slightly, swinging it towards the motionless figure. A few degrees higher, a few degrees across, and it would have been aimed at the centre of his chest.

'No need to get heavy,' said the alien.

He raised one arm towards his face, and his hood fell back. His head was narrow and oval, ochre and hairless; his lips were thin, his mouth small; his nose was narrow, his ears large; his eyes were dark red slits, vertical slits.

And he was an alien.

'This is a real bummer,' he said, glancing up at the sun.

'Too hot?' asked Abdenga.

'Too cold. It's midwinter, man.'

'Is it?' Abdenga wiped sweat from his face. 'It seems very warm.'

'I ain't here to rap about the climate,' said the alien, covering his head again.

'Ask what he wants,' said Rajic.

'Ask who he is,' said Ewart.

It was his spaceship, his expedition, he gave the orders. He felt at a disadvantage because the alien knew who he was. It shouldn't have bothered him, he supposed, because billions of people knew Ewart's name without him knowing theirs. But they were Terrans.

'"Ask what he wants. Ask who he is",' echoed the alien. 'Is this dude your interpreter?'

Abdenga was his interpreter, Ewart realized.

Although if all the alien's sentences had been as intelligible, the slate would have been enough.

'He's my lawyer,' said Ewart.

'Groovy, baby,' replied the alien.

Ewart looked at Abdenga, and Abdenga shrugged.

'What do you want?' Abdenga asked, and Ewart was annoyed because that had been Rajic's question.

'Galactic peace, harmony throughout the universe, love between all races,' said the alien. 'Same as everyone else wants, man.'

'What do you want from Mr Ewart?'

'Zero.'

If that was true, he was the first person who'd never wanted anything, so naturally Ewart didn't believe him.

'Who are you?' asked Abdenga, which had been Ewart's question.

'Moonflower,' said the alien.

'Does this world have a moon?' Ewart said to Rajic.

'How should I know?' Rajic glanced around the arid landscape. 'Does it have any flowers?'

'If you want to know where it's at, man.' Moonflower continued, 'I'm hip to the scene.'

'He appears to be offering his services as a guide, sir,' said Abdenga.

So the alien did want something, and it was the same something that people on Earth always wanted: Ewart's money. It was reassuring to know that humans and aliens were exactly the same in this respect. No matter what planet in the galaxy, they all wanted to cut a deal, to turn a profit.

No one could do that better than Ewart. He was the

ultimate entrepreneur, and the universe was his for the taking.

'How much?' he asked.

'Sir,' said Abdenga, 'as your lawyer, I advise that you should allow me to negotiate a contract of employment with the alien.'

'How much?' Ewart repeated.

'Zero,' said Moonflower. 'Do I look like a bread-head?'

'Does he?' asked Ewart, who wished the alien hadn't reminded him of food. He waited for the translation.

'Er . . .' said Abdenga.

'I ain't no capitalist pig,' Moonflower said. 'I won't rip you off, man.'

'I'm glad to hear it,' said Abdenga, and it was hard to tell if he knew what the alien meant. 'But if you wish to become an employee of Mr Ewart, then I suggest you adopt a more suitable manner of address. You should call him "sir" not "man".'

'"Sir"? How about: "Oh great potent warrior from the sky who rode down to our lowly world upon a magic chariot of flame and honours us with his supremely magnificent presence"? Where you from, man? You think we're savages?'

Abdenga did think they were savages, but at least he didn't say so.

'You're offering your services as a guide, free and gratis, for neither reward nor favour?' said Abdenga. 'Is that correct?'

Ewart knew he couldn't be wrong. No one did anything for free, not on Earth or GX486/33–D, nor any other planet in the galaxy. Anything that was free wasn't worth having.

'If he won't name a price,' said Rajic, 'it probably means he expects some kind of exchange. A favour for a favour.'

It was that way on Earth, thought Ewart, and it was the same everywhere else.

He didn't need a guide because his visit to the surface of GX486/33–D was almost over. He'd already seen more than enough and needed to get back to the *Demon Star* to eat. But his bargaining instincts were as keen as ever, and it was hard to resist making a deal even though he didn't want what was on offer.

'If you did become my guide,' he said, 'there must be some small token of gratitude which you'd accept.'

'I've got the sun, the sky, the air,' said Moonflower. 'What else could turn me on?'

'Whatever you want.'

'Glass beads.'

Ewart looked at the alien. The alien looked at Ewart. Then Moonflower pulled back the top of his robes to reveal a necklace, a string of multi-hued glass beads which glinted in the alien sun.

'A bunch of fab beads would be a real gas, man,' he said.

'Right,' said Ewart. Fab beads? Beads could be fabricated on board the *Demon Star*, he supposed, although it didn't matter. If he didn't pay, what could the alien do? 'What's there to see around here?'

'On this dung dump? Zero. Until tomorrow. It's solstice. Man, do we party!'

'Do you?' asked Ewart.

'Tripping from sunrise till sundown. Way-out music and wild jiving. Blow your mind with the smokes and booze.'

'And food?'

'Eats! We've got the ace macrobiotic joint in the whole world.'

What did a macrobiotic joint taste like? There was one way to find out.

'Can I book a table?' asked Ewart.

'We just liberated a table, man!'

'Is that an alien "joke", sir?' asked Abdenga.

Ewart ignored him. 'How much to go to your party?'

'It's free, a free festival. Ain't that why you're here, man, to turn on and tune in?'

'Right,' said Ewart.

'Be there or be rectangular,' said Moonflower, and he walked away.

'I don't know. I'm a busy man.'

'He must have been the local chief,' said Ewart

'Or warlord,' said Rajic.

Ewart glanced at him, but Rajic was looking towards the Algolans. Something was happening, but it was hard to tell exactly what because Grawl was almost invisible in his camouflage outfit. He seemed to be running, although not very fast. Then Ewart realized that he was being chased. One of the Algolans was after Grawl, who was running around in circles.

'What's going on?' asked Ewart.

'Looks as if Grawl's found someone his own size to play with,' said Rajic.

Grawl was twice the size of the Algolan, but Rajic was right. Marysmith was chasing Grawl, who would almost let her catch him before speeding up again. After several seconds, Grawl suddenly halted and turned. Marysmith stopped and quickly spun around, and it became Grawl's turn to chase her.

Watching the psychopathic bodyguard playing games with the little girl was an unnerving sight, and Ewart felt an icy shiver down his spine.

The little girl.

Alien or not, that was all Marysmith was. A little girl. Not much different from . . .

Ewart squeezed his eyes tightly shut. It was easy not to see, but it was impossible to forget.

'Is it true?' he asked, opening his eyes.

'Is what true, old bean?' asked Rajic.

'Don't talk about food! Not when I'm starving. Is it true that Janesmith intends to kill Marysmith?'

Rajic looked at him. 'Yes.' He nodded. 'It's true.' He nodded again. 'It really is.' And again.

'I could have her killed first.'

'Would you?'

Ewart shook his head. Even if he believed Rajic, he wouldn't do that. Especially to a woman.

A woman? No. Janesmith wasn't a woman. She might resemble one. She might even be female. But she was an alien.

Although Ewart prided himself on being totally ruthless, assassination had never been one of his strategies. He had many enemies, however, none of whom had his high business standards. Which was why he needed constant protection.

Ewart believed that neither would Larnvik have resorted to murder. They were deadly rivals, but not literally. Things might be different now, when Larnvik discovered what he was left with after Ewart's escape from Earth.

Violence was the first resort of the incompetent, and Ewart had more subtle, more powerful weapons in his armoury. The only killings he'd ever made were corporate, and no blood had been spilled as the price of victory.

It hadn't always been like that. At one time, he had become violent. Very violent. When his world was destroyed, all that he'd lived for capriciously annihilated, he no longer wanted to live and the rest of the world had to be destroyed with him.

Instead, he'd survived. Life was hard, the world was cruel, and the only way to succeed was by being even harder, even crueller.

That was when he become William Ewart and began to avenge himself against the whole universe, taking and taking, forever taking whatever he could, accumulating more and more wealth to insulate himself from the past and ensure that he had a future.

'Where's she going?' he said.

Janesmith had been watching as Grawl allowed her sister to ambush him, then she suddenly turned and made her way down into the valley.

'It looks like she's heading for Moonflower,' said Rajic. 'Maybe she wants him to show her something.'

'Show her what?'

'Something alien, I suppose. How should I know?'

Ewart looked at Rajic. From his tone, he probably did know. They watched as Janesmith and Moonflower stopped in front of each other.

'Another great moment in galactic history,' said Rajic. 'The first meeting between an Algolan and a – what? – GX486/33–Dian. Probably.'

One of the autocams hovered nearby, recording the event for posterity.

'He could be inviting her to the festival,' said Ewart.

'Could be. When I first saw him, I thought he was trying to sell you his sister.'

'Does that really happen? Isn't it a myth?'

'Myths are based on fact. You wouldn't believe the number of "sisters" I've been offered.'

'Right.' Whatever Rajic said, Ewart wouldn't believe him.

'They were just trying to sell local goods to the tourists. And what's the most basic of all urges?'

'To eat.'

'I thought you didn't want to talk about food.'

'That's the answer. The most basic urge is to eat.'

'No. It's sex.'

'Food is more of a necessity than sex.'

'For the survival of the individual, yes. But not for the survival of the species.'

Ewart glanced at Zena. 'What did you say was the purpose of life?'

'The human race exists in order to procreate, sir, to produce the next generation which will then in turn reproduce itself.'

'Right.' He looked at Rajic. 'And that's what you mean. Reproduction.'

'Yes.'

'But reproduction isn't the same as sex.'

'Sex is the traditional form of reproduction.'

'Right, but sex with an alien doesn't lead to reproduction. Does it? It can't do. The genes are all wrong, the chromosomes completely different. Fertilization can't take place. Can it . . .?'

'I've never heard of offspring being produced from such liaisons,' said Rajic. 'But there are still plenty of volunteers carrying out practical inter-species experiments.'

Ewart shuddered at the idea. He was prepared to accept that aliens were the equal of any human, any Terran. But to have sex with one of them . . .! It was totally unnatural. Anyone who was attracted to an alien was perverted.

He glanced over at Moonflower, thinking how the females on this world must be very similar in appearance. It wasn't that they were ugly, because no such standard was applicable. Humans were ugly, humans were ordinary, humans were good looking. But aliens, they were just . . . different.

Compared to Moonflower, even Janesmith was attractive. In fact, she could almost pass for a Terran. Even her colour wasn't too unusual, although it was a decade since skintint had been all the vogue.

Having done his best to ignore the Algolans, Ewart found himself wondering what Marysmith would look like when she grew up.

'On any planet in the galaxy,' said Rajic, 'selling sex is the oldest profession.'

'And that's the oldest phrase in the galaxy,' said Ewart. 'There are two types of basic sexual equipment, and everyone has one or other. They come as standard fittings with the rest of the body. Right? The skills are instinctive, easily learned, and an enthusiastic amateur can perform as well as a professional.'

'Speaking from experience, are you?'

Ewart turned and looked at the other three, at Zena, at Abdenga, at ... who was he, the one with the autocams?

'Off,' he said. 'No more filming. I don't want this recorded. Take your cams somewhere else.'

'Whatever you say,' said the auteur.

'Go away, Joe.'

'Where to, sir?'

'Anywhere. This is a private conversation.'

'As your lawyer, sir, I should be present in order to—'

'Get out of here.'

'Yes, sir.'

Abdenga walked slowly away. The auteur also left, his autocams hovering around him.

'What is the oldest profession?' said Rajic.

'Chef?' Ewart suggested.

They both laughed.

'Are you going to the festival?' asked Rajic.

'Right. After coming all this way, you think I'd miss the chance of a meal?'

'Good show. If you don't try what the galaxy has to

offer, you might as well have stayed on Earth. Try the food. Try the women.'

'What? Moonflower's sister?'

'Not necessarily. But maybe on the next world we reach.'

'*We?*'

'Yes. We could travel together. Sometimes, you know, I almost think of you as a brother.'

Ewart laughed for a moment. He'd forgotten how charming and persuasive Rajic could be, but beneath the surface he was cool and calculating – almost as much as Ewart was.

'If you're willing to try alien food,' said Rajic, 'why not alien sex?'

'They're completely different things.'

'Yes. And no. You don't eat purely for nourishment, do you? You eat because you enjoy it. Because the wonderful aroma of each dish first teases your nostrils and stimulates your appetite, then the intricate texture of every mouthful yields to your lips and teeth, its complex flavours sensuously caressing your palate. The sweet and the savoury, the sharp and the spicy, all of these take turns to tantalize your taste buds. Fish or fowl, flesh or fruit, fat or fibre, each fabulous offering is shared with the rest of your body, every delicious morsel slowly sliding from your reluctant tongue and down your eager throat.'

'Stop it. Stop it!' Ewart's mouth was watering. He could almost taste what Rajic had described, and his stomach growled in anticipation.

'Or you can live on bread and water. Food isn't just for

survival, is it? It's for the pleasure it gives you. And it's the same with sex.'

'Pleasure? Sex with an alien? Pleasure?'

'You should try it. You should try everything once. Except suicide. Why not? You're already married to an alien.'

'She's four years old!'

'But she's got a sister.' Rajic glanced away, but he couldn't hide his smile. 'Forget it.'

'Forget it! How can I forget it? You're depraved, that's what you are. Depraved! You were always weird, even as a kid.'

'Me? What about you?'

'What about me? What do you mean? What about me?'

'I'm just offering you the benefit of my experience. Travel broadens the mind, and given time ...' Rajic shrugged. 'But I suppose at your age it's too late.'

'At my age? I'm two years older than you are!'

'From your lack of interest, I thought you must be too old for sex.'

'Too old? Never! It's just that I don't happen to fancy aliens. Or fish. Or animals. Or insects.'

'What about simsex or mindlay? You must have tried them.'

'I've tried them. I've tried the best of everything. You're right, I'm old: old-fashioned. I like the real thing.'

Rajic looked from Ewart to Zena, and he nodded.

'Must try that again myself. How about it?' he said to her.

Zena smiled invitingly, and Rajic began to return her smile. Suddenly, the gun barrel was against his mouth, pressing his lips hard against his teeth and freezing his half-smile.

'I think that means "no",' said Ewart. 'You must forgive him, Zena. He isn't used to talking to a real lady.'

'Should he be punished, sir?'

Rajic stood immobile, his eyes wide with fear. Ewart remembered what Rajic had done to him years and years ago, parsecs and parsecs away. He had been a weird kid, there was no doubt of that. Ewart still hadn't taken revenge, but now it was more appropriate than ever.

'Right,' he agreed. 'But only minimum disruption, and when I give the word.'

Rajic dared not move a muscle. All he could do was blink his eyes, begging.

'Talking about food,' said Ewart, 'remember when you used to make me sick?'

That had happened several times before Ewart became suspicious. Rajic loved cooking, Ewart loved eating, which should have been the perfect arrangement. He enjoyed countless great meals, but every so often one of them made him throw up. It was only later he realized this was the idea. Rajic must have mixed a really bizarre concoction of ingredients, something Ewart couldn't stomach, something no one could stomach. Except Rajic. Because whenever Ewart made him swallow it, it had no effect.

'Remember?'

Rajic rolled his eyes from side to side.

'Is that a negative response?' asked Ewart. 'I'll ask you again, because it's always best to confess. If a criminal pleads guilty, the sentence is often less than it would be. Remember?'

Rajic rolled his eyes up and down.

'But not in this case,' said Ewart. 'I've waited over half a century to get even. Zena.'

The barrel of her gun was still up against Rajic's mouth. She squeezed the trigger. Then the weapon was gone. Zena quickly backed away.

Rajic frowned, opened his mouth as if to speak – and every delicious morsel which had earlier slowly slid from his reluctant tongue and down his eager throat suddenly reversed course and erupted from his mouth and splattered on to the alien ground.

Ewart turned his head and moved away, not wanting to see what Rajic's gastric processes had started to do to his share of the wonderful banquet he'd served earlier.

Holding his stomach as he heaved, Rajic bent double, spewing up every last atom of his meal. Slowly, he stood upright, wiping his lips and chin with the back of his hand. He opened his mouth wide, inhaling deeply.

'What a waste,' said Ewart

'Not on some worlds,' Rajic muttered, as he staggered away. 'Regurgitated food is a necessity.'

'Right.'

'I mean it. The elite on Capella have slaves who do everything for them, even eat for them. They can't chew, because they've had all their teeth pulled out.'

'So they eat vomit? Right.'

'They also have to be carried everywhere. The ruling class have their legs amputated. And their arms. A head and a torso, that's all they are.'

'Right, right.'

'I can also think of at least one race that considers totally digested food a great delicacy.'

'What? You mean . . .?'

'Yes. It gives a whole new meaning to recycling, doesn't it?' Rajic managed a smile.

Ewart shook his head, trying to empty his mind of the awful idea. Rajic was lying, of course. Wasn't he?

'But they'll have real food here,' said Ewart. 'Natural ingredients. Won't they?'

'Depends what you mean by "real" and "natural". If the natives can eat it, you can. None of it will do you any harm. I've had to eat plenty of things I'd prefer not to remember and, guessing what's been nixed from my memory, plenty of things I'm glad I don't remember.'

'Anything . . . alive?'

'Depends what you mean by "alive". Back on Earth, you've eaten live oysters. Did you bring any for your honeymoon?'

'This isn't my honeymoon! That child, that alien, isn't my wife. In any case, I've never needed oysters. I eat them because I enjoy it.'

'But do the oysters enjoy it?'

'Probably not as much as they enjoy simsongs, artdiving and meeting new oysters. Enjoy it! The whole reason for their existence is that they get eaten.'

'They'd have been really disappointed if they died of

old age? Like all the other animals that were slaughtered so you could eat them?'

'If animals aren't meant to be eaten, why do they taste so good?' asked Ewart. Those who appreciated genuine meat had a duty to maintain the old culinary traditions. 'If they aren't eaten, they'd be extinct.'

'The ones you've eaten are extinct.'

'Still talking about survival of the species?' said Ewart, and he smiled. 'But they weren't killed, you know that. Most meat is grown in vats.'

'Not the kind you eat – or ate.'

'Right. But if I chose a leg of tiger, the tiger would regenerate another one.'

'And what would happen to the new leg? It would get eaten. What a life!' Rajic shook his head, then quickly put one hand to his mouth again.

'No sudden movements for a few minutes,' said Ewart.

'Thanks for the advice.' He took a few deep breaths, then continued, 'Very few races eat live creatures. It's usually considered a bit primitive, although they might make an exception for ceremonial occasions.'

'Here, you mean?'

'Maybe. Or the locals might honour you by chewing your food first. It would be a great insult if you refused to eat it.'

'I've insulted better than these.'

'Whatever you're offered, just chew – if you have to – and swallow. You've got your bugcollar.'

Ewart stroked the thin strip around his throat, which was a smaller and more specific version of his bugbelt.

Whatever he ate would be immediately rendered inert. Although he could choose to enjoy the taste, the texture, the flavour, nothing that was incompatible with human physiology would be absorbed.

They should have sold alien bugcollars on Earth, he thought, so that Terran food wouldn't be digested. It would have been an ideal way of ensuring a balanced diet.

'This will protect me tomorrow?'

'It'll protect you against anything you eat, although it won't be any protection if they decide to eat you.'

'What?'

'You want to eat alien food, try something different. It could be the same with them. You're different, something new to eat. But don't worry. If anything happens to you, you've got Galentic Xploration's guarantee. They'll wipe out every local within ten kilometres as reprisal.'

Ewart had known Rajic longer than anyone else and should have been able to dismiss his lies; but even when he knew they were lies, they could still make him feel very uneasy. Galentic Xploration would have issued a warning if there were any danger. Wouldn't they . . .?

'If someone from one planet ate someone from another,' said Ewart, 'would that be classified as cannibalism?'

'The victim probably wouldn't care what it's called. Some aliens do practise a form of cannibalism, eating their own people, or part of them. Perhaps as a mark of respect when one of them dies, or else it—'

'Why did you look over there?' Ewart interrupted.

'Where?'

'You looked over at Marysmith.'

'Did I?'

There was no sign of Janesmith, or of Moonflower, and Marysmith and Grawl had ceased chasing each other. They were sitting side by side, apparently talking in sign language. Ewart watched them in bewilderment.

'Are Algolans cannibals?' he asked.

'How should I know?'

'Because you spent so long talking to Janesmith.'

'You think she'd have told me? "Hello. I'm very pleased to meet you. I'm from Algol. Yes, it's very nice there. We eat each other, you know."'

'Have you ever heard of aliens eating other races?'

'You name it, I've heard of it.'

'Aliens eating other races.'

'There are stories. I've heard of trophy hunters who visit every known world to hunt and kill one of the locals. Maybe what they kill, they eat.'

'If they eat it, there won't be anything left as a trophy.'

'Other aliens are abducted by different races for zoos, because some worlds try to collect one of every species in the galaxy.'

'Only one?'

'Or two. A breeding pair. Or perhaps they're abducted for scientific purposes, for vivisection. Or to become slaves. Or for sex.'

'I wondered when you'd mention sex again.'

'Alien sex is a lot safer than alien food. OK, not safer. The bugcollar makes food safe. But with sex at least you

242

know what you're getting. Or you don't.' Rajic smiled. 'That's what's so great about it.'

'Abduction, slavery, cannibalism. Admit it, it doesn't happen. It's all made up, a legend, just like … space pirates.'

'That isn't a legend.'

'Really? They exist? And so do aliens who eat other races?'

'Yes. No. I don't know.'

'What do you know?'

'I know that on Mira the men duel to the death. The victor becomes the prime male, with a harem of wives to serve him. One male, lots of females. But I'm sure that doesn't interest you.'

'It does. Imagine the meals all those different wives could cook.'

Rajic laughed. 'I'm beginning to feel hungry again,' he said.

'You can't be.'

Rajic glanced back over his shoulder, to where his vomit was scorching under the heat of the alien sun. 'That isn't my kind of food. When it first went in, I mean. I only ate it to be sociable. If you deal with fancy food all the time, you prefer something plain and simple.'

Fancy food, or plain and simple, Ewart could have eaten either – or preferably both – right now. Because Rajic probably knew it, he didn't say so.

'You are what you eat,' said Rajic. 'Do you want to be an alien?'

'What? I'll become an alien if I eat their food?'

243

'There must be some reason why every alien race looks different from us, different from every other race, and my theory is it's because on different planets they eat different food. It's obvious.'

'So I eat a meal here and end up looking like Moonflower? You're crazy.'

'Check out the evidence. If anyone stays on an alien world long enough, they begin to change, both physically and mentally. That's a fact.'

'You haven't changed. You're older, uglier, but you still look human. More or less.'

'I've never stayed on any one alien planet long enough for it to affect me. But given time, people change. Stay here long enough, and you'll begin to look like them.' Rajic glanced around. 'I'm going back to the lander. You?'

Ewart needed to eat, and he'd intended to return to the *Demon Star* as soon as possible. But he didn't want Rajic to think he was scaring him away from the surface.

'Later,' he said.

'Abyssinia,' said Rajic. He turned and walked back down the slope, towards the valley and the lander.

'What did he say?'

'Abyssinia, sir,' said Zena. 'It is a former name of a former country in north-east Africa.'

North-east Africa? Maybe Rajic had once been there and was referring to the similarity of the landscape. Perhaps he was Earthsick. If there was such a thing.

'He was lying, wasn't he?'

'About what?'

About everything, thought Ewart, but he said, 'About people changing.'

'No, sir, Mr Rajic was not lying. A human, or any other being, will begin to change if they spend long enough on an alien planet.'

'It can't be.' Rajic couldn't have told the truth.

'A person, human or alien, will inevitably be affected by all the various influences of a new planet and its star. Such physical changes are comparatively slight at first, taking many years until they become apparent.'

'What influences?'

'Gravity, climate, atmosphere. Mass, size, density. Number of moons. Size, mass and orbits of moons. Ditto other planets within solar system. Distance from primary or primaries. Size, type, temperature, electromagnetic spectrum of primary or primaries. Sidereal revolution period, axial rotation period. Mean orbital velocity. Ellipticity of orbit. Angle of inclination of equator to plane of orbit. Geological composition, geographical composition, geophys—'

'Food?'

'One meal will not turn you into an alien, sir.'

That was all he needed to know.

'May I ask you a question, sir?'

'Of course.'

'How should I address your new wife?'

'What do you mean?'

'She is a princess, sir. Should I call her "your majesty" or "your highness"? Or should that be "your royal majesty" or "your royal highness"? Or, as Algol has an Empress as head of state, should it be "your imperial majesty" or "your imperial highness"? Or is there some other appropriate title of which I am unaware?'

'If there is an appropriate title, Zena, the slate will translate it. I think.'

'And how do I curtsy, sir?'

'How do you what?'

'Curtsy. It is how a female of lower social status genuflects to a member of a royal family, the equivalent of a male bow. I have practised, but it does not look right.'

She crossed her right leg in front of her left, bent at the waist, and lowered her head as she leaned forward. And it didn't look right.

'You don't have to bother with that, Zena.'

She stood upright again. 'I think I should, sir. She is a princess.'

'The word loses something in the translation.'

'Then she is more important than a princess?'

'Gains something, I mean. On Algol, Marysmith is a princess. Anywhere else, she's just a little girl.'

'She's your wife, sir.'

Ewart shrugged.

'As you are married to a princess, does that mean you are a prince?'

'No.'

'Not even on Algol, sir?'

'I doubt it.'

'But you are already an Algolan warlord.'

'Not exactly.'

'And there is a possibility that Marysmith will become Empress?'

'So it seems.'

'Would that make you Emperor of Algol, sir?'

Ewart had never considered this, but he had something much more important to think about.

He wondered what his first alien meal would be like.

Compared with what he'd seen Rajic prepare, tomorrow's food might well be disappointing. But he hadn't fully appreciated many of his favourite dishes the first time he'd tasted them; his palate had needed educating.

Whatever it was that he ate on GX486/33–D, it was bound to be different from anything he'd ever eaten before – and not because it was alive or pre-chewed.

The art of gourmet cooking probably hadn't developed very much here, but the natives would provide the very best of whatever they had for their guest.

Moonflower's story of a solstice festival was just an excuse, and the real reason they were celebrating was obvious. It was in honour of their famous visitor.

Ewart's arrival was the most important thing that had happened to this insignificant little world since it had been discovered.

CHAPTER FOURTEEN

'Go away, Joe,' Ewart had said, and Abdenga wished that he could have done exactly that: gone away, all the way back to Earth.

But there was nowhere to go, and now he was down on the surface of GX486/33–D again, standing on one of the slopes above the village, watching as the savages prepared for their primitive and doubtless very unhygienic solstice ritual.

The previous day, there had seemed to be very few aliens, and they had acted in a slow and quiet manner. Today, there were thousands of them, and they were all very busy, very noisy. The crowd milled around and around as everyone talked very loudly to everyone else. They had to raise their voices to make themselves heard above the incessant beat of dozens and dozens of drums.

Because there were more of them, the foul stench of alien bodies had become more intense, and his bugbelt was unable to protect him from the smell. Didn't they ever wash? How could they tolerate being close to each other?

Then Abdenga wondered if it was the burning torches which most of them carried that gave off such an overpowering stench.

The savages had been clad in dark robes yesterday, but now they wore different colours, all very bright. Reds mixed with yellows, yellows intermingled with blues, blues blended with reds, creating a fractured rainbow of orange and green and purple.

All except one, who was still in dark colours.

Abdenga might not have noticed the difference if the alien had been amongst all the others, but he stood some distance away, like an outsider. He was smaller than the rest, his movements slightly incongruous. Perhaps he was a child, or maybe a cripple, and he didn't walk like the other savages because his limbs were in different proportions.

In fact, Abdenga realized, he was totally different. The reason he was acting like an outsider was because he was one, and there were only two suspects.

Abdenga started to make his way down the slope and across the valley to confirm his suspicions. It took four or five minutes until he was standing behind the dark figure. By then, he'd decided which of the two it was.

'Carrillos,' he said.

Carrillos spun around. It had to be him, even though his face was hidden by his hood. Abdenga was unable to read his expression, but the archaeologist was so surprised that he didn't issue his automatic correction: Dr Carrillos.

'It's only you,' he said, his head quickly turning from side to side as he looked around.

He must have been looking for Ewart, who was meant to deliver him to the third planet. And he didn't want to go.

Carrillos tugged his hood forward in the hope of ensuring anonymity, clasped his hands together so that his sleeves didn't hang below his knees. In case that wasn't enough, he sat down on the ground.

Whatever he did, it would make no difference. Ewart could easily have found him if necessary. Carrillos would be as visible from the *Demon Star* as he'd been to Abdenga. In fact, Ewart could well have had them both under observation at this very moment, which was why Abdenga had to be careful what he said.

Not wanting to get his suit dirty, he remained standing. The alien dust on his shoes was bad enough.

'You can't hide,' he said.

'I'm not hiding.'

'Just as well, because you're the only one wearing yesterday's colour. It seems that fashion changes overnight here.'

'Only for the festival. But there weren't any other threads for me.'

'Threads?'

'It's the native word for clothes.'

'Why are you wearing that stuff?'

'So I can blend in.'

'You're not blending in. You look ridiculous.'

'Have you seen yourself?' said Carrillos.

Because he'd left Earth so unexpectedly, there had been no time for Abdenga to pack a change of clothes and he still wore his legal robes. Although not his wig and cloak, of course, which were strictly for court appearances.

He had nothing else to wear. Anything from the ship's wardrobe had probably belonged to an alien. Not that this seemed to bother Ewart, who had lost every trace of sartorial sense since leaving Earth and now dressed as if he were on holiday.

Abdenga's outfit was cleaned every day, but Carrillos didn't seem to care how he looked.

'You should be ashamed of yourself,' said Abdenga.

'What for?' said Carrillos.

They might have been far away from Earth, but decent standards had to be maintained. There were two bulwarks of civilization. The rule of law was one, and pride in appearance was the other. Civilized societies were orderly societies, where personal grooming was as vital as a neat and clean environment. Take away the dignity of the law and respectable clothing, and the result was anarchy.

'As the superior race, we have to set these savages a proper example. You must know that, Carrillos, you're an intelligent man.'

'You make the word "intelligent" sound like an insult,' said Carrillos, looking up at Abdenga. He tugged off his hood as if to see more clearly. Although his grey beard was gone, he still looked as old as he'd pretended to be.

'When you're in court,' he continued, 'you have to wear the appropriate outfit. An old-fashioned suit. I'm an archaeologist, so think of these robes as a very, very old-fashioned suit. I have to wear this to do my job. Understand?'

'This isn't your job. And archaeologists don't wear cattleperson uniforms when they dig up Old New York.'

'Dig up? Why does everyone think that's all archaeologists do? We study people. But because the people we study are no longer around, we learn about them and their culture through what they left behind: their buildings, their artifacts, their writings.' He shrugged. 'Their bones.'

Abdenga gestured down into the valley. 'But these savages are still around.'

'I know! For someone in my profession, this is living history, a unique opportunity to study a primitive society at first hand. I can actually talk to the people, question them about their lives. If it weren't for Ewart, I'd never have discovered my true destiny: to produce the first comprehensive treatise on the natives of GX486/33–D. Such a pioneering anthropological work is certain to become the definitive authority. And, because he brought me here, I intend to dedicate my magnum opus to William Ewart. When will he be back? I want to thank him.'

Abdenga looked at Carrillos, wondering what he was up to. He hated Ewart as much as Abdenga did. And, like him, he wanted to return to Earth. No one in their right mind would prefer to stay on a barbaric world such as this.

Carrillos knew that the *Demon Star* was directly above, watching, listening. Everything that happened on the planet's surface was monitored, and any mention of Ewart's name prompted a recording of whatever was said. He was evidently hoping to appeal to Ewart's vanity, that the promise of having some obscure scientific dissertation dedicated to him was enough to let Carrillos stay here.

But Ewart probably no longer cared about delivering Carrillos to GX486/33–C. It wasn't that he'd forgotten about his original agreement with Mac's Mineral Moons, because he never forgot anything. Having been paid in advance, however, there was no extra profit to be made from the deal, and MMM was hardly in any position to sue for breach of contract.

Abdenga saw no advantage in telling Carrillos this, so he said, 'Mr Ewart will be here, I imagine, in time for the feasting.'

Why was Ewart so enthusiastic about the festival? He prided himself on being a gourmet, but what possible enjoyment did he expect to derive from the kind of food eaten by savages?

Yesterday, Abdenga had been given the opportunity to try a variety of alien meals which Rajic had prepared. The other Terrans seemed to believe that he was prejudiced and would refuse to taste anything. He didn't want to offend Ewart's brother, who might be useful to him, and so he'd sampled a number of different dishes which came from the more advanced races. As he'd expected, nothing had been as good as even the worst food from his own planet.

'That's this afternoon,' added Carrillos. 'All the natives have fasted since sunset. This morning there's a procession all around the valley, around the fields, when they pray to the sun that it will cease its drift towards the horizon, that it will turn back and end the winter.'

'How do you know so much?'

'It's a solstice festival. They were held in almost all early Terran societies. The Maya, of whom I am the leading authority in the universe, used to—'

'How do you know so much about this place?'

'One of the natives told me. Moonflower's been of great help. When I needed a pad to crash out, he found one for me.'

'A pad to crash out? That's more of the alien lingo, is it?'

'Yes, in the local idiom it means a cave in which to sleep. Or it could mean a place in which to hide. I'm not sure exactly.'

'You slept in a cave?'

'Yes.'

Carrillos was definitely going native.

'Are you still wearing your bugbelt?'

'Yes.'

But he hadn't gone all the way. Yet.

Abdenga wondered if Moonflower was the same savage he'd spoken to yesterday. It wasn't very likely that they all had the same name. Unless it was the slate which had given it to them, as a result of a translation glitch.

'What else did Moonflower tell you about the festival?'

'When the sun's at its zenith, that's the climax of the ceremony. Look, they've started.'

Abdenga looked. The parade had begun. Those in the lead were climbing the slope at the near end of the valley. Thousands of voices ritually chanted, twice as many thousands of feet kicked up clouds of dust, all stamping down in rhythm with the drums which were finally beating in unison.

'Then with all the solemn stuff over,' Carrillos continued, 'they start eating, drinking, dancing.'

'The climax? What happens at noon?'

'Didn't I say? That's when the priest carries out the sacrifice.'

The sacrifice...

Abdenga had known that the inhabitants of GX486/33–D were primitive, but to discover they practised sacrifice made him shudder.

'Savages! How many do they kill?'

'Just the one.'

'Just the one! Isn't that enough?'

'It doesn't seem many.'

'Doesn't seem many! You're already like them!'

'I don't know what you mean.'

'They sacrifice one of their own ... *people*! And you say it doesn't seem many!'

'No, no, no.' Carrillos laughed. 'You've got it wrong. It's not a human sacrifice.'

'I know that. How could it be? They're not *human*.'

'It's a chicken. They sacrifice a chicken. One chicken.'

An important pagan ceremony like this, an annual festival in which the whole village took part, and they sacrificed only one chicken ...?

Carrillos was right. It didn't seem many.

'They're poor,' said Carrillos, 'Sacrificing one chicken is probably a great ... well, sacrifice.'

'I hope there's more to eat than one chicken,' said

Abdenga. 'There won't be much left when Ewart gets here.'

Carrillos laughed again, and Abdenga wondered why.

'The chicken doesn't get shared out,' said Carrillos. 'It's a gift to the sun god, its blood mingling with the waters which give life to the valley, the village, the people.'

Abdenga glanced towards the savages marching up the slope, wondering if Moonflower was with them. The Moonflower he'd talked with had been sent to Ewart by Lamakinto. What had the missionary said to the alien? And had they spoken to each other since?

'Have you seen Lamakinto?' Abdenga asked.

'No.' Carrillos shook his head. 'If I never saw him again, it would be far too soon.'

Far too soon wasn't very far away, because Abdenga saw Lamakinto approaching them. He was still in his Terran clothes, but he probably had a number of identical outfits. Even if they were his United Religions vestments, it was better than being dressed like a tourist or wearing native threads.

Carrillos hadn't noticed, so Abdenga nodded towards the priest.

'Talk of the devil,' he said.

'You aren't going to interfere,' said Carrillos, breaking the long, long silence.

'Is that a question or a statement?' asked Lamakinto.

'It's a threat.'

Lamakinto had the whole planet to choose from, but

he'd decided that the best place to sit was right next to Carrillos.

It was as if the missionary were haunting him. Last night, he'd even dreamed that Lamakinto had entered his cave to talk with him – or at him. Carrillos couldn't remember what was said but, trapped in his sleep, he'd been unable to get away.

He could have escaped now, but why should he? He was here first.

'I've told you before,' said Lamakinto, 'I'm here to observe.'

'Only because you want to see what you can change.'

'Not at all. People are the same on every world.' Lamakinto glanced towards the procession, the head of which was now returning, entering the far end of the valley. 'Their beliefs have much in common with those of United Religions of Terra.'

'You'll change whatever is different.'

'Not change, adapt. This world has a very different calendar to our own, for example. Today's pagan ritual is a celebration of one of their most significant dates. In the fullness of time, such ceremonies will become the same holy days which we all share.'

'You want to destroy their culture, make everyone the same.'

'Their culture began to die the day Galentic Xploration's first ship landed here. And that was the best thing that ever happened to them. Modern medicine will prolong their lives, and contemporary technology will give them better lives. Pain and poverty will be wiped out.'

'Pain and poverty? That's only just beginning. Galentic Xploration will exploit the natives almost as much as United Religions of Terra will!'

'You're an archaeologist, Carrillos. You live in the past, what do you know of the future?'

'I know these people have no future, not now.'

'I suppose famine and disease must be very interesting for you to study. But not for them to endure.'

'They're not starving. They're not ill.'

'They live in ignorance, enslaved by their witch doctors.'

'Witch doctors? Why use such a derogatory term? Why not call them priests? They're no different from you. If they're witch doctors, then so are you!'

'Your profession and mine are so alike, Carrillos. The very first priests were scientists. You could say that the witch doctors here – very well, the priests here – they're scientists. They're astronomers. They predict the solstice, and knowing precisely which is the shortest day is vital to an agricultural society such as this.'

'The priests keep their knowledge of the calendar to themselves. If everyone here knew how to calculate the solstice, there would be no need for this whole charade.' Carrillos pointed towards the parade. The drums were still beating, the chants as loud as ever. 'The declination of the sun has reached its greatest angle, the days will become longer.'

'"The declination of the sun has reached its greatest angle." Blah, blah, blah. How dull! Isn't it better if they think of the solstice as the return of their god? The sun is their god, their life. What better reason to celebrate?

The sun goes away. The sun comes back. They know what they see.'

'And I know what I see,' said Carrillos, looking at him.

Archaeology needed patience, and Carrillos had always considered himself very tolerant, willing to listen to every side of an argument. Lamakinto had an answer for everything, and he could sound so reasonable, but that was part of his job, to make the unreasonable seem plausible. Carrillos wished that he could kill him.

Murdering the missionary would be a great humanitarian service to the inhabitants of GX486/33–D, even if they weren't humans, but he knew that he wouldn't do it. He wasn't a violent man. Even if he had a gun, he couldn't pull the trigger, and he certainly couldn't put his hands around the ghastly priest's slimy throat and squeeze and squeeze while he begged for mercy and keep on squeezing and squeezing until the arrogant bastard was dead . . .

Lamakinto was to stay on this world, allowed to do his worst, while Carrillos was to be banished to a dead world, where he could do no good. Wasn't that perfect proof of the non-existence of a supreme benevolent deity?

Or perhaps the opposite was the case. This was exactly what Lamakinto's god wanted: for United Religions of Terra to be recreated here in its own image.

Carrillos planned to remain. What he'd said to Abdenga was partly correct, because it would be interesting to study a primitive society which had many parallels with various early Terran cultures. But he was going to make sure that he carried out his research on the other side of the world from Lamakinto, even if he had to walk there.

'The return of the sun brings more light to this world,' he said. 'And science is liberation from darkness. In the course of time that will happen here. Science is knowledge, religion is superstition. You want the darkness to continue, replacing native superstition with your own, and with you as the high priest instead of him.'

The figure leading the procession had to be the high priest. He was one of the few clad all in white, the others being those immediately behind him who were carrying a . . .

A table? It was the table on which Rajic had served yesterday's meal, Carrillos realized. Turned upside down, it was supported on the shoulders of four natives. Another of the white-robed locals sat on the inverted table, surrounded by all manner of pots and containers, including the dishes Rajic had used for his alien banquet. Carrillos supposed that all of these must have held gifts to the sun god. There were several more objects on the table which didn't appear to be of local origin, and at first Carrillos wondered what they were. Then he realized that Ewart's envirosuit had been dismantled and lay amongst the offerings.

'Where's the chicken?' asked Abdenga.

Carrillos turned and looked up. Abdenga had been standing there so long that he'd almost forgotten him. Ewart and his party had arrived in the lander a while ago, and Carrillos expected Abdenga to go and join them. He hadn't.

'What chicken?' asked Lamakinto.

'I can see all kinds of things on the table stolen from Mr Ewart,' said Abdenga. 'But there's no chicken.'

'What's he talking about?' asked Lamakinto, as if he were suddenly an ally against this outsider.

'I know it's an alien chicken,' said Abdenga, 'so it must look different.'

'Is he Earthsick?' asked Lamakinto.

'But I can't see any kind of animal,' said Abdenga. 'Or bird.'

'He means the sacrifice,' said Carrillos.

The high priest had reached the oasis which was the heart of the village. There was a low wall around the water, making it seem like a deep well. All the irrigation channels radiated from here, some of them flowing through tunnels carved into the sides of the valley. The procession slowed down, as did the drumming and the chanting, while all the locals encircled the priest and the upturned table on which sat the figure clad in white.

'You think they're going to sacrifice a chicken?' said Lamakinto.

'That's what Moonflower told me,' said Carrillos.

'What exactly did he say?'

'He said, "We off some chick, man."'

'I think you misunderstood. "Off" indicates a termination, which must mean to kill or sacrifice; but a "chick" is a young female.' Lamakinto nodded towards the figure seated on the table. 'That young female.' He glanced up at the sun. 'Any minute now.'

'Oh,' said Carrillos.

'They *are* savages,' said Abdenga. 'I knew they were.'

'We're witnessing an ancient local tradition,' said Lamakinto. 'This is what they always do at the winter solstice to stop the sun flying off and never coming back.'

'Even if they didn't do it,' said Abdenga, 'the sun wouldn't fly off.'

'We know that,' said Lamakinto, 'but they don't want to take the risk. It's always worked before, so they presume it will work again. What harm does it do? It doesn't hurt anyone. Apart from the victim, I suppose. But everyone else has a great time.'

In the valley, the crowd was no longer moving, the chanting had ceased, the drums were silent. Only the priest was speaking, head tilted upwards, both arms raised towards his god – and holding a curved knife in each hand, the blades glinting in the sunlight.

'I'm only here to observe,' said Lamakinto. 'I can't interfere, can I?'

Carrillos kept staring at the awful scene below, watching as the table was lowered to the ground and the victim led towards the well. Her fate was inevitable, and she didn't even try to resist. The high priest turned towards her.

'But you can,' added Lamakinto.

'Yes,' said Carrillos, and he stood up.

He hadn't made himself stand up, and he didn't make himself start running down the slope. But that was what he did.

Trapped deep within himself, a prisoner no longer in command of his own body, it was as if he were again ensnared by last night's dream. He was alone but

Lamakinto was still with him, still talking, still making no sense.

Another part of Carrillos felt like an outsider, that he was watching himself run towards the sacred well.

He was nothing more than an observer. An observer who was about to interfere.

'Where's he going?' said Abdenga, staring in amazement as Carrillos hitched up his robes and hurried towards the floor of the valley.

'He wants to get a better view, I suppose,' said Lamakinto.

'You made him go down there.'

'I didn't do anything.'

'I heard you. I'm a witness. You said, "But you can." That was some kind of code to let you control him.'

'I'm not controlling him.'

Lamakinto was lying. The first thing Abdenga had learned as a lawyer was that everyone lied, some more than others. But Lamakinto's whole life was built upon a foundation of lies: he believed in the existence of God, despite the fact that there was no evidence which would have satisfied even the lowest of courts.

'They'll kill him,' said Abdenga.

'I hope not. If they do, Galentic Xploration will wipe out my new congregation.'

There was only one reason why Lamakinto would have sent Carrillos down there – to prevent what was about to happen.

He reached the edge of the crowd. Their backs were turned and they hadn't seen him until now, but the savages made no attempt to halt him. Carrillos slowed, weaving his way through their ranks towards the well.

The victim was neither held nor tied, but was willingly kneeling at the priest's feet. The chief savage was still praying to the sun god, twin knives raised above the low well – and the sacrificial offering's white-hooded neck.

Carrillos was getting nearer and nearer.

Abdenga was also getting nearer and nearer. Without realizing, he'd begun walking down the slope into the valley. Now that he realized, he didn't stop.

It was best to be as far away from Lamakinto as possible, even if that meant being closer to the savages.

'Come back!' shouted Lamakinto.

He hadn't tried to stop Carrillos, but he didn't want Abdenga involved. All the more reason for him to keep going.

By now, Carrillos had almost reached the high priest. Then he was grabbed by two of the savages who had carried the table.

After completing his long and arduous legal training, Abdenga had hoped to dedicate his career to helping his fellow men. Until now, the only one he'd ever helped had been Ewart.

Here was Abdenga's chance to help another man, another human. This would be a great test of his legal skills: persuading the aliens not to take reprisals for the way Carrillos had interrupted their barbaric ceremony.

Whatever happened, neither of them would be in any real danger. The savages must have known they'd be punished if they hurt an off-worlder. Or did they know?

And did they care? They might do whatever was necessary to ensure that the sacrifice took place.

Carrillos shouted out something as he tried to shake off his captors. The priest became silent, then turned towards him, twin blades still raised high.

Things didn't look very promising, thought Abdenga. Perhaps it would be too late for legal argument.

That was when the shooting started.

A series of explosions burst amongst the aliens, thick swirling smoke erupting from the ground.

Halting, Abdenga glanced across to the other side of the valley. Zena and Grawl were firing into the crowd. As the savages began to scatter, he discovered that alien screams didn't sound much different from human ones.

Through the dust and the crush, Abdenga saw that Carrillos was no longer being held captive. He stood by the well, and the high priest lay at his feet.

Abdenga was about to turn away, but what was there for him if he went back?

The explosions continued, and he hoped that Zena and Grawl were aiming carefully, not simply firing at random. He began walking towards Carrillos again.

After a number of paces, he suddenly shouted, clutched his chest and dropped to the ground.

'Are you all right?'

The voice was faint, as if from a great distance.

Carrillos didn't know the answer. All he knew was that he was sitting on the ground and couldn't stop coughing. When he looked around, he still could hardly see anything. But at least he was no longer totally blind and deaf.

'Who's that?' he asked.

'Father Lamakinto.'

The voice still sounded far off, but Carrillos could make out the priest's silhouette standing a few metres away.

'What's going on?'

His voice was hoarse, and there was a sour taste in his mouth, as if he'd been sick. When he wiped his lips, he found that he had been. His eyes were dry and very sore, and his ears ached and hummed, the echoes of distant thunderclaps still reverberating deep within his skull.

As his eyes slowly focused, he saw he was next to the sacred well. The high priest had been about to sacrifice to the sun god, he remembered.

'How did I get here?' he asked.

'It seems you were unable to maintain cold scientific detachment,' said Lamakinto.

And it hadn't been a chicken which was to be sacrificed, but a native girl.

Carrillos started to rise, putting his hands on either side to lever himself up. His right hand touched something, and he drew back quickly, sliding away. It was a white-clad body.

'The victim?' he asked.

'A different victim. It's the witch doctor who's dead. And Abdenga.'

'That's terrible.'

'Yes. I'll have to find another village. All this for nothing.'

'All what? What have you done? You've only been here since yesterday.'

Carrillos could see much better by now, but he wished he couldn't. All around him lay hundreds of natives, the dead and the wounded.

'Excuse me. Is this heaven?'

One of the aliens was leaning up against the edge of the well. He was dressed in white robes. No, *she* was dressed in white. She was the one who was to have been slain by the high priest. At least she was still alive. In fact, Carrillos now realized, almost everyone seemed to be alive, all of them coughing or vomiting or trying to crawl away.

'This doesn't look like paradise,' said the native.

'That's because you aren't dead,' Carrillos told her. 'But the priest is.'

He noticed a movement which seemed out of place amongst all the mayhem. It was Grawl. He and Zena must have used non-lethal weapons, and now he was making his way through the casualties. He halted by a supine shape which also seemed out of place. It was Abdenga.

'I say, that's a bit much.' The native coughed, and the white hood slipped off her face. She looked like Moon-flower. 'I always dreamed of dying, and now I've been cheated. Oh dear.'

'Aren't you glad to be alive?'

She raised an arm, indicating the village, the whole valley. 'My word, no! Would you wish to live here?'

'It's better than some places.'

'I was promised immortality.'

'How can you be immortal if you're dead?'

'I was going to be an angel and live in heaven for ever.' Slowly, she stood upright. Although not as tall as Moonflower, she was still taller than Carrillos. She stumbled towards the high priest. 'You stole my place in paradise.' She kicked his corpse. 'You absolute beast!'

Because Carrillos's eyes and ears had half recovered, he could watch and listen to all this. But because his brain wasn't fully functional, none of what he saw and heard made any sense.

'My friends were all so jealous, my parents so proud.' The unsacrificed sacrifice walked unsteadily away. 'What am I going to tell them? They gave me such a splendid farewell party. This was to be the greatest day of my life. I'll never get another chance. It just isn't fair.'

'There's no gratitude,' said Lamakinto.

Although Abdenga didn't hear a single footstep, he sensed someone coming closer, closer, until they halted next to him. He stopped breathing. Something touched his throat, but he'd already tensed himself and kept absolutely still.

It felt like a stick and was pushed harder and harder against his neck. He remained frozen, his eyes firmly closed. Then the object was withdrawn. There was total silence, but he knew he was still being watched.

His throat felt raw, and he needed to cough, but he clenched his teeth and fought back the urge.

A warm breath of air blew over his face, then another, and he realized it wasn't air. It was warm breath. Something was breathing on him, some kind of wild alien beast was about to bite into his flesh, eat him alive!

Abdenga opened his eyes.

Grawl was staring at him, his face only fifteen centimetres away.

Abdenga had always been scared of Grawl, but now he felt differently. He felt absolute terror.

Grawl looked down impassively for several seconds, then he stood upright. Standing above Abdenga, he seemed like a giant. He was holding his gun, and it was the barrel which had been pressed up against Abdenga's throat – because he did it again, lightly resting the muzzle beneath his chin.

Too paralysed to move a muscle, Abdenga knew this was the end. Grawl was about to finish him off.

The bodyguard mouthed two words: *You're dead.*

Although Grawl was as expressionless as ever, it was the first time Abdenga had ever seen his lips move.

Abdenga wanted to close his eyes, but there were muscles in his eyelids and he couldn't even blink. His heart was racing, as if aware that it didn't have much time left and had to get in as many extra beats as it could.

He waited for the inevitable.

Then Grawl backed silently away. And vanished.

Abdenga stared all around, then raised his head to look further all around, but there was no sign of him.

He'd gone, really gone, and Abdenga remembered to breathe again.

He closed his eyes and tried to relax, which wasn't very easy.

Of course Grawl hadn't killed him. Why should he have

done? The only reason he'd have killed him was if Ewart had ordered his death. Why should he have done?

But why hadn't Grawl hauled Abdenga to his feet and dragged him back to Ewart?

Perhaps the bodyguard hated Ewart as much as everyone else did.

Abdenga lay in the dust, gazing up at the green sky. The *Demon Star* was not the only ship in orbit around this backward world, and somehow he had to find a way of boarding one, of getting back to Earth, back to Miss Yasmerel. She would be so worried, not knowing what had happened to him.

Being a lawyer was all that Abdenga knew, so he had to make the most of his skills and talents. On a lawless world such as this, the opportunities were infinite. Once he'd found a pad to crash out, he could start devising a whole new judicial system . . .

Trapped on a barbaric planet, surrounded by savages, Joseph Abdenga felt more optimistic than he had in a long time. The whole world was filthy, smelly – and so was he. His outfit was dirty, stained with vomit. It couldn't be properly cleaned, not here, and he would never be decently clothed again. He'd have to find some alien threads to wear, and the only thing to eat would be native food.

But it was far, far better than having to work for William Ewart.

'You're not dead,' said Father Ahmed Lamakinto, staring down at the unmoving figure of Abdenga. 'I'm very glad.'

'So am I,' said Abdenga. 'But would you go away, please. If Ewart sees you talking to me he might suspect I'm not deceased.'

'He'll just think I'm saying a prayer, which is what I came to do.'

'That's very good of you. I don't wish to seem ungrateful, but I'm not a believer.'

'You should be. God has saved your life.'

'My life was never in any danger. I wasn't hurt, or not until the nausea gas hit me. I pretended to fall because I want to remain on this planet. Please go away.'

'This is a long prayer. Why do you want to stay?'

'Because I want to get away from Ewart.'

'So do I,' said Carrillos, as he came and stood on the other side of Abdenga, looking down at him.

'I quite understand,' said Lamakinto. 'Mr Ewart is not my favourite person, I must admit, although he was chosen by God to bring me to this heathen world.'

Until a minute ago, Lamakinto had thought that he'd failed, that because Abdenga had died the whole village would be annihilated in reprisal. Had that happened, of course, it would have been God's will. But Abdenga was alive, and that was also His will.

'Will you please both go away,' said Abdenga. 'You're attracting attention to me.'

'Whether we're here or not,' said Carrillos, 'Ewart will soon know you're not dead. You can't lie there for ever.'

'I'll lie here long enough for you to dig me up if I have to.'

'Archaeologists don't dig—' Carrillos began, but his words dissolved into a fit of coughing. It seemed to be infectious, because Abdenga also began to cough, although he tried to do it silently and with his mouth closed, which made him cough even longer and louder.

'The autocams will be watching you,' Carrillos said, 'and listening. Just like they'll be watching me.' He glanced up, and one of the auteur's units was hovering above the well, studying the high priest's body. 'There's nowhere either of us can hide.'

'You can never hide from God,' said Lamakinto. 'He sees everything.'

'So does Ewart,' said Carrillos.

Lamakinto looked down at Abdenga, who had closed his eyes again, as if believing that if he couldn't see them neither could he be seen.

Abdenga's presence during the ceremony had been unexpected, but his appearance had proved timely. Because Ewart owned the lawyer's contract, his body-guards had tried to protect their investment and started shooting. This had been very useful, and events had reached a satisfactory conclusion much more rapidly than Lamakinto had hoped.

He was grateful to both Carrillos and Abdenga, but of course their intervention was all part of God's plan – although Carrillos had needed prompting to play his role. Perhaps, in return, Lamakinto could be of service to them.

'Neither of you wish to leave this planet, it seems,' he said. 'And there's one certain way that you can stay.'

'If we're dead?' said Carrillos.

'If you become my assistants.'

'No,' said Carrillos.

'No,' said Abdenga, opening his eyes.

'Even this far from Earth, Ewart wouldn't dare cross United Religions of Terra.'

'He would,' said Abdenga. 'He had you locked up.'

'I needed solitude and a period of contemplation,' said Lamakinto, which was correct. Although he hadn't realized it at the time. 'As the head of URT on this planet, I have the authority to confer holy orders on you both.'

'Become a priest?' said Carrillos. He laughed without humour, then looked over towards Ewart and the others, who were still on the opposite slope of the valley.

'It is God's will,' said Lamakinto. 'He chose you to rescue that unfortunate wretch from becoming a ritual sacrifice.'

'?'

'You were possessed by the spirit of God.'

Lamakinto noticed that Abdenga's eyes were still open, and he was looking up at him. He seemed to know it was through Lamakinto that the holy spirit had possessed Carrillos, but that made it no less true.

'What would we have to do?' Abdenga asked.

That was one, thought Lamakinto.

'You'd become a priest?' said Carrillos.

'It can't make things any worse,' said Abdenga.

'Can it be done quickly?' Carrillos asked.

And that was two.

'Years of study and religious devotion are usually required,' said Lamakinto. 'But under these circum-stances, an exception can be made. Stand up, Abdenga.'

'I'd prefer to stay like this. I'll stand up when Ewart can no longer give me orders.'

'You'd rather take holy orders, you mean?' said Carrillos.

'If you're not serious,' said Lamakinto, and he made as if to leave.

'I'm serious,' said Carrillos. 'And Abdenga's always serious.'

'You are both certain about this?' said Lamakinto. 'You have to enter the clergy willingly.'

They looked at one another.

'Yes.'

'Yes.'

'Very well. Please memorize these few lines, which I will ask you to repeat. "Being pure of heart and filled with the spirit of God ..."'

Neither of them was sincere about becoming a priest, or so they believed. They both thought they were agreeing for their own benefit. Lamakinto knew differently. Once, when he'd desperately needed sanctuary, a similar opportunity had been offered to him. The alternative was a very long period of corrective rehabilitation. He had no intention of ever keeping to his religious vows and planned to go his own way as soon as it was expedient. But that had never happened. Like Abdenga and Carrillos, he had been chosen by God.

A decade later, he was on a brand new world, his task to bring the word of God to its heathen inhabitants. Who better to lead such a mission than a convert?

He said, 'This is indeed a wonderful day for you, my new brothers, for myself, for United Religions of Terra, for this world, and for everyone God has put upon it.'

'It's not a wonderful day for the high priest,' said Carrillos. 'He's dead.'

'God gives life. A life taken is a life returned to Him. Although not in the case of the witch doctor, of course, who is doomed to spend all eternity in purgatory.' Lamakinto paused, then added, 'And this village wasn't big enough for both of us.'

'You make it sound as though you killed him.'

'I did.'

The witch doctor was the leader of a pagan creed. He had to die to prove that his was a false religion, that the only true God was infinitely more powerful than all of this world's primitive deities. The priest's death at the height of the solstice festival was a necessary symbolic gesture.

'How did you kill him?' asked Carrillos.

'He was slain by the wrath of God.' Lamakinto reached into his robes.

'You shot him!'

'I was only the trigger. God guided my aim.' He slid the gun back into its hidden holster.

This was the first of many battles they would have to fight. The one true religion needed defending with blood as well as with faith. They carried a sword in one hand, the sacred texts in the other.

'Shall we begin your ordination before Ewart decides to visit us?' Lamakinto suggested. 'Please repeat the holy oath which I taught you.'

The two novices recited, 'Being pure of heart and filled with the spirit of God . . .'

Lamakinto listened as their voices rose upwards.

One of them would take slightly longer to reach God, because Abdenga was still lying horizontal on the ground.

Everything was happening so fast, which must be the way that He wanted it. Lamakinto had only arrived yesterday, and already he'd eliminated his main rival and recruited two priests. The new brothers were not his equals, of course, and a hierarchy needed to be established.

Today was a great day in the history of GX486/33–D, a date which would become one of the most holy days in the sacred calendar.

This was only the beginning, however. After all the villagers had been converted, the real crusade would start when URT spread the one true message beyond the valley, when they came up against all the other alien religions which had sent their unholy missions to this planet.

But God's will would prevail, Ayatollah Ahmed Lamakinto had no doubt of that.

When Grawl returned, he shook his head.

'What does that mean?' asked Ewart.

'It means he's dead,' said Rajic.

'Dead?'

Rajic looked around. He kept thinking there was someone behind them, but there was no sign of anyone or anything. If there were, Zena would have noticed.

'It's the same as not being alive,' he said.

'But he's broken his contract.'

'I'm sure it wasn't voluntary. And his future employment prospects are very limited. With or without a reference.'

Ewart gazed down into the valley. Lamakinto was standing over Abdenga's body, and Carrillos was slowly walking towards them.

One of Jarker's autocams hovered high above, taking in the whole scene; another was over the oasis and the body of the high priest; a third had followed Grawl as he went to inspect Abdenga's corpse, and now it was focused on Ewart.

Ewart appeared unaware of Jarker most of the time. Part of his ability to hide his true identity was to make himself as inconspicuous as his cams. Acting as an auteur masked his role as Larnvik's agent, which Rajic guessed was a cover for yet another purpose. But Jarker's talent seemed very limited, because only Ewart appeared oblivious to him.

'Did you kill Abdenga, Zena?' asked Ewart.

'No, sir.'

'Are you sure? You keep asking if you can. I didn't ever say I wished he was dead, did I? You didn't use that as an excuse to shoot him?'

'No, I did not. It is inherently dangerous to use any kind of weaponry, sir. The human body is easily damaged. Even when uneuthanasiastic charges are fired, accidents can happen.'

'What was he doing in the middle of it all?'

'He wasn't in the middle,' said Rajic. 'That was Carrillos.'

The question was: what was Carrillos doing in the middle of it all?

Abdenga and Lamakinto had been easily recognizable on the other side of the valley, watching as the ceremony began. Rajic had assumed that one of the locals was with them, perhaps Moonflower. But Zena had identified the third figure as Carrillos. Dressed in native robes, he'd suddenly jumped up and run down to where the priest was about to decapitate one of his congregation.

Rajic had no doubt that Lamakinto would have been able to give all the answers, but he had no intention of asking any questions. Whatever happened, it was too late for Abdenga. He was another victim of religion, and there would be no resurrection for him.

'I feel bad about Abdenga,' said Ewart.

'Not as bad as he feels,' said Rajic, thinking it odd he should seem so upset. 'He's dead, but that's life.'

'Death is the purpose of life,' said a voice from behind them.

It was one of the locals. Rajic realized that he'd been standing there a while, silent and unseen. It had to be Moonflower. Today he was clad in pale green robes.

Zena and Grawl spun around, their weapons raised. Even they had been unaware of the native. His deceptive skills were far more sophisticated than Jarker's.

'No, it isn't,' said Ewart, not bothering to glance back. 'And Abdenga had no right to die without my permission. He still owes me eighty-seven years, and he doesn't have any relatives I can claim off. I've been cheated.'

Rajic was reassured to find this was what Ewart had felt bad about.

'Where there is life there is death,' said Moonflower.

'Renewal and rebirth. The death of a star, but the birth of a galaxy. The death of a man, but the birth of an amoeba. Weighed on the cosmic scales, everything balances out.'

He wasn't talking the same way as yesterday, and there was something else odd about his voice. It hadn't come through the slate.

'What's one death,' said Rajic, 'as long as it isn't mine? Although it's two, not one. The priest's also dead, and he was only trying to do his job.'

He kept talking, not wanting to stop because that would mean having to consider the implications of his discovery. Whoever Moonflower really was, Rajic knew he wouldn't like it.

'There are billions of humans on Earth,' he continued, 'trillions of people throughout the galaxy. However many die, they're all easily replaced by unpaid, unskilled labour which enjoys its work.'

'Who are you?' said Ewart, as he finally looked over his shoulder and noticed the newcomer. 'Take off your hood.'

Zena and Grawl were still aiming their guns at the alien, while one of the autocams was focused on him.

It wasn't only the hood which he removed. The green robes seemed to dissolve and melt away, while the figure within became smaller, his shape uncertain for a few seconds, then resolving into that of a Terran male.

He was totally average, wearing ordinary clothes, with nothing about his appearance to differentiate him from millions of others. Rajic knew that he'd make even less of an appearance on the autocam: he would be totally invisible to electronic scanning.

His eyes flickered across Zena and Grawl, and they lowered their weapons.

'My name is *******,' he said, in a very normal voice, 'and I'm taking over the ship.'

PART THREE

Dinner

Hideaway

CHAPTER FIFTEEN

Ewart was glad when Janesmith went in the opposite direction. The short journey in the lander was the first time he'd been close to either of the Algolans, but she'd completely ignored him and spent the whole ride to Hideaway staring at Grawl.

But now she spoke to the nearest alien, a squat, yellow creature with an enormous head and short arms.

'Did you hear what she said?' said Ewart. 'It sounded like "Show us your genitals".'

'That's what happens when you overhear something not directed to you,' said Rajic. 'With so many slates around, the signals get mixed up.'

Ewart noticed that Zena was also watching Janesmith, checking that she didn't try to return to the *Demon Star*. Orders had been left that she wasn't allowed back alone. Marysmith was still on board the ship. Hideaway was no place for a four-year-old.

Grawl had done his duty, and Janesmith's sister was

still alive. That was probably why she'd been glaring at him all the time, hating him for protecting her rival to the Algolan throne.

Could it have been Janesmith who'd given Grawl a black eye and a new break in his nose? Ewart didn't believe Zena's story, that he'd walked into a door which hadn't opened soon enough. Although it seemed very unlikely that Janesmith could strike faster than Grawl's reflexes could defend him, Ewart could think of no other explanation.

His sister-in-law vanished down one of the corridors which led off the entrance hall, and he was glad to see her go.

'Why's it called Hideaway if you could find it so easily?' he asked.

'I didn't find it. The captain did. He was following your orders.'

'I didn't give any orders. Did I?'

Ewart still hadn't met the captain, although from what Rajic said evidently there was one.

'You must have done,' said Rajic. 'Why else are we here? It was your idea. After GX486/33-D, you wanted a vacation.'

'No. It was your idea. I'd never heard of this place.'

They looked at one another, and Ewart could tell that Rajic was as confused as he. But, like him, he wouldn't admit it.

What had really happened on GX486/33–D? They'd been on the planet, now they were on a pleasure satellite, and Ewart had no clear recollection of anything in between. How had they got here?

The *Demon Star* had brought them here, obviously, and he could even remember various details of the voyage. But it was almost as if he hadn't experienced them, that instead he'd been told about everything. Each minute of the time he'd lost during the journey was locked away in the vaults of his mind, but the key to his stolen memories was too elusive and he couldn't quite focus on it.

'Do you ever get the feeling that your life isn't your own any more?' he said.

'Yes,' said Rajic. 'Ever since I discovered you'd bought the *Demon Star*.'

It wasn't that Ewart felt as if events were taking him over, because he knew they were. And it had begun as soon as he'd left Earth, when the ship had headed towards GX486/33 even though he had no real reason to go there. Why had he given priority to Lamakinto and Carrillos? It had just happened.

The missionary had been delivered and the archaeologist was only one planet away from his original destination. Abdenga had also remained behind, or his remains had. He'd owed Ewart eighty-seven years, but that was no great loss. Neither was Abdenga. Away from Earth, his knowledge of Terran law had been totally redundant. Every world had different laws, if they had any at all.

Ewart had always been a leader, a decision maker. But now he'd taken a back seat and become a passenger on his own ship, with no idea of his destination.

He tried to remember, but the hours and days spun around and around, the Möbius strip of memory bringing him back to the present. Trapped helplessly on a whirling cosmic roundabout, never able to get off.

Then he realized that he could have got off. If he wanted, he could turn around and take the lander back to the *Demon Star*. But he didn't want to. Now that he was on Hideaway, he might as well take advantage of what the artificial planet had to offer.

Or at least he thought that was what he wanted. What if whoever had brought him here wanted him to want to stay here . . .?

No. No one had brought him here. It was his own idea. He'd just forgotten. A touch of Earthsickness, that's all it was.

Rajic said, 'We're here now—'

But were they? Ewart could be imagining all this. He was still on board the *Demon Star*, ensnared by faulty engine technology. And Rajic was part of his hallucination, his role to say what Ewart was thinking.

'—so we might as well enjoy ourselves.'

He might be caught up in a delusion which could at any moment dissolve and leave him floundering in a puddle of embarrassment.

Rajic added, 'I'm going—'

To have some fun, thought Ewart.

'—to have some fun,' Rajic concluded.

Ewart watched as Rajic turned and began making his way towards another of the wide corridors into the interior of the satellite.

It wasn't the first time he'd heard him say that, seen him do this. The seconds replayed themselves exactly the same as last time.

'Where?' asked Ewart.

'Gambling.'

'You've been here before,' said Ewart, as he realized what was happening.

Rajic paused and looked back. 'I've been everywhere.'

This was different from *déjà vu*. The reason everything was so familiar was because he was sharing Rajic's experience. Somehow.

'If you can afford to gamble,' he said, once again, 'I'm paying you too much.'

'You haven't paid me anything.'

'Right. And that's too much.'

'Are you coming?'

'I'm a businessman. I don't gamble.'

'That's all you ever did. That's why you had to leave Earth.'

'No. I took calculated risks.'

'See you later.' Rajic turned away again, reaching the end of his script. 'Maybe.'

Maybe? Wasn't Rajic worried that the *Demon Star* might leave, that he'd be trapped here? Ewart supposed it was a much better place to be stranded than GX486/33–D.

'Where can—?' he started to ask.

'Ask at reception,' said Rajic, and then he was gone.

Ewart took a good look around. If this were all a hyperlusion, he had to admit that it was very impressive.

Viewed from orbit, the asteroid had shone like a star, radiating its own inner fire. Planets glowed with reflected light, but Hideaway was all on its own, far from any solar system which might try to claim it.

An artificial asteroid with a power core at its very heart, this source of energy also fuelled its propulsion unit. Smaller than any planet, Hideaway was larger than any spaceship, and could slip into falspace and travel to the far side of the galaxy in search of new customers.

There seemed no need for that at present, judging by the number of craft which circled the pleasure satellite.

People kept coming and going through the entrance, striding and strutting, shuffling and swaggering past Ewart. No, not people. Humanoids of every possible shape and size and variety.

Aliens . . .

He'd seen thousands and thousands of images of aliens, had already travelled across space to GX486/33–D, but that was only an appetizer and had barely hinted at the overwhelming main course.

Nothing had prepared him for being zillions of kilometres from his own world, surrounded by creatures as impossibly strange as these. They were all completely different from each other, even more bizarrely coloured and weirdly shaped than Ewart had ever hoped. He could see them all, hear them all, even reach out and touch them if he wanted. This had been his childhood dream, and he didn't care whether it was real or not.

It was simply, complexly, magnificent.

He could have stood there for ever, watching the inhabitants of the galaxy walk by. Some of the newcomers headed straight down the various tunnels.

(Except they weren't straight, there wasn't a straight line anywhere on Hideaway. Every floor and wall and ceiling followed the curves of the asteroid.) Others entered the booths at the side of the vast entrance hall, only to emerge a few minutes later and then disappear around one of the passages leading towards the various unknown attractions.

'Let's find out where to go,' he said.

Rajic had told him to ask at reception, and he must have meant one of the booths. Zena led the way, with Grawl taking the rear.

They had been disarmed before Ewart's group was allowed on to Hideaway, and something else had happened. What was it? Who was it? Janesmith and Rajic, Zena and Grawl, himself and – someone else. Right, the auteur.

Ewart was pleased that he'd remembered. The auteur's autocams and equipment had been removed before he'd been permitted entrance. But where was he now? Like Janesmith, like Rajic, he was gone and so it didn't matter.

The booth had seemed small, but it was much larger within; it had seemed featureless, but as soon as they stepped inside it was suddenly transformed into an enviroscape. Above, the blue sky was flecked with pale clouds. To the left was a shoreline, the edge of a turquoise ocean lapping over the sandy beach; to the right was a dense forest, all the trees very tall, with branches so thick they blocked out the sky; and straight ahead was a distant mountain range, jagged peaks white with snow. Between the sand and the forest, the ground was covered in thick grass.

It was meant to be a representation of Earth, Ewart guessed, or Earth as it must have been a few centuries ago. But how did they know where Ewart was from? Or had his biogenetic structure been analysed, a calculation made of the kind of planet he must have inhabited, and an ideal version of such a world produced?

Standing in the centre of the scape was what appeared to be a man, a Terran, but he was neither. He was a holographic simulation, given a composite appearance to make Ewart feel welcome. Noticing how his size, shape and features were entirely average reminded Ewart of someone, although he couldn't remember who. The memory was too elusive and had gone before it could be retrieved.

'Welcome to Hideaway, milady,' said the host, as he bowed.

The computer controlling him had made a mistake, greeting Zena instead of Ewart. Two mistakes, because she was no lady.

'It's always a particular pleasure to greet a woman as beautiful as yourself,' he continued, speaking without need of translation. 'How may I be of service to you, milady?'

Ewart said nothing. He might learn more this way. Because he remained silent, Zena took the initiative.

'This is my first time here,' she said, 'and I would like to know what services and facilities you have to offer.'

'It all depends what services milady requires,' said the host, and he glanced at Ewart and Grawl. 'These two are your sex slaves? A dwarf and a fatso, how amusing. We can find something far more interesting and stimulating for milady's pleasure.'

'What did you call me?' said Ewart.

The host looked at Ewart. 'A sex slave, sir. You are obviously so virile that it was a natural assumption. I profoundly apologize for my mistake. Welcome to Hideaway. It's always a pleasure to welcome a man as handsome as yourself, sir. How may I be of service to you?'

It was no use getting angry with a computer, but Ewart had to put him right – *it* right – on one thing.

'These are my bodyguards,' he said.

'Whatever you wish to call them, sir. But we can find something far more interesting and stimulating for sir's pleasure.'

'Are you offering me sex?'

'Not personally, sir, although it's kind of you to consider me. Hideaway specializes in supplying sensual sensations from every solar system.'

'You mean sex with aliens?'

'Yes, sir. You name it, Hideaway has it. If we don't, it's not worth having.'

'I don't want sex with an alien.'

'This would be a real sexual encounter, sir, although genuine sensynth is available. You can't tell the difference. Would you prefer that?'

'No.'

'I'm glad to hear it, sir. A man of such evident experience as yourself could tell the difference.'

'"Evident experience"? Are you saying that I'm *old*?'

'Not at all, sir. Although perhaps you are more

291

cautious, and that is very wise. Alien sex is perfectly safe if you take precautions, sir. A bugbelt for any environment. A bugcollar for any food. And a bugstrap for any sex.'

Ewart had heard the key word, and he repeated it.

'Food,' he said. 'I'd like to eat.'

'Yes, sir. You can have any meal that you wish. And would you like to gamble? Every game of chance in the known universe is played here.'

'No. All I want to do is eat.'

'But eating isn't illegal, sir, although of course some foods are prohibited on various worlds. You want to eat something which is illegal on Earth?'

'No.' said Ewart, as he realized that the host did know where he was from.

'Hideaway provides a unique range of services to the deprived people of the galaxy.'

'Space travel costs a fortune. Anyone who can afford to come here isn't deprived.'

'There's more to life than money, sir. People may be wealthy, but they can still be deprived of their natural rights. Whatever is legal on one world may be illegal on another, and it probably will be. On Hideaway, the sum total of the galaxy's illegality is available.'

'And that's what it comes down to? Sex and gambling?'

'Many worlds have taboos which seem very strange to more rational beings such as ourselves, sir. There are planets where it's illegal to talk, for example, or to use perfume, or to wear shoes. Hideaway doesn't offer special facilities for these activities, although of course they are permitted. Everything is permitted. If you don't wish to participate in alien sex, sir, you can watch a performance of your choice.'

Ewart shook his head in bewilderment. Aliens having sex? Was that supposed to be erotic? It would be as dull as watching goldfish mate. Probably less so, because he found himself wondering how goldfish did mate.

Rajic had kept talking about alien sex. After being in space for a while, was that all that anyone ever thought about? Perhaps Earthsick meant that the whole hormonal balance of the body became altered, and the same kind of thing happened to other races.

Ewart enjoyed sex. Usually. It was a great leisure activity, and ideal for a busy man such as himself because it didn't last very long. But if he spent too much time away from Earth, would he also turn into an addict, craving sex with any kind of alien? When would he begin lusting after fur and feathers?

'I know,' he said patiently, 'that I should try everything once, everything except suicide, but—'

'You can try suicide here, sir. Temporarily, of course. The after-life experience isn't to be missed. You haven't lived until you've died.'

'And I suppose I could try this while having sex with half a dozen assorted aliens of my choice?'

'Yes, sir. What better moment to die than at the peak of ecstasy? Is that what you want?'

'No, it isn't what I want.'

'Correct me if I'm wrong, sir, but I get the impression that you're reluctant to take advantage of all that Hideaway has to offer.'

'Right. No aliens. No sex. Just food. Right?'

'I'm employed to make sure everyone enjoys themselves, sir, and I believe—'

'Let me eat and I'll enjoy myself, I promise.'

'Of course you will, sir. Everything here is the best, and we have the best food in the galaxy.'

'None of it's regurgitated?'

'You mean recycled, sir. Regurgitated means bringing forth undigested food from the mouth, but recycled means—'

'I know what it means, I know what end it comes from, and I don't want either.'

'Only the finest and newest ingredients are used, sir.'

'Good. Can I book a table at your best restaurant?'

'After which you'll have sex with an alien?'

It seemed there was only one way he'd ever get a meal, and that was by saying, 'What about sex with a female of my own race? Is that possible?'

Something like that was probably too normal to be available on Hideaway, and Ewart hoped it was.

'Yes, sir. Would you like a Terran female who looks like an alien or an alien who looks like a Terran female?'

'Looks like? You mean people deliberately make themselves into aliens?'

'Bodymod is very popular, sir, and is one of the many services which we provide on Hideaway. There are various degrees of adjustment, from minor alterations to complete rebuilds. Why should anyone be restricted to how they were born? Anything can be changed. Would you be interested in such a service yourself, sir? You

294

could change sex, for example. That's relatively simple. If it isn't to your satisfaction, you could change back.'

'No!' Then Ewart thought of something. 'A whole new body, you said? A young body?'

'Of course, sir, as young as you like. With any modifications and improvements you want.'

'And would it last as long as a new body?'

'There is a slight temporal disadvantage, sir.'

'You mean "no".'

'We could do a lot with you, sir.'

'What do you mean by that?'

'Nothing, sir, nothing. You have so much potential, that's all.'

'What do you mean by "so much"? You called me "fatso", didn't you? You think I'm fat?'

'Not at all, sir. Compared to many races, you are little more than a skeleton.'

'I will be soon, unless I eat.'

'Of course, sir. Allow me to say one more thing. Although I seem to be Terran, that's only because my appearance is designed to make you feel more comfortable. I am, in fact, an alien.'

'I've nothing against aliens. I just don't want to have sex with one.'

'You are male, sir, and so am I. Because of that, although we are from worlds which are hundreds of light years apart, you and I have more in common with each other than with any female. It has been said, and I believe it's absolutely true, that there are only two races in the galaxy. Males and females.'

'Are you trying to say that I've already had sex with

aliens, so I might as well do it again?'

'Females are the most alien creatures that exist. Do they think like us, react like us, behave like us?'

Ewart realized that the host was right. Women *were* aliens. That was why he'd always had so much trouble understanding them. Because they were totally different.

'The restaurant is waiting for you, sir.'

'Good.'

Ewart glanced back. Because the enviroscape wasn't total, he could see through to the entrance hall. An alien was being carried in on a stretcher by two more of his kind. He must have been involved in some terrible accident, because he had no arms or legs. But such injuries didn't seem to have affected him, and he grunted orders through his toothless mouth.

'If he's going to the restaurant,' said Ewart, 'make sure my table's as far away as possible.'

'No bodyguards in the restaurant. Get rid of them.'

Ewart looked at the alien who stood in the rounded doorway. Was he the head waiter? If so, the slate should have provided a more respectful translation, including a 'sir' at least.

The alien was smaller than Ewart, with very slender limbs. He had two thumbs and five fingers on each hand, and wore dark goggles which seemed to be part of his face. His nose was flat, with wide nostrils, his mouth small and narrow, and his large ears jutted out high from the sides of his hairless head. He wore a tight black outfit, which contrasted dramatically with a skin so pale it was almost translucent.

'In that case,' said Ewart, 'I won't eat here.'

'Don't. You think I care?'

'What about letting one of them come in?'

'No. This is an exclusive dining room, for Hideaway's special guests. Perhaps it's different where you come from, but the elite generally consider it undignified to dine while employees are present.'

Ewart didn't like the idea of going into an unknown place without protection; but he liked the idea of being one of Hideaway's special guests.

'You are safe here, Mr Ewart,' said the alien.

'How do you know my name?'

'You're famous.'

'Right.' He was famous. They'd heard of him all over the galaxy. He was one of the elite, allowed into Hideaway's exclusive dining room.

'Don't you trust us?'

'No,' said Ewart, and he smiled.

The alien's mouth moved slightly, but there was no sound. Ewart presumed that it was a smile, not a sneer.

If those who ran the asteroid wanted to harm him, they could do so at any time. He'd already accepted the risk by venturing on to their territory, and it would make little difference whether Zena and Grawl were with him or not.

'Wait for me,' he said.

Zena and Grawl waited, the alien stepped aside, and Ewart entered the dining room. He was the only person there.

'Very exclusive,' he said.

'You are my guest, Mr Ewart,' said the alien.

The door slid shut behind him, vanishing as it became part of the wall. The lights dimmed for an instant and the restaurant was suddenly transformed.

Ewart gazed around in total amazement. The room itself was circular, not very large, yet its surroundings were absolutely sensational. He looked up, looked down, and was almost too scared to move in case he was swallowed up by the infinite.

'Quite a place,' he whispered, still staring around in awe.

The roof was transparent, a window on the universe, with countless glittering stars scattered at random across the vast heavens.

The view beneath Ewart's feet was equally spectacular. It was as if he stood on nothing, that he was held suspended above the miniature star which burned with pure white brilliance in the absolute centre of Hideaway.

Ewart felt himself swaying back and forth, as if solar gravity were trying to drag him down and at any moment he would plummet into the inferno below.

'Your table is ready, Mr Ewart,' said the alien. 'This way.'

Ewart found it easier to walk if he kept his eyes on the alien and didn't look down, down to where his feet appeared to tread on nothing.

The room had appeared to be empty, but in the centre was a wine decanter and two glasses which seemed to be hanging in mid-air. As he came closer, Ewart saw they were standing on a crystal table. There was a seat on either side of the table, and these were also translucent.

Neither the table nor the seats seemed to have legs, appearing to float above the invisible floor. Ewart bent down as if to sit, holding his weight on his feet while he reached under the seat and searched for a support, but there was none.

To his surprise, the alien sat opposite him. Ewart also sat down, and the seat moulded itself to his body. He ran his hand along the edge of the table, discovering that it was oval.

The alien picked up the decanter and filled Ewart's glass, then his own, with what looked like red wine. He lifted his glass and drank.

Ewart raised the other glass, swirling around the liquid and sniffing at the bouquet. Under normal circumstances, he would never have tried an unknown drink before it had been properly analysed. These, however, were not normal circumstances. Although he was wearing his bugcollar, he wasn't fully confident that it would protect him. He had to trust his nose. The aroma smelled wonderful – and the taste was even better.

'Excellent,' he said, which it was.

Although the vintage was totally unknown to him, every aspect seemed very familiar. It was like a blend of many different fine wines, but whereas this often resulted in the destruction of every individual flavour, here the character of each unique taste was enhanced and complemented by all of the others with which it had been so exquisitely combined.

He drank again, savouring the full richness, admiring the strong but pliant body, adoring the appealing piquancy which amused his expert palate and made him smile.

'Where's it from?'

'A small planet we own. A long way away, you won't have heard of it.'

'Where?'

'Myrmyrym,' the alien told him.

He hadn't heard of it. Another mouthful was called for, and he slowly washed the liquid around his gums, letting it ooze through his teeth and then flow across his tongue, tantalizing his tastebuds before cascading down his throat. He looked at the alien, remembering what he'd previously said.

'I'm your guest, you said?'

'That is correct. Allow me to introduce myself, Mr Ewart. I am Dulsedech. I am female. I am the chief controller.'

'Chief controller of what?'

'Of Hideout.'

'Hideout? I thought it was called Hideaway.'

'We have different names for tax purposes.'

Ewart laughed. 'I can understand that.' He took another generous mouthful of wine.

Dulsedech also supped some more wine but made no other reaction. Her race obviously had a different sense of humour, or perhaps none at all. Ewart felt uneasy in her company, not because she was an alien, but because he couldn't see her eyes. Hidden behind the dark lenses, he couldn't tell if she was staring at him or not. He glanced away for a moment, watching the white ball of fire beneath.

'Most of the light from below is reflected back,' said Dulsedech, 'otherwise we'd be instantly blinded.'

'You wear those goggles in case something goes wrong?'

'My ancestors were nocturnal. Even the faintest of light is too bright for my eyes.' She looked upwards. 'The stars are optically enhanced so they can be seen despite the illumination in the room.'

'All this must have cost a fortune.'

'An artificial asteroid of this size seems unique. Its makers are believed to be a very ancient race, probably extinct, perhaps even from another galaxy.'

Ewart looked all around once more, while Dulsedech refilled both glasses of wine. Another galaxy . . .

'I've taken the liberty of choosing from the menu for you, Mr Ewart. I'm aware that you're not familiar with the variety of food available away from your native planet, and so I've ordered a meal suitably appropriate to a man of your wealth and reputation.'

Ewart raised his glass in thanks.

If the wine were anything to go by, the meal would be absolutely superlative. He wondered how long it would be until it was served, but it might be regarded as impolite to ask.

Dulsedech was fully aware of his status, and he was very pleased to be accorded the respect to which he was entitled. But how did she know so much about him? Rajic must have told her. After all, it was Rajic who had brought him here. Wasn't it?

And what was Dulsedech really after? Despite his importance, Ewart knew he was only being treated so well because they wanted something from him. But who were they? Dulsedech claimed to be the chief controller, but what did she control chiefly? Ewart didn't know what planet she was from, and he didn't want to ask in case she regaled him with her unexpurgated biography.

Perhaps she was wining and dining him for personal rather than professional reasons. It wasn't unknown for a male to entertain a female guest lavishly in the expectation of being rewarded with sexual favours. Was it the same with Dulsedech? Was she as obsessed with sex as every other space traveller seemed to be?

Ewart sipped at his wine again. Sex was a form of communication, he supposed. The most intimate type of dialogue there was. He'd spent most of his life in the communications industry, but was there any better way of getting to know an alien race than by having sex with one of its people?

And why was he suddenly thinking like this . . .?

Was it the wine? Was it an aphrodisiac? Could it be that his human physiology was attracted by Dulsedech's alien female pheromones?

Was she even a female? She could have lied, and there was no way of telling. Or there was a way, but he hoped he wouldn't have to find out.

He tried to think of something else, anything else.

'Have you had this place long?' he asked.

'It was a recent acquisition. We took over Hideout as payment for a debt.'

'It must have been a very large debt. Who owed you so much?'

'Space pirates.'

Ewart almost choked on his wine. He glanced at Dulsedech. Maybe she did have a sense of humour. But her expression hadn't changed. She was serious.

'It was owned by space pirates?'

'Yes. Hence the name: this used to be their hideout. They would go on raids, return here, then escape to another part of the galaxy.'

'Are you sure? That's not all a legend?'

'Space pirates existed.'

'They don't any more?'

Dulsedech gestured with her wine glass. 'The pirates must have stolen this asteroid centuries ago, and it took a long time until they realized it was their prime asset. They turned Hideout into a pleasure satellite, offering whatever the peoples of various races wanted.'

'Let me guess. Sex with aliens?'

'Dreams. They claimed to sell dreams. And the dreams of most people can be satisfied by a few simple pleasures. The pirates gave up looting and murder, discovering they could earn more from victims who were willingly robbed of their wealth. Hideout became very successful, but it was never a legitimate enterprise. They didn't pay their taxes.'

Ewart almost laughed. Instead, he shivered.

'What happened?' he asked.

'We took over. They went back to their old ways, trying to operate an illegal business, but we'll make them pay for their crimes.'

While she spoke, a round hole appeared in the table top, as nearly invisible as the oval surface itself. Dulsedech reached in, her hands vanishing in the nothingness, and she lifted out a huge plate, the contents of which were hidden by an ornate golden lid encrusted with jewels.

'Your meal, Mr Ewart,' she said. 'The best that you can afford.'

He'd been waiting for this so long, his first alien meal, and he eagerly raised the cover. For a second he thought that the food was as translucent as nearly everything else in the room. He could see nothing, he could smell nothing. There seemed to be nothing on his plate. That was because there was nothing on his plate.

'Where's my meal?'

'That is your meal, Mr Ewart. As I told you, it's the best you can afford.'

'I'm a wealthy man. I've substantial investments on various planets.'

'No,' said Dulsedech. 'All your assets now belong to us. And you're still in debt.'

Ewart stared at the alien. His skin was damp with sweat, but his blood ran cold.

'You're a vampire!'

Dulsedech was a tax official. No wonder she had no sense of humour. Although maybe that was why her race had two thumbs and five fingers. For counting money.

'No,' she said. 'I'm vegetarian. We take no artificial stimulants. No drugs. No alcohol.'

Ewart glanced at his glass. No alcohol? She was lying.

The wine couldn't have tasted that good without alcohol.

He tried to stand up, but his chair wrapped itself around his legs, restraining him. He clenched his left fist, summoning Grawl and Zena. Although they'd been disarmed, that was little handicap. The invisible door would be shattered at any moment. Ewart waited to be rescued.

Nothing happened.

'Your bodyguards are otherwise occupied,' Dulsedech told him.

'Right, I admit it, maybe I do owe the Terrestrial Taxation Authority a few hundred rupan, perhaps even a few thousand. But that was there. Now I'm here. It's over. What's it got to do with you?'

'It's got everything to do with us. We own the Terrestrial Taxation Authority.'

'You *own* it . . .?'

'Another recent acquisition, although naturally our ownership has been kept secret. The first thing we did after the takeover was begin to collect all of our new subsidiary's outstanding debts. You owed the most, Mr Ewart, and therefore you were our top priority.'

'But who are you?'

'We are the largest financial organization in the galaxy, but we prefer to maintain a low profile. We have no name. And we have many names.'

'It was you who took me to court?'

'Yes, and we were very displeased when you ran out on your debts.'

'I can pay.'

'With what? We've sequestered all your assets.'

'The *Demon Star*.'

'The ship was owned by Solar Transit Leasing, which in turn was owned by Sol Global Network, but is now owned by us.'

'By you? What happened to Hiroshi Larnvik?'

'He went bankrupt.'

'Right!'

Larnvik had succeeded in taking over Ewart Communications Corporation, but it had ruined him. Such great news called for a celebratory drink. Even a non-alcoholic one. Ewart tried to reach for his wine, but the chair held his arms immobile.

'During your absence, you've become the most hated person on Earth,' said Dulsedech. 'On most planets that position is held by our organization, although totally without justification.'

'Me? Hated? Why? Because I ruined Larnvik?'

'Because you destroyed the entire economy of your planet. Which does seem a totally justifiable reason for hating you.'

'No ...'

'Yes.'

'Everything is connected, Mr Ewart. Your planet's financial system was built upon a foundation of credit, each debt supporting all the others. With one link in the chain broken, the entire edifice came crashing down, and Earth's economy was plunged into a deep recession.'

Ewart's various companies had passed the same securities back and forth between themselves to give the illusion of a solid financial base, although the whole organization was supported by its massive debts. But that was sound business practice. It was credit which made the world go around, which made the galaxy turn on its axis. Ewart Communications Corporation was like a coin spinning on its edge, smoothly and swiftly going around and around and around. While it moved, it remained upright.

If the coin ever slowed, it would fall. It had fallen. And it wasn't only Larnvik who had been crushed beneath.

'You owe us a great deal of money, Mr Ewart. Not only the relatively minor sums originally due to the Terrestrial Taxation Authority, but also the massive losses which we have incurred through so many companies going into bankruptcy and being unable to pay their taxes, as well as all the sums which they would have paid us in the future had you not sabotaged your world's entire financial and economic structure. Because of you, it will be a very long time before our investment in the Terrestrial Taxation Authority becomes profitable. If ever.'

'How did you find me? Who brought me here? It was Rajic. Wasn't it?'

'You brought yourself here, Mr Ewart, and that will be a mitigating factor when we decide what to do with you. Does your planet impose the death penalty for tax evasion?'

'No!'

Ewart tried to free himself again, more desperately this time, but his limbs were firmly held. He looked at the wall, but there was no sign of the doorway.

'There's an old saying on our world: "Set a cheat to catch a cheat",' said Dulsedech. 'We are prepared to let you work for us.'

'Me! Become a taxman . . .?'

It was the craziest idea Ewart had ever heard. Everyone else worked for the tax authorities, he supposed, paying most of their income to parasitic blood-suckers whose only function was to leech away the wealth created by others. But he'd never been like everyone else, which was why he'd never paid tax.

'How much will I earn?'

'Is that meant to be an amusing remark? You'll be paying off your debt to us for ever.'

Ewart couldn't join the enemy. But there was no alternative.

Until the door opened.

Rajic and Zena and Grawl and someone else walked in. Ewart recognized the fourth person, even though he had no recognizable features. They'd met on GX486/33–D, Ewart remembered. It was he who had brought the *Demon Star* to Hideaway.

'Who are you?' demanded Dulsedech.

'*******,' said the man.

'You can't be!'

'Would I lie?' He turned to Ewart. 'We're going.'

'Where?' asked Ewart, and he found that his arms and legs were free.

'He's not going anywhere,' said Dulsedech. 'None of you are. You're all under arrest.'

'We've got to get back to the *Demon Star*,' said Rajic.

'If you steal that ship, you're all pirates!' said Dulse-dech.

'Tell us we'll never get away with it,' said *******.

'You'll never get away with it!'

'And that we'll be hunted down to the ends of the universe.'

'You'll be hunted down to the ends of the universe!'

'Shake a leg,' Rajic said to Ewart. 'We've only got a few minutes. Didn't you always want to be a pirate?'

'No.' It was his head that Ewart shook. 'I'm staying.'

'What for?' said Rajic.

'To pay his debts,' said Dulsedech.

'How?' asked Rajic. 'By washing up for trillions of years?'

'We don't need him,' said *******.

'We can't leave him here,' said Rajic.

It was good to know he thought so, but Ewart said, 'Get away while you can. Grawl, Zena.'

'Yes, sir?' said Zena, who stood by the entrance with Grawl.

'Go with Rajic. He's your new boss. I want you both to serve him as well as you've served me.'

'Yes, sir. Is there any one last thing I can do for you? Shall I kill the alien?'

Ewart glanced at Dulsedech.

'No,' he said. 'Just go.'

'Yes, sir,' said Zena.

She turned and went out through the doorway. Grawl looked at Ewart for a moment, then he also left. ******* followed.

'It's not too late,' said Rajic.

'It is,' said Ewart.

The brothers gazed at each other for a few final seconds.

'Chin up, old man,' said Rajic.

Then he was gone, leaving Ewart alone with Dulsedech.

Anything was better than having to travel in the *Demon Star* again. Except maybe becoming a tax collector.

But Ewart knew when he was beaten. He was too old to run. There was nothing to be gained by risking his life. At his age, he should be taking it easy.

So he remained on Hideaway. He never discovered the name of the organization for which he toiled and slaved every waking hour, and neither did he find out what planet Dulsedech was from or whether she really was female.

Every day was the same as the previous one. Long and boring. With nothing to look forward to, all he had left were his memories. And right up until his dying day, William Ewart always wondered what would have happened if instead of refusing the chance of escape he'd said:

'Right. Let's go.'

AN END

Ewart couldn't join the enemy. But there was no alternative.

Until the door opened.

Rajic and Zena and Grawl and someone else walked in. Ewart recognized the fourth person, even though he had no recognizable features. They'd met on GX486/33–D, Ewart remembered. It was he who had brought the *Demon Star* to Hideaway.

'Who are you?' demanded Dulsedech.

'*******,' said the man.

'You can't be!'

'Would I lie?' He turned to Ewart. 'We're going.'

'Where?' asked Ewart, and he found that his arms and legs were free.

'He's not going anywhere,' said Dulsedech. 'None of you are. You're all under arrest.'

'We've got to get back to the *Demon Star*,' said Rajic.

'If you steal that ship, you're all pirates!' said Dulsedech.

'Tell us we'll never get away with it,' said *******.

'You'll never get away with it!'

'And that we'll be hunted down to the ends of the universe.'

'You won't get that far,' said Dulsedech. 'You think you've nixed Hideout's security web, but . . .'

******* started to turn, then suddenly froze. Rajic and Zena and Grawl also became still, and Ewart's limbs were once again immobile.

'As I told you,' said Dulsedech: 'You're not going anywhere. None of you are. You're all under arrest.'

'Who is he?' asked Ewart. Even as he stared at the

stranger, there was nothing memorable about him.

After masquerading as one of the natives on GX486/33–D, ******* had somehow taken command of the *Demon Star* and guided it to Hideaway without anyone on board realizing what was happening. Although they had only arrived an hour ago, ******* already intended to leave.

But now he'd been stopped. Literally.

'We don't know,' said Dulsedech. 'There might only be one *******, or he could be part of a whole race. Why did you come to Hideout? What did you do while you were here?'

******* said nothing.

'He used you and your ship, Mr Ewart, and he planned to use you again. You're fortunate we caught him.'

'Used me for what?' said Ewart.

'That's what we'll find out.'

'You won't,' said *******.

Then he exploded.

Within a nanosecond, the whole room and everyone within it was totally annihilated.

Within a microsecond, all of Hideaway was absolutely obliterated.

Within a millisecond, every ship in orbit around the satellite was completely destroyed.

All that survived the cataclysm was the small white sun which had been the core of the asteroid.

Its enigmatic origins puzzled hundreds of generations of astronomers from thousands of races across the galaxy.

The tiny star remained deep within the interstellar wilderness for countless millions of years, by which time every one of the thousands of races had become extinct and there was no one left to do the counting.

ANOTHER END

Ewart couldn't join the enemy. But there was no alternative.

Until the door opened.

Rajic and Zena and Grawl and someone else walked in. Ewart recognized the fourth person, even though he had no recognizable features. They'd met on GX486/33–D, Ewart remembered. It was he who had brought the *Demon Star* to Hideaway.

'Who are you?' demanded Dulsedech.

'*******,' said the man.

'You can't be!'

'Would I lie?' He turned to Ewart. 'We're going.'

'Where?' asked Ewart, and he found that his arms and legs were free.

'He's not going anywhere,' said Dulsedech. 'None of you are. You're all under arrest.'

'We've got to get back to the *Demon Star*,' said Rajic.

'If you steal that ship, you're all pirates!' said Dulsedech.

'Tell us we'll never get away with it,' said *******.

'You'll never get away with it!'

'And that we'll be hunted down to the ends of the universe.'

'You'll be hunted down to the ends of the universe!'

'Shake a leg,' Rajic said to Ewart. 'We've only got a few minutes. Didn't you always want to be a pirate?'

Ewart remembered when they'd been kids, the stories Kosmos had told them, the games they used to play. Sometimes they'd battled against fleets of space pirates, and sometimes they'd been pirates themselves.

He glanced at Dulsedech, then shook his head and smiled. William Ewart working as a taxman? Never!

He picked up his drink. It wasn't wine, but it tasted almost as good. He drained the glass, then cast it aside. It smashed invisibly against the transparent floor.

'Right,' he said. 'Let's go ...'

NOT ANOTHER END ...

... just the beginning!